9-91

		DATE DUE	
		JUL 03 2012	

F

8-91 BT 1995

Published by:
  Black Heron Press
  P.O. Box 95676
  Seattle, Washington 98145

ISBN 0-930773-17-9 (cloth)
ISBN 0-930773-18-7 (paper)

TYPOGRAPHY BY DATAPROSE, SEATTLE.
COVER DESIGN BY MARY A. FOOTE
PHOTOGRAPH BY JUAN SEBASTIAN AGUDELO

The Confession
of
Jack Straw

a novel by

Simone Zelitch

BLACK HERON PRESS
Post Office Box 95676
Seattle, Washington 98145

FOR KEN McNEIL, IN ANSWER TO
YOUR LETTER, AND FOR BECKY

Truly, truly I say unto you unless
a grain of wheat falls into the earth
and dies, it remains alone; but if it
dies it bears much fruit.

John, 12:24

But while I pondered all these things,
and how men fight and lose the battle,
and the thing that they fought for
comes about in spite of their defeat
and when it comes turns out not to be
what they meant, and other men have to
fight for what they meant under
another name— while I pondered all
this, John Ball began to speak again
in the same soft voice with which he
had left off.

William Morris, *A Dream of John Ball*

June, 1381

How the insurgents planned to destroy the realm is proved by the confession of John Straw, the most important of their leaders after Walter Tyler. After Straw had been captured and sentenced to execution in London by the Mayor, the latter spoke to him publicly: "Behold, John! You are certain to die soon and have no hope of saving your life. Therefore, to ease your passage from this world and for the health of your soul, tell us in all honesty what plans you rebels pursued and why you stirred up the crowd of commons." After Straw had hesitated for some time and refrained from speaking, the mayor added: "I promise you, John, that if you do what I ask, I will make arrangements for the sake of your soul and will have many masses celebrated for it during the next three years." Many citizens who were present promised the same thing, one mass from each person. Straw was so moved by such fine promises that he began . . .

Walsingham, *Historia Anglicana*

ONE

1. The Confession of Jack Straw

Don't write Jack Straw—They called me that but they were wrong. This cell is sopping and if I'd been made of straw I'd have rotted long ago. Or if you want clean proof look twice when you cleave my head free tomorrow. Lord Mayor Walworth: will you hit straw or bone? I'll feel bone crack, that's certain, but as your neck won't feel the ax, you'll have to take me at my word—I'm not Jack Straw. My Christian name is Michael and you'll want to bear me to sweet Heaven as a Christian. We're all Christians here, true? Dear brother scribe, write Michael, Michael Row.

Yet few who marched on London knew me Michael. Will Nettle did, and I could twist this history around and blame my fate on Nettle and a letter. The letter's the more likely of the two. Will felled me with a jug of turned cider and a tale about a Maidstone tiler.

He crossed the croft through low May fog, a jug in either hand. It was more heat haze than fog, truth told; it was untimely hot, and the grass cooked like cabbage. My cottage floor cooked too, and baked my stockings. The Sunday mass had been said early on and the hardest workers mowed their acres in the common field but I'd spent a fortnight sowing white beans and I couldn't press myself to work that day. I sat in my front room with my elbows on the trestle table, long legs stretched out, watching Will cross with his jugs. The late sun hit him full in the face and he blinked it out of his eyes like water, turning to the open door, bellowing: "Michael! News!"

I nodded him in and he slammed his burdens on the table and rubbed his hands.

"I'm Marshal of the Whitsun Ale!"

He laughed, rubbing his blue shirt, working the cork out of the sweating sow of a jug with joy. He'd wanted to

be Marshal since he'd come to Gravesend years before.
They were wise to choose him. He was a brewer and he
had a brewer's heart, just the sort to worry over Whitsuntide for half the season with no mind to his own brewing.
He'd empty the Thames and fill it with good ale.

The cider was good, mind you, thick as pudding,
strong as brass. He brewed it like a southerner, threw
everything from bones to boots into the pot to quicken it to
fire. He passed the jug in the way of a toast to his new
title, and I felt it burn a line down my throat.

He shook the second jug. "This one's for Jenny." He
settled, searched the room. "I guess she's by the river,
with the heat."

Jenny was in the back bower, roasting herself like the
goose she was. She had a lame leg, but she was no gentle
cripple; she might as well have swung it like a whip. I
leaned back and called her.

She hobbled out, savage and snarled as the flax in her
drop spindle. Her light hair was a tangle, and her brown
skirt hiked up round her bum right leg. Will's eyes were
on her, but she never met them. It was Will who'd lamed
her, years before. She'd taken a fall in his chalk ditch on
her way home from Dartford market, and he'd set her
sprain backwards and snapped the bone. Will told her he
was sorry so many times that Jenny stopped forgiving him.
He nursed her, feebly, still. He pushed the second jug of
cider toward her.

"This is strong stuff, Jen. It'll ease you."

"I don't want to be eased, thank you, Will." She
worked at the spinning, glowering, as though flax held a
grudge against her.

"This cottage is no place for you today, dearie. Why
don't I fix you a nice spot by the river? You can't see the
grass for the blue pimpernels." He grinned like a dolt and
ran a big hand up and down the jug. He looked at the
hand, and ran it through his hair. Jenny spun on.

She said, "I have to cast my brother's fine white
clothes for Whitsuntide, though I don't see the sense in
them."

That made Will laugh. "No sense?—well, you're right!

He'll dirty them up soon enough. There'll be cheese rolling and sport and dance and Michael'll be in the thick of it."

I smiled. "I don't think so."

He wagged a finger. "I'm claiming you—I'm Marshal now, and you're my man! You're going to lead a mime."

I raised my brows and took a cautious mouthful of cider. "I don't lead."

"Ah, but you tell tales, and I've got a wonder of a tale —just right!" He opened his tunic and scratched his chest, grinning. "Got it from a beggar heading north. He wanted to trade news for ale and it seemed a good bargain. You're a man who likes a story."

I nodded. The cider took hold now, and the hot, thick air turned rosy. Even the rough stool felt friendly, like a hand. I liked Will because he asked little of me and he listened like a lad. I turned lad then; I could have listened to Will's silly voice forever.

"It's just about a Maidstone tiler." He paused and drew the jug to his lips. "It's about him and one of those clerks, Hales's men, the tax collecters."

I broke in. "If this is about trouble I want nothing of it!"

"Ah, simmer down!" Will looked hurt. "By heaven, you're touchy. It's all good fun."

I felt Jenny's sullen eyes on me. "For some," I said.

He shrugged and didn't press me. He took another drink for courage. "Now tell me if this isn't a tale worth telling: the returns aren't what they should be. They never are. So Rob Hales sends more clerks and makes a second go at it. They try to figure who's past fifteen and old enough to warrant taxing, and one clerk gets the bright idea: he'll tax girls who've lost their maidenheads!"

He smiled in triumph. I shrugged: so it was another bawdy story. I dropped my guard and glanced over my shoulder. Jenny seemed intent on spinning.

Will went on. "There was one girl. She was supposed to be fourteen, you follow? But she was well built, and the clerk started to lift her skirts to check when BAMM!—" He whacked his fist on the table. "Tiling hammer through the head!"

"The Maidstone tiler, I expect," I said. "Did the clerk die?"

Will nodded. "And the tiler—his name's Wat—he isn't even hiding. They say that every house in Maidstone has a shingled roof. I guess clerks aren't popular in Maidstone."

"Are they anywhere?" I was on my fourth round of cider. "Here's a tale for you, Will—" But then Jenny pushed by and her charmless eyes caught mine. There'd be no tales. She turned sharp as a soldier on her one good leg and sparked the cooking grate. Her face was lost in smoke. Nettle yawned.

"You could turn that into a story, now couldn't you?"

"It is a story," I said.

"Not a proper story. Not the way you tell them." Nettle smiled and set his head in his hand, moony with the cider. "You could call it something like the Tiler and the Clerk or the Man Who Tested Maidens." He was tickled now and begged until I swore I'd pass the tale on properly and set it into verse for Whitsuntide.

Content, he took the empty jug and left the full behind. I might have walked him home, but his brewery lay Thamesside. Too many ferries docked there, and too many strangers pushed toward Watling road. More, heat made the pigs bold. Our council hired a boy to shoo the common swine back with a birch rod, but our Lord wanted his own pigs to wander at their will. They wore bells round their necks to mark their freedom and they nosed slop over chalked cobbles till wharf housefronts held naught but snort and stink.

Yet my cottage held smoke and Jenny. Worse, I wore a face she'd seen before. Soon it would be Whitsun and there'd be an empty week for prayer and feasting. Till then, one only had to weed, to tend the garden, to grease and patch a cart to hold a burden of hay. I'm a good worker when I have to work; I put my heart into it. When my hands are idle my heart has to find something else to do.

Jenny knew this well. When Will had gone, she looked up from the bacon on the grate, and said, "Why aren't you at Billing's?"

"It's early," I said. "With the little patch I work there

it isn't worth drubbing it dead."

"Better you drub it to straw." She speared a hunk of bacon. "You talk about taxes and lawyers and it gets into your blood."

"I keep you stocked in food and drink," I said. "If you're not pleased with me, marry."

"Become Will Nettle's ale-wife?" She laughed into the smoke and started coughing. "Oh, oh, wouldn't that leave you free of limping Jenny right enough! Heaven on earth!" She spat. "You'll leave me again."

"Leave you?" I snorted through the grease and gloom. That room turned laughter sour. "Last time, I left you with mother, father, two sisters, three brothers—and Jen, I was fifteen." Yet I'd returned to find her in that room alone, bone-thin and lame. I added, "I didn't exactly profit from that old adventure, Jenny. I came home half dead."

She looked back then, clean through me, at the far wall. It had been white; it was warped now, and mottled grey. She'd pegged a few long shelves there, but two of the three were bare; the third held half a sack of barley flour. Once upon a time a wall-loft had been heaping, and the cottage had held nine. She'd seen plague take two sisters. Two brothers fought in France; they'd likely died there. Another death would be no wonder. She shook her head. "You'll want to be a hero in a tale."

I laughed in earnest then. "Do I look like a hero?"

"There's Essex," Jenny said. And she bowed her head. Essex lay a mile away, across the Thames; we can see Tilbury from our own wharf on a fine day. Still, the word hung between us like trouble. Essex was where the serfs, the bound men were, where paupers hated Lords enough to kill them.

"Oh, Essex," I said, "but not here. Not in Kent. Or at any rate," I added, thinking of the Kentish Maidstone tiler, "not in Gravesend. There hasn't been a bound man here since the Plague, and there's freeholders like Rob Billing— and now he's going to marry that old money-bags, Jill Campe." Jenny didn't fancy Billing. Neither did I, but as I have no land of my own I took work from him when I could, and spent my evenings drinking with him.

She smirked. "Billing wouldn't—no—but you might!"
She showed a few bad teeth. "Not for love of Essex, but so
you can talk about it afterwards." And so I talk now,
scribe, mayor, my brothers, yet Jenny knew nothing of
bargain and confession. She said: "I saw your face when
Will told his stupid, bawdy story, and for all your talk, I
see it now. You saw yourself with the tiling hammer—"

"Some folks say Rob has three hundred pounds." I
flashed a full smile. "You're tight enough with his son, Joe,
the idiot! Quite a match that would be!"

That drew her up. She stood, all weight on her good
leg, a pronged fork raised for striking. "Joe has nothing—"

"A shrew and an idiot are a heady match. I wonder if
England's ready for your children!"

Down went the fork! I turned the stool up like a shield
and battled my lame sister back.

"Dopey Joe—Jenny's Beau—Ha!"

She made a quick stab and I seized her oaken staff
and armed myself. It wasn't long before she threw her
hands up, and knew the battle won. "You cursed fool!"
she said. "You've got me out of breath, and burnt the
bacon."

She sighed and poked the ashes on the grate, giggling,
flushed and almost pretty. I felt pleased with myself, and I
poked my head out for a breath of air. The wind was like
fresh water. My head cleared so quickly it hurt.

In truth, I felt unsettled. Something had stirred that
day, with Nettle's story. I remembered too much. I'd only
left Ball three years before. If empty hours and small woes
hadn't brewed with news from Essex, I wouldn't be in this
cell now, confessing. As it was, I left Jenny to her cooking
and went to the bower.

The bower was dark and close; the kitchen smoke had
blown in till the bedding smelled of bacon. The wheat-straw
thatch hung loose and shed a little; it let in some grey
light. I freed the latch on the oak cabinet. I sought a thing
I'd hidden with care, and I threw a dim, high heap down
till I held it in my hands.

It was a Bible. I opened it with two fingers; it had
seen hard wear and I tried not to tax it. It was a Latin

scribe's work, cribbed in a wandering English. It pained me to see how little I'd retained of Latin, but I wasn't interested in Latin then. The letter rested on the back page, where I'd left it.

I'd found it by my hoe in the garden a week before. I didn't know who put it there. I'm sure you've seen a copy.

> Jakke Mylner asketh help to turne hys mylne aright. He hath grounden smal smal; the kings sone of heven he schal pay for alle.

I took it to my bed and tilted it toward light. "Turn his mill aright . . ."

> Loke thy mylne go aright with the foure sayles, and the post stande in stedfastnesse. With ryght and with myght, with skyl and with wylle, lat myght helpe ryght, and skyl go before wille and ryght before myght, than goth oure mylne aryght.

"And if might go before right . . ." I leaned back.

> And if myght go before ryght and wylle before skylle; than is oure mylne mys adyght.

This was my second reading and I still knew nothing more than what I'd known the first time I had seen the letter's writing, the same script that ran above the Bible's Latin. I picked the words apart and wondered why I felt such bliss to know Ball working and alive. We hadn't parted well and I hadn't given him thought since I'd come home. I'd told Jenny only of our seven years together. Who'd given me the letter? How did Ball get it out of Canterbury jail? What did he expect of me? I knew well what he expected of me. All the while the notion of a living Ball made me blush for joy and shame. I didn't show the letter to a soul. I knew Ball well enough to know it wouldn't be the final message, and that I'd soon know the messenger.

I slipped the letter back into the Bible. It was John

Ball's Bible, John Ball who'd taught me to read. The memory of my time with Ball is clearer than the memory of that hot, strange Whitsuntide that brought me back to him.

---

2. Parson John Ball

I'd met Ball ten years back, before my family scattered. It was Lent, then, and we'd labored through the first plowing. The weather was a better match for Easter—bright and swollen, thawed clear through. Sunday mass was always warm with bells but that first hot Sunday the bells fought with spring birds. We heard the robins even through church walls, and it was hard to kneel and bow our heads when every drop of blood boiled with the weather.

Yet for all that, I see Saint Mary's now, clear as your face, scribe. I see rood nestled in loft, under its white Lent veil, to be revealed, like Christ, come Easter. I see the whittled figures of the seven sacraments set just below, an awning over Parson Wells' head. I smell the wood, the fresh chalk walls, and our own moist Sunday smell. Then on the wall there's paint and plaster: Jonah in the Whale, a bubble of a hollow fish and little Jonah curled inside her like a lamb. I knew that painting better than I knew my own face.

We sang our Ave and our Pater Noster like good Christians, and we sat through a sermon with one eye on the door. Then, dizzy with prayer, we rose and stormed out, laughing.

Mayor, spend winter with nine packed between four walls of wattle, floor deep in sour rushes smelling too much like you smell. Then step out and see flowers! There's maidenpink, catchfly, monkey orchid and the long, flowering grass. You stick some cat mint between your teeth to clean the taste of winter from your mouth, and you gather sprigs of everything!

Our elders met over the holy water and wandered off to drink or mulch and turn their fields for sowing. Children followed, hoping for a free hand with the ox goad, maybe,

or more likely bound for Gravesend wharf to beg a ferry
ride to Tilsbury. I might have done the same, I guess, but
that day I heard music.

The music wasn't comely. It croaked like rusty hinge
and ran the wrong way. That was the marvel of it; I'd
heard troubadors enough but most who made their living
piping knew their business. The tune broke the sweet air to
pieces, and it made me laugh. I cocked my head and
listened: it came from Watling crossroads, far from Gravesend center.

The children didn't think it worth much notice. They
guessed at the tune.

"Robin Hood and Little John!"

"Bide Lady Bide!"

"Ha! Bawdy one! It's Lent—"

They tossed their notions back and forth like apples,
and were done with it. I stayed put. At fifteen I was
neither man nor child, too idle to be one and too shame-
faced to play the other. A walk to Gravesend wharf
wouldn't do then, and neither would plain work, or idle
gossip at the tavern. So I stood there, gawking like a
hound. Jenny stood near, a babe then, shoeless even on a
Sunday. She nibbled her finger, nodding with the music.
Then she seized my arm and pulled me south. I shrugged
and let her lead me.

We reached the crossroads; what a disappointment! The
piper was dour as a parson, long and lean. His face was
the same piss yellow as his pipe and he didn't look the
sort who'd pipe out "Robin Hood and Little John." He was
parson indeed, though his hair was too pale and sparse to
form a proper tonsure. He wore black, and three lumpen
sacks swung round his waist. A few pale hairs hung from
his chin like roots on a radish. We stared at him, rose red
and mute. Jenny caught my hand and made me stay.

The parson lowered his pipe. His little eyes passed
over us, toward town, and fell on our faces like two drops
of vinegar. I heard him mutter: "Ah, Ball—suffer the little
children."

I found my voice. "I'm not a child," I said.

The eyes met mine. "Boy," he said, "can you read?"

I stammered and found wit enough to shake my head.

"You must learn." He tugged at the hairs on his chin. "You must read the Bible and become a winnowing fan. You must separate the wheat from the chaff!" Then he asked, "Is your father a bondman?"

Again, I shook my head.

"Well, none who know their Bible can be held in bondage." He stretched out, waving a long arm. "Nor can they abide bondage!"

I nodded.

"They know the rich and poor have one master and must be one condition." He frowned deeply. "You know that Master?"

I thought, sweating and longing for an honest ale to wash the blush away. I answered: "King Edward?"

"Christ!" The parson spread the word like mustard. "He bought all freedom with his blood."

He turned down toward Dartford, pipe to his lips again. I turned too, toward the tavern, the King's Arms, but Jenny caught me fast.

She pointed. "Look!"

Ball was some distance off, still torturing his pipe, eyes on the hedges, men and sheep due west. His melody had drawn crows and they flew toward him, cawing in chorus.

"I'll bet crows feed him," Jenny whispered, "Like Elijah." Then she said, "Let's ask him to dinner."

I groaned. "Let the crows feed him."

"Nonsense." It was an odd word for a babe to use, but it came out sweet and the charm worked on my will like shears on a hedge. "Ask him what he's piping."

I let her lead me on. The crows passed Ball, I guess off to a more likely Elijah. Ball had stopped short; his eyes looked up and down and settled in on nothing in despair. Noon sunlight turned his bald pate dazzling. Then he looked and saw me. I mumbled out the question.

He paused. "The Ballad of Robin Hood and Little John." He cleared his throat. "Where are the grownups, boy?"

I answered, "In the tavern or the church."

"One day they'll combine the two, boy," he said.

"Heaven and Earth are one!"

That made me laugh, and I liked him well enough to urge Jenny forward. She asked him to dinner.

"Blessed are the pure in heart," he said. He was so solemn that I laughed again. He gave me a fierce look. "After we've supped I'll begin to teach you how to read in both English and Latin."

I laughed and laughed—what was more laughable than Mike Row reading Latin? We walked together, and his every move was queer and endearing, the rustle of the coarse black cloth on his long, powerful legs, his strange eyes that moved along the Thames as though it was something finer than a river. I saw us doubled there and thought—there's a picture! I'll be a priest like Parson Ball. He was stiff and fast, and I pumped along gleefully, proud to keep pace. Jenny lagged, and once we had to stop and let her catch us. She huffed up, beet-faced, and her slow seven-year-old toddling addled me like poison. I tried to lose her again, but she clung to me till we got home, and even after.

Ball stayed for dinner. Back then, our cottage buckled out with life. The thatched straw smelled of aging onions and the salted ewe we'd slaughtered when her teeth had worn too low to graze. My father came home from our thirty acres with a burnt face and a sweat-soaked smock. He saw Ball, perched on his best four-legged stool, and he was overawed. He looked at his black hands and hid them behind his back. My mother smiled and gave Ball bread and cheese and lent-herring. He took them with a nod and a blessing.

My father asked Ball where he came from.

"Essex." He didn't look at my father; he had eyes only for the bread. My mother poured out milk and set it in his hand. Ball bolted cheese and added "Colchester." He addressed the milk.

My father nodded, drawing up a smaller stool. I stood, Jenny on my leg like a fungus, watching Ball with pride of ownership. Ball looked at the stool beneath him. "A nice piece of work," he said sharply. "And the cup holding the milk's no pauper's cup. Have you a trade?"

My father was abashed. "I'm a tenant. I work the land I'm leased, though I'll confess, father, that times are better than they were when I was young. More land for fewer tenants since the plague—may God spare us—and labor's scarce enough for sons to earn a good day's wage." He paused. "Between you and me, the stool's another matter. Plague empties some fine cottages—"

"Has it ever occurred to you that God sets temptation in your path to test your will and faith?" Ball ran his long hand through his beard. "You're a free man?"

"As I said, I get by." My father searched the room for other suspect trifles and a sly hand bade my mother stow them in the loft. "Not as well as some, but then a big family needs to stay on with a lord. We can't pick up and move to greener pastures. Now if all the boys were working like men . . ." He frowned and shook his head. "Michael's got a strong back, but—"

"I'd like to speak to you about your son," Ball said.

Then my brothers trooped in. Their boots were caked in earth. Frank and Peter, arms draped round each other, threw a heap of daisies on my mother's lap. Then Alf, the eldest, set a bundle on the table.

"First crop in," he said. His hands weren't used to carrying anything heavier than a ledger, and they rubbed against each other to recover. He could cipher, and already had the clerkly, narrow eyes you see in merchants. Ball sat, quiet as his stool, and for a time my parents forgot him in their pride in the cabbage and beans. They layed them out along the table, drunk with bounty. My mother minced some salt mutton and swore we'd feast, for all it being Lent.

Alf turned once, spotted Ball, and turned twice more. He kept on looking, closing his eyes the way he did when he recounted figures fresh from London. Ball suffered that suspicious gaze through dinner and supper; in fact, Ball stayed the night. That evening, the two older girls, Ann and Marjorie, walked off our heavy supper by the river. Frank and Peter wandered off to shoot their longbows in the dark. My mother and father followed, intent on a dark talk—later I knew myself the subject. Alf sat in the back bower working his figures; I could hear his nasal voice, so many groats owed and groats paid. Ball took a thick book out of one of his sacks and set me to sounding out letters. It was the first time I'd held a book on my knee; all I could think was that the binding and parchment were pressed hide. They felt warm-blooded, still. Jenny sat at my feet, mouthing along. When the light failed, we moved close to the hearth despite the smoke; Jenny moved with us. At last, Ball wearied of me; he wanted a blanket. I crossed back to the bower where we kept bedding. Alf caught my shoulder.

He drew me back hard till the edge of the oak cabinet caught my hip. I started to cry out but he set a firm hand over my mouth. He whispered, "You know who that is? That's John Ball, the one they call the Mad Parson of Kent. He's not even a priest—defrocked."

I felt a cold rush. "I don't care."

"Well, I just thought you ought to know who you bring home."

"He told father he wants me to go with him."

"Michael, you're not about to." Alf frowned. "The man's notorious. With every piece of news from London there's another tale about John Ball. It's bad enough you—"

"But you haven't heard him. He's funny." I looked askance, through the door. Ball was leaning far back on the big stool by the fire now. The three sacks lay in a circle round him. His head was back and he was snoring softly. "Besides," I said, "he's right."

"About what?"

"Heaven and Earth. Why is the world the way it is, Alf?" I thought about the cabbage that we'd feasted on that night and sighed. "For months, barley bread, that bum stuff we called barely bread, and today we eat till we're sick. One bad harvest, and no cabbage will save us. One bad harvest and Lord Simon can take everything but this stinking cottage, for all the sweat we pour into the land."

Alf suffered this until I'd finished. Then he said, "Oh, change the rain and sun—make every harvest golden! We live well, Michael, and if you worked you'd learn to appreciate—"

"Bound men work," I said. "Will their work set them free, Alf?"

"Grandfather was a bondman and father is a free tenant and you're apprentice to a madman." He shook his head and smoothed his soft, new beard. "Our family's fortune's rising."

I smiled a little. "I'm going to seek my fortune . . . like a good younger son."

"Younger sons and devils and Giantkillers." He smiled at last, with testy love, an elder brother's smile. "Don't tell me about Heaven and Earth, Michael. You want to go off and do things. You don't want to tell your tales to sheep forever."

All the while, Jenny had crept in behind us. She threw her arms around my middle, then, and cried: "I want to go with you!"

I turned and laughed. Her big pink head seemed too big for her shoulders and her feet were pigeon-toed. I'd never seen her look more of a babe in swaddling than that night. I took her hand. "You'll wait here and watch my place in bed."

"I want Heaven now!" she shouted. "I want Heaven on Earth!"

I turned; Ball was still dozing. I prayed to Holy Mary that he hadn't heard my sister. Alf smiled, sly, as if to say: she's no more fool than you. To Jenny, he said, "What's the hurry, little Jen?" He picked her up and slung her on his shoulder. "A bit of sleep's heaven enough for you, this time of night."

He carried her, kicking, to her corner of the bower. I was left to gather bedding.

I wasn't sure what Ball wanted of me. I threw two goat-hair blankets on his knees and set to working off his boots. I pulled, feeling a fool, and he woke in time to see me fall backwards with a boot like a hunk of straw and tar in my hands. He frowned.

"Now I'll have to trouble with getting it on. If you really want to help, get a night's rest and wake me before dawn."

I nodded.

"Your father doesn't seem to think you worth your board here. He's promised you to me as an apprentice and we must be off before he has second thoughts." He looked at me as I crouched, still. "There are things about me that he doesn't know, I think."

I said, "I know them."

He nodded absently and seemed to doze again, but then he said, "Boy, have you ever seen a windmill?"

"We have a watermill here," I said, "but there's a hill called Windmill Hill. And I know a tale about a windmill."

"The mill of God grinds slowly, but it grinds exceedingly small." I'd heard the saying somewhere, in church, maybe, yet I didn't know, nor do I know today, if Ball was talking of Earth, Heaven, or the hard dry turning of his own thoughts. Then he took my hand in both of his and shook hard. "Welcome."

3 . The Miller and the Devil

Once there was a miller who gave short weight on grain. He saw nothing wrong with this and he was fond of saying "Piety never filled a stomach." He lived well, and his wife and children never knew want, but he thought himself a pauper if he didn't have what belonged to his neighbor.

The miller's daughter fell in love with a poor plowman named Jack. Jack asked the miller for his daughter's hand, but the miller turned him out of the house.

"They say you're very clever," said the miller, "but you don't have a penny in your pocket."

"I'm cleverer than you are, miller," said Jack. "I know that for every penny I lack here I'll have a thousand in Heaven."

Such talk didn't make the miller like Jack any better. He would walk off, muttering "Piety never filled a stomach," and go about his business.

One night it stormed, and the arms of the windmill broke to pieces. The miller couldn't bear the thought of a day's loss so he spent the long night setting the splintered wood in the dark. As he worked, his mind wandered and he thought of the new horse he was going to buy and the new coat he was going to wear and it seemed as though he had those things already. He became impatient. Then he remembered what Jack had said about a treasure waiting for him in Heaven. If Jack the ragbag, without a penny to his name, was rich there, certainly the miller would have something waiting for him. What use would he have for a new coat in Paradise? Why couldn't he get his portion now?

The thought stirred him, and he found himself whispering out loud: "Yes . . . I could do with my portion now . . ."

Then he looked up and cried "Oh!" for there was the Devil.

"I've come with your portion," he said, "and you must come with me."

The miller shook till his hat fell off.

"Come now," said the Devil. "You chose me long ago. You never expected good of Heaven, and you were always fond of saying that piety never filled a stomach."

The miller said, "It was just a figure of speech. I never meant it."

"Ah—" said the Devil. "Then let piety grind you bread by morning."

The Devil disappeared, but the miller knew he'd return.

He hurried home and found Jack with his daughter. He passed without a word.

Jack was startled. "What's the matter, old man?"

The miller told Jack about his encounter with the Devil. "If I don't grind wheat into flour through piety by morning then I'll have to go with him," he said. "Jack, I'm told you're clever, and if you can save my soul you'll have my daughter and share the mill."

Jack agreed to the bargain, and set the family to work.

First he made the miller's wife set a bag of grain by the broken mill. Then he led the miller to an abandoned church. The two of them found a crucifix as broad as a bridge and as high as two men. They heaved it up on their shoulders and they were hard put to carry it back to the mill.

Then, they worked together for the rest of the night, and by morning the cross was affixed to the post and turning, grinding wheat into flour. The miller's daughter baked the flour into two loaves.

The Devil returned but when he saw the cross grinding the wheat he turned white and disappeared.

Jack married the miller's daughter, and helped keep the mill in repair. The family prospered, though the new mill tended to stop when the miller tried to short-weight his customers. Its flour baked the sweetest bread on Earth.

4 . Abel Ker

But you don't want a tale—you want confession. Lord Mayor, scribe, I'll let a fortnight pass for both our sakes. Now you'll hear dark talk and conspiracy; you'll meet young Abel Ker. I saw him at the King's Arms and he gave me a look that soured my beer. The eyes snapped through a gap in swaddled yards of homespun capped by a high hood. His nose poked out too, dagger-sharp. I can't, in truth, say I disliked a face I couldn't see, but those eyes and that nose told their own story; he was set on talking to me. I tried to go on talking to Billing and Nettle, but he walked straight over and he said, "It's hot in here."

Will said, "You could try pulling down your hood. You know, if your head's hot—"

The hood twitched. He said, "I'll be outside."

He left us in a cloud of his own stink. Billing made a face. "Now there's a man from Essex! What did I tell you? Shoddy cloth comes from Essex, thin ale, and men like that. It's all the bound men there, setting the good cloth on fire so we free Kentish can't get to it!"

"And women?" Nettle smiled.

"Ah—the shrew cloisters they keep there! Twelve years of apprenticeship, the girls have. I'll tell you, men!" Billing sat straight, raising his cup. "Keep a good eye on your brides, when you get them, lest they be replaced with Essex changelings!"

"Watch your own bride, Rob!" Nettle called.

"Ah, there are shrews enough here in Kent!" He pointed his sharp finger round the room and shook his head. "Some women pay less mind to their men than those Essex serfs do to the law."

I looked out the window. I could just mark the tip of the man's hood in the moonlight.

Will turned his empty cup. "Hmm . . . Tell me, Michael. Could you get Jenny to speak the part of tiler's daughter in the mime?"

I said, "Jenny? She'd sooner take the tiling hammer to me."

"And Jenny's no Kate Tyler . . ." Billing rubbed his white chin with white fingers. "They say Kate looked a woman at thirteen . . ."

Will laughed, then. "Rob, you're getting married in a fortnight! Keep your mind on Jill Campe!"

Rob shrugged. "She's an old girl, Will, but I can't complain. The money's kept her young, praise God." He drummed the table, smirking. "I'm thinking of selling Joe to the priesthood. They always seem to have a use for idiots." He gave me a pinch. "Isn't that what your father did, Michael?"

The hood was gone now, and my heart sunk to my toes. The man had been the messenger from Ball—why else the secret look? I'd missed him. The window was as empty as my cup. Then clouds broke; the moon spilled into the court, and I saw the hooded man. I saw him pace and I felt myself rise to meet him.

Nettle tapped me on the shoulder. "How about another round while you're up?"

I nodded, and I crossed the crowded tavern. I stepped out, and the cold air made me gasp. I loosed my tunic at the shoulders, sighing, thinking: it *was* hot in there. There was no messenger. Then I turned and saw him looking at me. His back was to the window, and his face was lost to me, but light spilled round legs wound with cokers till they looked like shapeless piping. He walked toward me and moonlight caught on his sharp nose like milk. Then, slowly, he unwound the homespun and drew off his hood.

"Abel Ker," he said. I didn't know him. His bare face was raw red and pocked. It topped a neck thin as a walking stick. It would have been a comic face but his eyes had no fun in them. They were the eyes I'd seen, bitter little bird-eyes. He couldn't have been older than nineteen. He said, "Do you have the letter with you?"

I shook my head.

"You understand it?"

I hesistated, but I nodded.

"You have a voice?"

I almost nodded on, but I stopped short and said, "Yes, I've a voice."

He drew me out of the light and pulled me toward him. "The time for silence is over," he said. "You've been silent for three years, I'm told."

I didn't answer.

"Can we trust you to act quickly?"

"Ker . . ." The voice came from my stomach. "Leave me be."

He laughed. "Leave you to what, then? Drinking ale with fools? Why did you come out here? To tell me to leave you be?"

I pulled away and bowed my head. "I wanted news of an old friend."

"I hope you treat your friends a little better these days, *Row*." He dragged the name into a taunt. "You're needed in Essex, or at least in Erith, in your own county."

I said, "I'm needed here."

"Oh, stop playing Piers the Plowman and listen to me. The fire's spreading and if you don't come to it, Row, it'll come to you."

I looked up then. "Not here." I tried to look past him, at hedge and meadow, far cottages, roaming sheep. "Not in Gravesend. Gravesend's safe from fire." Ker's lean, keen face made me uneasy; six years ago it could have been my own. "There's a man in the tavern, son of a serf, who has three hundred pounds!"

"I'm not talking to the man in there," said Ker.

"I'm not the man I was. I know my loyalties."

"You own nothing but your cottage now, I hear. Lame sister—very sad. Maybe one sick sheep left of your family's flock. All thirty acres taken by your Lord Simon while you roamed. Well, maybe you can live with hunger." He nodded, and the head bobbed like a pump. He pumped out this: "You can live with it or you can sling your sister over a pony and move on, but real bondsmen can't move an inch. In Essex, they have to look beyond their noses or even the little they have is stolen. In Essex—"

I said, "I'm loyal to my family and my friends. I would fight for the sake of a friend, I think. Nothing grander, Ker, not anymore."

He turned away and wrapped his face back in its bundle. He pulled his hood up like a friar done with a sermon. I'd figured he'd say something like: please think of Abel Ker as your friend, Row, but he said no such thing. He said: "We'll see each other again." He walked off before I could answer.

I stepped back into the tavern, shaking like a man out of cold water. The quick heat made me sweat and I called for two ales, praying my voice didn't tremble. Ferrymen shouldered through and took their mugs in pairs, smelling of Thames-water. A man stood by, holding a hound by the collar, singing an old, loud song with a thousand verses, knit by a refrain:

> Oh she betrayed him in the morning
> And he forgave her at the noon.
> The rival's floating in the river.
> The babe is sleeping on a stone.

The ale-wife brought the man a plate of pork and peppers and he fed half to the dog. My two ales came with weak, warm heads and I crossed as Nettle and Billing tossed pennies for the next round. I wanted to go home.

Nettle sat me down and started on the beer with spirit. "So, who ought to be the Lord and Lady of the Whitsun Ale, Michael? Who ought to lead the Whitsun lamb?"

I shrugged; I couldn't think of one blithe soul, then, for my heavy heart. The tavern spun with drink and talk and fellowship, but it was as if it was happening elsewhere, as if I was watching a mime, knowing all the while I'd have to leave and seek my own death.

Yet they gossiped on, blind as two bobbins. Billing rattled the stool, raging against hired men. "Trouble with these wage laborers," he said, "no stake in the harvest. Too much work for too few men since the Plague. Those

fools can ask for a lord's portion for a day of work. There
was a time when a man was paid with a herring and a
good rye loaf."

"Oh, go work your own land and pay yourself," Will
said. Our ale is nought to your strong wine, my brothers;
it's like boiled water. Still, if you drink enough of it it's
bound to do something. Three pints made Will merry, and
four made him thoughtful. He was on his sixth. I think
he'd caught my humor; his eyes were hard and wet, like
stones.

Rob Billing said, "Mike—how about a tale?"

"I just gave you The Miller and the Devil, Rob," I
said.

"Something with a wedding in it then." He pumped
Nettle's hand. "Will, you think you'd take on me and Jill
for Whitsun Lord and Lady? Or how about my Dopey Joe
and Jenny?"

Nettle's eyes turned on me then. "I guess you haven't
set the tale to verse. I don't suppose I could ask Jenny
about . . ." He propped himself on one arm, faced the
door. "In fact, I'll go give her my regards in person."

"Not just now, Will Nettle." Billing sat him steady.
"Force yourself on her tomorrow, boy. You can't wake a
maid and expect her to thank you for it."

"In two weeks I'll be haying. This is the time for
courting, Rob." He rubbed his face and frowned. "And in
the autumn there's the brewing and—"

"Sweet Saints—you have time!" Billing pounded his
grey chest and laughed. "Look at me! I'm no young man!"

"But you've already married." Will set his head in his
hands. "I should have asked her before it happened, Rob,
before she fell into the ditch. She was warm to me then,
and there was life in her, but she was too young. Now
she's gotten old all at once—and it's my fault!"

"And if she can't forgive you, let her rest—"

And on it went on like that: weddings, Jenny, all well
soaked in ale. I slipped off unnoticed. I hugged the road's
edge, walking like a full cup, slow, for fear of spilling.
What filled me? I'd know when it spilled over. As I walked
I wondered why I clung to men like Billing, who cared no

more for me than a beggar for a louse. It was because
some deeper love had soured, I thought, and now that love
was left to birds of prey like Abel Ker. Better to forget the
meeting. Better, maybe, to go where Ker couldn't find me.
A cold wind skipped the Thames and made me shiver. I
faced Essex, Tilbury wharf, the ferryman's window keen as
a star. I walked back to my cottage, and I slept.

Gabriel's bell woke me. Jenny was up already. She
stepped into her black skirt, hair undone. I liked to watch
her when she thought me sleeping; she seemed a sweeter
sister then. Her face was lost in something as she plaited
her fair hair. She pulled her stockings up, whistling about
as well as Ball had piped. Then she saw me.

"Well, brother," she said. "Today you'll be working."

I lolled, laying with my arms back like bolsters. "Ah,
no. I'll practice for Whitsun."

"Whitsun!" Jenny leaned on her walking stick and
rolled her eyes. "And what will you be wishing for this
year?"

Mayor, each Whitsunday we wish on the turning
summer sun; I guess Mayors and old scribes never see a
true Kent sunrise. The sun carries the wishes up to heaven.
I didn't know what I would wish for, then. Jenny frowned.

"You want to be rid of me, don't you?"

I sat up and threw off my blanket. "Jenny," I said,
"I'm at a loss."

"You want me to marry Nettle!"

"Marry him if you want to." I rubbed my head. "Or
be in his Whitsun mime."

She snorted. "In the mime? Is there a village gimp in
Maidstone?"

I sighed and stared up at the thatch. "He wants you
to play the tiler's daughter."

"So Nettle can look up my skirt, then?" She gave her
plait a tug. "You were with him last night, weren't you?"

I nodded.

"Did he tell that tale again?"

"How many times can a man tell a tale?"

"He wants you to get it right," she said. She frowned
and smoothed her skirt back. "Something happened last

night. I can read your face as sure as you can read a Bible, brother."

She crossed to the front room and I followed, on knife's edge. I said, "Jenny, hear me out."

She set a loaf of brown bread on the table and sawed through. "About your going off? Well, you've done it before, Michael, without my leave."

I sighed and gnawed a crust. "There's nothing for us here. It's not a matter of my leaving, Jenny. I want us settled in, so you won't feel your life hangs on my staying. I could go off and earn a better living, send a few pence home to you. I could go off and find Alf in London, filch a pound—he has enough."

Jenny wiped the bread knife on the table. "That's not what I mean, Michael."

"But that's what I mean." I frowned. "Jenny, why won't you take Nettle?"

"If you like Will so much, marry him yourself!" she snapped. "Why can't I be the one to go off? I'm the one who stays here and you figure that'll make me settle for . . ." She stopped and looked at her hands, eyes low. "For what I see."

I sighed, sorry I'd spoken.

But she hadn't finished. "I figured you'd know, Michael. Didn't Ball ruin it for you?"

"Ruin what?" I asked.

She looked back with uncertain eyes.

"Heaven and Earth," I said. "They count not a rush, Jen, when you measure them against an empty maw."

She shook her head. "No, your belly means nothing when you measure it to Heaven. That's the trouble." She brushed bread crumbs into her hand.

"Heaven and Earth are one!" I turned my voice on edge, a neat match for John Ball's voice, and I climbed the stool and turned my chin up. "Claim Heaven here! A man has a right to bread!"

I'd hoped to make her giggle, but her eyes were moist and she looked up with no more good cheer to her than young Ker. "Heaven's not here, Michael. Till you know that you'll have one foot on the road."

"So you wouldn't want to follow me this time, Jenny?"
I climbed down, voice still full of mischief. "You wouldn't
have me take you on my back to dance for alms?"

"I couldn't go, could I, with my lame leg." She sighed.

I crossed my arms. "Jenny, I was fool enough to talk
of leaving, but I really want you to think about . . ." I
wasn't sure what I'd wanted her to think about. "Think
about speaking the part of tiler's daughter."

She rose and gave me a queer look, half cross, half
pained. "I don't want to, Michael. I don't like the tale."

"Play out the story here," I said, "and maybe you
won't be set on the notion that I have to wander off in
search of tales. I'll make a bargain of it!" I'd found my
power over her and I was loath to lose it. "Play the part of
daughter and I'll stay."

She shook her head, "I can't . . ."

I grinned. "Afraid you won't pass the test?"

She hesitated. Then she said, "No, I'll do it. But I
don't like it. I don't like the story, and I don't want some
lousy head under my skirt—Not Nettle's!"

"The hammer'll clean your skirts soon enough," I said.

"Then let Joe Billing be the clerk!" Jenny looked up
then, with a full warm smile. "That's my will in the
matter, Michael. I'll have none but Joe!"

"Dopey Joe?" I spoke through bread.

"He'd look up my skirt and he wouldn't know what
he was looking at." She poured out ale to seal the bargain.

"So you want to marry Joe Billing?" I asked.

"Marry?" If my mischief drained away she'd soaked it
up like rain. "Ha! Well maybe I will, Michael. At least he
gives me no trouble!" She gave me a full cup and raised
her own. "A bargain then. I'll play the tiler's daughter and
you'll play tiler and stay and protect your lame Jenny!"

I drank, wondering what little joy this news could give
to poor Will Nettle. Jenny emptied her own cup, blithe and
rosy. As ever, Dopey Joe had turned us friends, and it was
friends we parted. I rose and walked off to tell Nettle of
the bargain.

Jenny stood by the open door, still laughing, waving.
"Michael! Joe has more wit than we think!"

I called back, "Then he'll make you a fine husband!"

"No—he knows about Heaven, Michael. We're daft enough to care for Earth—Joe isn't!"

My laugh turned dull, and I hurried on. Why did my Jenny waste her love on Dopey Joe? Rather, did she wish to turn idiot herself? I remembered when I'd come home, found her with her leg up and her hair in strings, eyes pebble-dead, full of a fog like plague. Far better I stay put, risk another message, and tend her as we'd bargained than return to find her in like state again.

I walked the chalk road toward the Thames, and tried to see myself working leased land, with long, worn weeding hooks. I'd plank a tumbrel well and wheel wheat chaff to my pair of oxen. I'd twine half a dozen weighty tools together and bear them till they'd wear a deep nick in my shoulder. For all my fancy, I had neither land nor good tumbrel nor oxen. It was a tale I told myself. The white, sharp sun beat on the road. Grass was sparse, on chalklands, and the old town that rounded Gravesend wharf looked grey and lone.

The wharf was packed. That in itself was baffling. It wasn't market-day and the ferry wasn't due in port for three full hours. Wives and craftsmen clustered round the baker's door, and more pushed up the street. I ran into a woman Rob might call a shrew, a widow named Faith Corning. She was a big, proud gossip, and she met me, hands on hips, with a broad smile. "I wouldn't think to find you here, Michael. A beggar's trading news for bread and he's just down from Essex."

I staggered, turned to leave, but Faith seized my shoulder.

"This man's seen things, Mike. There's been trouble—a proper story, this is. Hales sent John De Bampton's men to collect taxes, but they were attacked. It wasn't just a tiler this time. It was a hundred men and women with scythes. They cut the men like corn! Bampton set soldiers on them and the serfs chased them off and set the clerk-heads on poles. Bampton's in London." Her smile turned long and hard. "Some say the armed folk mean to follow."

My heart buzzed up and back like a horse-fly in a jar.

That's why I'd kept myself from Essex news. It took me over like a devil and I had to stand firm—let it pass. But there was Will Nettle, slapping Faith on the shoulder and seizing me, shaking, shaking . . . "By the Saints! By Thomas, what a story!" He grinned and mussed my hair with a big hand, and cried, "Could we work it into the tiler tale?"

I brushed him off and tried to lose him, but there was no losing Essex news. I saw the canny beggar, swathed all over in rags, unreadable, with five good loaves under his arm. For a time I'd have sworn it was young Ker, but this rude nose was round and greenish and this beggar wasn't young. There was no conspiracy there, save a conspiracy of stories. It was a tale which brought the fire across the Thames to me.

5. The Man From Essex

The beggar was stuffed stout with bread and cheese and ale and wrapped in Gravesend's best wool blankets. "Ah—the blessed serfs—" he'd say. "Now they have a life, don't they. They walk round with bent backs like green shoots with no sunlight and they eat what Bampton can't give to the pigs and when they tend their common land it's called trespassing and ach—" Here he'd thump his hard, plump hand on his knee, "—they burnt the charters and the fire was bright as the morning star, bless Holy Mary."

My neighbors round him praised the sacred Virgin and waited, baby-eager, for the beggar to speak on.

"There was a boy named Tom Baker in Fobbing, a youth in first flower, he was, a baker's boy not past sixteen, and he spoke in town squares like Saint Paul and rode all round the country, rousing the people!"

A lad looked at him with eyes like stars. "Did he ride a big horse?"

The beggar nodded. "Yes he did, little boy. It was as big as—" He pointed to a broad oak we called Magog. I walked away.

The day was wrong, too bright, and evening came on late and pale, like an afterthought. The beggar had been with us for two nights now. He spent the first at Nettle's, tucked between his two apprentices. They'd complained about snoring and he spent the second night at Faith Corning's, where he ate the cheese she'd saved for Whitsun rolling. Still, none tired of him, save one—Mike Row.

When he spoke at the wharf, I worked for Billing. I'd weed out red corn cockles from his wheat and cut the twining nettles. Acres off, across barley, I'd hear the beggar coming. He'd stand on the ridge of turf that marked the

bounds of the strip holdings and he'd point north, toward
Essex, chattering till the field hands filled his arms with
bread and cheese they'd brought for supper.

North I went. I set out nets for perch and drew them
empty. After an hour of watching a low ferry punt the
Thames, I read the faces of its passengers and knew each
one a man from Essex. I dropped the tangled nets and left
the shore before the boat could dock.

I found myself in the common garden. The lord took
all the Row holdings, but he'd left the garden patch fallow
and Nettle had worked it in Jenny's name until I returned.
Still, it didn't hold enough to feed a hermit. Gardening is
women's work, and I felt wrong and lonely, kneeling
among stout, gay women. They knew gardens. They'd
sown cress, patience, fennel, mint, and mustard seed
among the leeks and beans. The herbs grew thick and
strong; the beans were full to bursting.

I looked at the white beans I'd sown. I'd worked the
half-acre of garden like a crofter, and plowed and mulched
the chalky earth into grey dung, but nothing had sprouted.

Tess Drew, the ferryman's wife, took her hat off and
waved. She shook a peck of radishes. "Good Whitsuntide!"

I stared at the soil, and scooped up a palmful.

She trooped over, and knelt beside me. "Lad, that seed
was sown too shallow!" She picked at the wrinkled seed-
beans, smiling. "I'll show you how it's done." Her eyes
looked out from her loose, crooked wimple and she turned
and parted the earth with her hands. I watched her; all at
once I took a clot of seed and sod and tossed it toward the
meadow in a fury. I shook, and drew my cold hands to
my eyes. I took it for an omen, and it was an omen I had
neither wit nor will to read.

I stomped off, cuff to coker grey with mud. That
afternoon, I'd promised Will I'd hear the Whitsun mime
straight through. Bless Nettle, he was too busy to bother
with the Essex beggar. He was clearing a yellow barn to
house the Lord and Lady, weaving bowers, washing the
Whitsun lamb, and brewing pudding-ale to seep his hopper
cakes. For his sake, I kept my word and walked to the oak
grove where the players gathered for the mime.

He'd brought a dozen cakes there. Jenny waited, staff over her knees. She looked pellet pale out of the cottage. She shivered, pulled her shawl close, despite the sun, and took her cake with a bitter nod. She took a second cake for Dopey Joe.

Joe lolled in the blue mud by a chestnut tree, rubbing his dirty hands on his green stockings. I'd found two men, Billing's field hands, to speak the clerk parts and force Dopey through his piece. They'd come from work, and wore their tattered breeches. We looked a dreary company.

Will handed Jenny a third hopper cake. "Steeped in my best ale," he said, shy and proud. He kept his hand on hers a little longer than he had to; if Jenny noticed she didn't let on. "Currants in this batch as well, Jenny. Finer than the ones we'll have on Sunday."

She nodded, dull, and turned back to the man I'd found to play the Father Tiler. "Hugh, please try not to hit me this time."

Hugh was a brown ape of a smith, with hairy arms which seemed to have a will of their own, but he had a good heart. He looked helpless. "If you'd just step back a little faster . . ." Then he remembered she was lame, and added, "The hammer's only made of straw."

Jenny picked a long strand of straw out of her hair and sighed. Nettle snarled at Hugh and ran back to his duties.

I stood back, and looked at my five players: Jenny, Joe, Hugh, Billing's two men. Hugh said, "Michael, let's quit this sorry mime: Tell us a tale! How about something with Jack the Giantkiller!"

I glowered. "You get tales enough from Essex."

Jenny called, "Let's have done with this, Michael!"

"I've a wise sister," I said. "Let's begin!"

Hugh stepped up with his straw hammer and rubbed his face. "I am a poor tiler," he said, "of Maidstone fair and free. I have a fine daughter." He pulled Jenny forward round the middle. She resisted, struggled free, stared at the ground. "My treasure is she," he said.

Jenny cleared her throat. "I am his pure daughter, or so people say."

"Ha!" called a mock clerk.

"And now the clerks take all our scant goods away . . ." she said, too softly.

"Not while I am with you . . ." Hugh said, and he tried to pull Jen back again.

The three clerics came, the two bearing Joe on their shoulders, singing:

> Oh we are jolly men of God
> Who empty pockets weekly.
> We do exactly as we please
> And go about it meekly!

One laborer said, "Here's one for taxing. Clerk—is she of age?"

The other nodded. "Brother, I know when a maid is a woman. A clerk is a clerk but a lusty and true man!"

They swung Dopey down—thrust him under Jen's skirt.

Jenny stood with Joe's head buried below; she stared through a circle of leaves, at the sky. I couldn't read her face, but I'd turned red. Hugh hit Joe on the back with the hammer and the two clerks caught his legs and tried to pull him out again.

"Come on, brother! The boy's made of stone!"

"I'm trying . . ." One dropped Joe's leg and wiped his forehead. "He must have taken root in the mud."

I called: "Step back, Jenny!"

Jenny looked down. "He's sleeping." She shrugged and hiked her skirt just high enough to show us Joe's soft head pressed against the grass. He snored.

Hugh scratched his head. "That would be a fine twist for the mime, don't you think?"

"Well, look!" a laborer said. He pointed at the road, and we turned, and stared. Nettle passed; he rode a yellow pony and behind him walked the Lord and Lady of the Whitsun ale. They were shy of fifteen, strangers a week before, or strange to one another as two village children can be, yet their arms were linked and they were covered with the gold ribbons of love-pledge. Both wore white; both wore garlands of daffodils. We knew it for show, knew in less than a week they'd be strangers again, yet that show was finer than the show we'd jangled through before they came. The lady led a lamb by a gold ribbon; its coat was milky white, and it wore a soft, green garland round its neck.

"Well," said a field laborer softly, "isn't that something."

Then the road was empty, though we felt a ghost of white, like a white shadow, on the earth. Then the beggar came.

He munched a heel of bread, and watched the toes of his stockings with interest. The stockings were new, likely traded for another tale. He saw us, stopped, and bowed.

"Ah, so you've seen them passing? Very fine, very fine, but not what we have in Essex."

Hugh scowled. "What do you have in Essex, then? The Fairy Queen herself dancing in the church square, I suppose . . ."

"And sets the parson's head on a pole!" a laborer added.

The beggar shook his head. "Oh no! Nothing so fine, but we do have the dance."

They looked up with new interest then. "We always like to see a new dance," Hugh said cautiously, "but I've nothing for alms, beggar."

The beggar grinned. "You have ribbons?"

All three had yellow ribbons in their pockets, ribbons they'd planned to give ladies.

"You'll get them back," he said, "but if this beggar will Morris dance he must wear ribbons."

The men gave him their ribbons, as though they were made of gold, and he bound them round his elbows, cuffs, cokers, stockings, hood. He took five strings of bells from his rucksack and wound them through the ribbon. Something fell out—parchment. A breeze blew it to my toes.

The script and even the shape of the parchment caught me fast. I didn't dare bend down to take it, though all eyes were on the beggar. I bowed my head; it was enough.

Jon Balle gretyth yow wele alle and
doth yowe to understande he hath
rungen youre belle. Nowe ryght and
myght, wylle and skylle, God spede
every ydele. Nowe is tyme. Lady helpe
to Ihesu thi sone, and thi sone to his
fadur to make a gode ende in the name of
the Trinite of that is begunne, amen,
amen, pur charite, amen.

Now is time. I looked up again, shaking so hard my
bones must have rung out like bells. As for the beggar's
bells, they were wound through the ribbons now, and he
looked straight at us, serious, crafty. "This isn't a new
dance, brothers . . . Oh no! This was danced at the first
Whitsun when the tongues of Christ's wit came and filled
the blessed apostles—filled them with the spirit of God!"

I shifted my weight, edgy.

"It was danced before they taxed us, before they took
our land, my brothers, before the lawyers and the robbers
came to sap our might and right and will and skill away!"
The beggar wiped his forehead. "We need a pipe and tabor
to do it properly."

Hugh had a pipe, but we lacked a tabor. As for me,
my knees were tabor enough for a troop of dancers. I
wanted to run, but I didn't have the nerve.

Hugh blew a note—a stomping, solemn dance began.
The ribbons jumped on the beggar's gray cloak and stockings, and his face turned in, eyes deepened. The pipe tune
followed, clumsy, at a distance, and if the dance was wild,
it was a deep, willed wildness. The bells alone played an
unmeasured, eerie tune. I thought of harts running on a
clipped meadow, or geese touching still water. It touched
me like those geese, till I felt ripples run clear to the heart.

I turned. Jenny was gone.

I left the three men and the idiot and found the path
she'd broken in the undergrowth. I didn't have to follow
far. She stood not twenty yards away, all tangled up in
broom-rape. I tore through, freed her, took a bunch of the
broom in my hand.

The broom smelled of cloves. She looked up sadly. "I saw you watching him."

"We were all watching him, Jenny," I said. "That's how he earns his keep."

"Well I didn't want to watch. I ran away." She steadied herself on the staff and said, "That's how you earned your keep, wasn't it? You did that, what he did."

I didn't answer. "Old Essex ought to be done by now," I said. "I'll carry you home. You've put too much weight on that bum leg today."

"Michael," She set her hand on my arm. "You'll keep your bargain, won't you? Because I'm not liking this, this tiler's daughter sing-song and worse—"

I nodded. Then I said, "For a friend, I told him."

"Because, if you leave, I'm not taking you back this time . . ." She stopped. "Told who?"

"No one." Blood rushed to my head and I shook myself. "Just talk in passing. I told a man I'd fight for the sake of a friend."

Jenny looked me up and down. She listened to the distant Essex bells. "Brother, tell me, who are your friends?"

6. The Oldest Story

I think of my first night away from home, the first with Ball. We two were off to Dover and the best road cut through Maidstone, but we seldom stayed a long stretch on the highway. Ball liked to poke into the odd cottage for alms. He pressed me up the boggy root-knit hills. We weaseled round, and tapped the door. Then we'd battle weeds and testy goats and find our way to Watling Road again, with a cheese rind, maybe, or a loaf. It was hard going for a man and boy, all mud and tangle. Once we met a river, and I bore Ball on my shoulders. When we'd crossed my shins were stuck round with fat leeches. So the first day went; we reached Maidstone that evening.

The parson lost no time. He set me in All Saint's green and handed me a big iron bell.

"Now son, you'll hear me preach," he said.

Then he took up his pipe and I swung the bell, keeping time. In truth, it clattered more than rang, but Maidstone knew it for Ball's bell, and Ball was known there. They gathered at once.

They called: "Old father! Keeping yourself out of trouble?"

Ball snarled. "There are some troubles men don't make themselves."

Then they hushed and listened to him preach.

Ball spread two books on a stool's edge and bent to read something we knew—he read the Bible. The color poured into his face and his back stiffened like a cat's, and his voice rang, all edge, a thresher.

"Parables!" he cried. "Allegories and parables! I've read you the holy words of Lord Jesus Christ and I will tell you what He meant, for He chose to speak in parables. You've heard of Dives, the rich man damned to darkness, and

Lazarus, the pauper who dwells with Abraham in Paradise."

All knew the tale; they'd seen it done at Corpus Christi. None knew the text, and as he read it out it felt raw, like he'd stripped away the skin. It made us hear the story for the first time.

"Dangerous words, brother, from a dangerous man." Ball opened the second book. "When a poor man comes to Judgement he dares to plead with God and give reasons why he should be treated kindly. And he claims by right, before a just Judge, the joy he has never tasted on earth! We dare to demand Heaven now, on Earth, to claim it! To throw Dives into the outer darkness!"

A baker, pink and soft as dough, waved out. "We can't bring down Heaven!"

Ball looked fierce. "Who brought down Hell? We all know about Hell on Earth—ask any poor soul here!"

The baker brushed a snow of wheat-flour from his chin and watched a swallow settle on a shingled roof. Some plowmen listened, and the lads and maids too young to see justice in hunger.

Ball pointed to the baker. "You work, and who do you work for?" Again, the second book—the pages turning. "You work for the rich and you give your goods to the rich. It's like dumping a bucket of water into the River Medway!"

"It's more trouble!" a woman called.

"You'd do better to take up arms and build your Heaven here—to clothe yourself and your family and do well, to clothe the poor and do better, to—"

"John Ball!"

Ball was caught fast in his sermon, fairly steaming, and he didn't see the big man till the crowd parted. The man wore a collar of squirrel fur, clasped in bronze, a fur hat, long free slashed sleeves dragging in the dust.

He called: "John Ball, in the name of the archbishop, I order you out of Maidstone."

Ball looked at him. "Well, Dives, you've stopped to listen to a poor parson." That drew a weak laugh from the folk. Some watched with interest as shamed and stricken as their laughter. Most started home.

"You're no parson," he said. "That title hasn't been yours for years, and you're a menace to Holy Church and to England." The man's pale, fine face caught the few who lingered. "These people have a right to know that listening to a heretic's against the law."

"Ha! Law! Whose law?" Ball's voice shook now. He rustled books. "A plague on your law!"

He cut himself short. The man had turned and the rest of the crowd followed. Ball spread his arms like wings.

"You ravage the church and rob the people! By God!" But then a stuttering boy snatched even the stool away, and Ball caught his two books before they hit the earth. He looked at me. "This isn't the first time."

I helped him clean the binding. Plainly, one was his Bible—the second book was too thin to be a Bible, and one night of sounding letters gave me wit enough to find a"P" or two in the long title. I said, "What can I do?"

"I'll find a use for you soon enough," he said. "We'll talk, son." Then he turned back, where the ragged youths were waiting. One approached.

"Beg pardon, father," he said. His red hair brought out the red veins round his eyes; that was the only color to him. His smock was rank, seamed hastily with thick thread, and he wore no stockings. The red hair on his grey legs was very horrible. "We want to know . . . what can we do? My father died in the Great Plague, and the lord, he's taking our holding and won't let me leave Maidstone for fear he'll lose my service." He took a breath, and a friend stepped out to support him. "And now they talk of taxing me. What do I have for them to take?"

"You have only one Lord," Ball said. "He paid all bond fees with his blood."

The boy nodded and seemed ready to go, but his friend asked again, "What can we do?"

Ball asked, "Can you use a longbow?"

This lad was proud and strong. He nodded as if he'd been insulted.

"Practice," said Ball. "Tell your friends to practice."

Then he took me aside and waved me onto Watling

Road.

"Imagine," he said as we walked on. "They train boys so they can cart them off to fight the French, and they never think these poor slaves might turn the bows on their masters." He sighed. "And what's worse, none think to turn." Still, he didn't seem downhearted. Later, I knew that Maidstone's folk had been better than most; just then I thought them cowards and traitors, and I was glad to be rid of them. We walked a good pace, eyes south and east, toward rising stars. The moon sapped color but the night seemed bright as noon. "I think . . ." Ball muttered. "Yes, we could start a chapter here easily."

"Chapter?" I turned to him.

"The Fellowship of the Great Society, they call it." He clasped his hands behind his back and swung his black sacks till they jigged. He bent out a whistle. "God's work and ours." He was full of cheer, then, and told me a tale for every bridge we crossed, every cluster of cottages. Were the families there good Christians? Would they give us a night's shelter? Had the fenced croft been a common field a year before? He knew the country well; he'd spent most of his life in Kent and Essex. He'd been trained in Colchester but when he'd lost his parsonage he'd wandered everywhere. He'd even walked as far as York when his wind had been better.

"Now I'm hard put to make twenty miles a day." He yawned. "We'll sleep in the open tonight."

He settled, felt the earth for roots, and stretched his lean legs out like walking sticks. He scratched his head. The camp could have been set in Gravesend, yet the grass seemed finer here, like fur, and the moon had a darker face. The quiet settled, heavy, and my head was packed so full with thoughts I couldn't get a thought out from under them.

After a time, Ball took his Bible out and we had a lesson. Letters didn't come easily to me, and Ball was a hard master. I stumbled through the first passage of Matthew, wondering, wondering why I had to bother with so many names. I tried three times, got it right the second time and wrong the third. Ball slammed the book down and he said, "What can you do well?"

I shrugged. "Well, not plowing, they tell me. But I know my psalms."

"And they say you tell stories," the parson said.

"Everyone does." I yawned.

"And each tells them for a reason. What is your reason, then?"

"Which one?" I laughed and shrugged. "Lord, it passes time, and it makes me friends and sometimes it makes some folk I don't like leave me be."

Ball set a hand on my shoulder. "Tell me a story, son."

"A story?"

"Tell me the oldest story you know."

I fidgeted. "I know the tale of the Normans and the Saxons."

He said, "That'll do nicely."

I looked at his sharp, gnawing eyes; what did he want of me? I turned to the gray hills and began: "Once England was a free place, where we all lived in fellowship under one King. The King loved the poor and he would always listen to them. They were no great lords—all men were lords. There were no great bishops—there were a lot of holy saints who owned nothing. There were no bound men, no serfs. The poorest in the kingdom would be welcome at the King's table. Then, the Normans came."

I turned to Ball. He looked at me with his wheat-grinding face on and his hood pulled low.

I sunk into the thin, unhappy story. "The Normans came from over the channel and at Hastings they took England from the Saxons. The Saxons were hardy, but they weren't men of war, and they tried to love their new lords but they knew they were no better, now, than slaves, under a yoke like oxen. Their King could never be one of themselves, a Saxon, and—"

Ball seized my shoulder. "That's not the oldest story."

The interruption addled me. "It's the oldest I know."

"You can read the oldest in it, son—and that's what you have to learn. Two in one!" He pushed his hood back and his scant hair stood like whiskers. "The story of the

Fall."

I hugged myself. It was early April, after all, and nights were cold. The weather woke me. Ball cleared his throat.

"Adam and Eve lived in peace with one Lord, that being God." He opened his second book, the book that wasn't a Bible, and thumbed through. "Falsehood entered the garden, and it was Falsehood that made Eve and Adam's children forget that they came from the same mother and father. He named some rich, some poor, and told them many lies that sounded sweet to them, until they forgot God and worshipped Falsehood. That sour apple was the end of Eden." He chewed a blade of grass from root to tip, and plucked another. "But my story ends differently, son. You see, the gate is open again, and the family is reunited. All goods are held in common. Heaven and Earth reunite—become one. Allegories!"

I said, "I don't understand allegories, Father."

"Here." He pushed the book toward me. "*Piers the Plowman*, written by a holy man named Long Will. I want you to sound it out if it takes you ten years." He must have seen me shiver; he took a layer of black cloth from his back and set it round my shoulders. It was lousy, but thick, warm from his body. "You're to be my second voice," he said. "When they keep me from preaching, tell them your stories and tell them what the stories mean. I'll spread news and fire their spirits and you'll amuse them and confound the law. Now you know your purpose."

I sat, bundling the cloth tight till I was swaddled like a babe. I wondered what I'd gotten myself into, brothers. I knew Ball had been thrown out of the church, and I wasn't sure if I wanted to be thrown out myself. I thought of the clean Gravesend church, the wood, the glazed, bright Jonah in his whale, and of the lousy cloth I wore, so far from home, that barely kept the chill from my shoulders.

"If you like," Ball said, "you can take a false name—protect your family."

"Father," I said, "I want to be a parson."

"This will make a parson of you." Ball almost smiled. "Now, what shall we call you?"

He seemed to make a game of it, and I wanted to bound off and leave him with his rusty laugh and dirty crawling cloak. Truth told, I might have gone, but I was cold, and I couldn't face the thought of walking into that strange night alone. Funny, brothers, how your petty fear can lead you into danger. Yet there was more to it: I liked that story, and better, his ending. I loved the ending because it struck deep, like the best tales do. It rounded my old story out like dough worked between hands into a loaf. It made the tale complete and true.

"What will I preach, father?"

Ball said, "The truth." He started to thumb through *Piers Plowman* again, but he stopped, and said, "Appeal to their hearts, son, to the natural knowledge in their hearts." Then, he took up his pipe and played.

The tune was melancholy. We both could have done without it. I said, "Play Robin Hood."

He shook his head. "I can't abide a robber. If you travel with robbers you don't travel with God."

"Why did you play it then, that day at the town cross?"

"To make you come to me," he said.

I seemed to see the two of us from far off, sitting out in that lone place, one playing the pipe badly and the other, head on knees, telling himself story after story to forget the cold.

7. At Pentecost

On Whitsunday we rise at the pealing of a round, low bell. Our lord, Simon De Burley, gave it to the parish. He'd called it Harvest Bell, and bade us ring it before dawn on harvest morning. Truth told, it could have woke the dead. That day it roused us for the Whit-sunrise, the rising sun that grants a heart's desire.

The moon set, and the sky was fresh milk. Dew froze on the meadow. We bundled in sheepskin and Jenny caught a deep fleece round her with a hemp rope, like a hermit. We crossed crofts, trodding down ice till it crackled. Six neighbors walked with us, Faith, her babes, two cottars, Ned and Lise, who'd brought an ailing ewe lamb, and a big plowman who bore a sack of seed for blessing.

Lise took the lamb up by its middle. She turned its dottle of a face on her black shawl and rubbed its chill away. They kept five sheep, the ewe the lone breeder. Ned led us down a hill, over hedge dark as dung. We walked in a silence like deep music. It broke when ice broke, when hedge snapped, sometimes by a lamb's bleat buried in a shawl.

It gave me new blood, brothers, walking steady with still neighbors round me, walking all together toward the Thames bank. I'd been a jangle since the beggar's dance, and this walk settled Mike Row certain as a firm hand on a bell. The bargain I'd set, the long dance that set me swinging like a clapper, all that faded till my dome went milk-white like the sky. Granted, my heart still dwelled on faith I'd broken, and on one I'd betrayed, but what's all that to dawn, brothers? I felt cold earth, the warm flesh of neighbors. The half dozen of us were deep as kin, made kin by cold, and by our wishes.

We reached the bank in fair time; there, half of

Gravesend waited for the sun. Thus runs the saying: What
you wish of God on Whitsun dawn, the instant the sun
rises and plays like a wheel, God will grant you. We faced
the river, bundles with red faces poking east. Jenny pulled
her hood low, and sucked her plait's end. I felt a hand on
my back, too hot. It was Nettle.

"What are you going to wish for?"

I rubbed my hands together, breathing down like a
forge bellows. He pushed in close; we watched for the sun.

Tilbury bank blackened, first, then melted down to
naught—out popped the sun. It played and turned, a fire
wheel too quick to hold a color. I wished my will before I
knew it. Nettle's hand moved down and met his side, and
that was all I knew: Will's drifting hand and the sun.

"Ah!" one man called, "What a playing turning wheel
he is! What a ship floating out there, taking our wishes to
Heaven!"

Light caught the Thames. Sparks tossed like stars. We
staggered back, and Faith's babe, Mary, cried.

Faith whispered, "Girl, wish now or God will think
you wish to weep."

Her whisper broke the charm, and I was among reeds,
some flowering yet, between Nettle and Jenny. The tongues
of fire that lined the turning sun were heat and light again.
The dew thawed; I was hot.

Lise shook her lamb. She and Ned had staked both
wishes on its life. It spit a spoonful of grey bile, and
bleated. Ned took Lise's hand and they nodded to the sun
and turned home to dress for the festival.

Nettle's round, grey eyes were still pinned high. Jenny's had long fallen and she plucked the white, frail
flowers from the reeds and sowed the water with them.
She gave me a look and turned home. I followed, and Will
spun round and asked, "Can I walk with you?"

His apprentices carped on about the kegs they had to
roll up the green before noon. They were cunning lads
who'd likely wished for pocket pence and were set on
getting them that day. Will sighed and let himself be
dragged back to the brewery.

Jenny pressed on. She leaned into her heavy staff and

pulled herself through roots and flowers. I might have borne her, but I stopped myself; she had to learn to walk alone. Her face was bone hard under all the sheepskin. At the first rise in the road she stopped and spoke. "I wished you'd keep your bargain—that's all." She stumbled on, though every step brought on another wave of pain. At last, I took her arm, and she bore down so heavily I staggered.

"I'll keep the bargain," I said. "I'll be the tiler to your tiler's daughter."

"Oh, then what did you wish for?" She gave a ghastly smile.

"For—" I stopped short, but I had to answer. "To keep faith, this time." I'd hoped she'd think I spoke of our new bargain, but Jenny was no fool.

Neither was she fool enough to press me. She knew it had to do with Ball and she'd never poke at that old wound. She pulled away so suddenly she stumbled, but she soon found her footing. We walked on, mute, till Jenny spoke again. "I think Will Nettle wished I'd let him marry me."

I said, "Jenny, would it be so hard?" We pushed round a turning in the road. "Is it the leg? You ought to forgive him."

"Forgive him?" She stopped, leaned on her staff, laughed. "Ah—Michael, you don't know your friend. He's like a mule—his great love's burdening himself. If I forgave him he'd nose round till he found a new shame to bear."

"It would make him happy," I said.

She turned her weight toward the sun. "It's like him to want a cripple, eh? A woman fallen in his ditch!" She leaned her head back and her hood fell so her little head lay lone in the dark mound of rug and fleece. "Maybe if he loved me whole—not just the leg he snapped. Maybe if I knew in my heart it would bring him joy, and wouldn't be another burden to him." She stood straight and turned up toward our cottage. "No sense, brother. There's no ridding yourself of your poor, lame Jenny."

I walked at her side, and I thought of Will, rolling his keg up toward Saint Mary's green, skipping up a storm of grass and turf as he watched the playful sun carry his wish to Heaven.

At home, we shed the sheepskin and I dressed for festival. I slipped my new white tunic on, and stepped into a pair of yellow stockings. Jenny sat in the same damp gray dress she'd worn under the fleece. She shook her plait and yawned.

I frowned. "You'll be a sorry sight."

"I look tiler's daughter enough," she said. "Would she wear finery to greet the clerks, then? You think she strutted like a Southwark whore?" She glared, and I backed down. When she rose to go, I rose with her, like we were a pair of fettered felons. The morning's peace had shattered, and I knew the festival would mean another Essex beggar's dance. Likely, he'd soon have all dancing Morris, tramping with him down the road.

If we'd been in high spirits it would have been a glory of a walk. The Whitsun Ale was held in Mary's green. The dank town by the Thames was latched tight, and even ferries were moored to the wharf for holiday. The chalk shone through dry grass and turned the earth to gold, and fresh-washed sheep munched there, cloudy and still. Our neighbors, dressed in white and yellow, walked through that new white and yellow world, eyes on the sun. Church bells rang unceasing. Well before we reached Saint Mary's we smelled cakes and ale. We saw the yellow barn, the court of the Lord and Lady. Jenny would have passed it by, but I stopped at the gate.

A mock guard with a white sword called out: "Bread and Cheese! Bread and Cheese for all good Christians!" He tossed a loaf and wedge to me and called, "Bless you, love! Good Whitsuntide!"

Saint Mary's green was mad with white. The chalk church had been scrubbed till a film of chalk dust topped the holy water. A few folk had whitened dogs with flour and one hound rolled flour off in the green grass and jumped up in a cloud. Three lads held cakes aloft on swords and danced them into slices; they sold the crooked pieces for a penny. On the west end, round cheese was stacked for rolling. On the east end, a mount had been built for our Whitsun mime.

I asked a boy, "Where's the beggar?"

"Bound for Essex this morning," he replied.

At once, I felt such wild relief I seized Jenny under the arms and danced.

She tried to pull away. "I'll drop the bread!"

"Oh, the bread be damned! Praise God! Essex is gone!" The dull ache I'd felt since the dance fell away like the morning's fleece and I thought: What the devil! There's no need to bother with any more than Mike and Jenny! I danced my Jenny up and down till I was drunk with it!

Rob Billing waved, and dragged Joe over; he'd dressed his son like a friar. "Ah—she ought to dance with my little clerkly son! Let her be, Row. We have to talk business."

I danced on. "No business now!" I shouted, though Rob stood near enough to hear a whisper. "It's Whitsunday!" I wanted to bind my joy by cornering the old, bland man and telling him exactly what I thought of him.

"Ah, always business if you don't want to be a poor cottar forever," said Billing. He took my arm and pulled me off. Jenny caught herself on her staff and sat back with Joe. Rob went on. "Why can't you learn from your own brother, Alf? He's got a soft life in London. You see? It's possible—"

I grumbled, munching cheese. "No sermon now," I said. "What is it?"

"Some crows are pecking up my seed. A flock of them. I need some men to chase them off." He whacked me on the back. "Now, Row, it won't take long."

The music started, then, pipes, tabors, bells. "You're mad," I said. "Chase your own crows."

He smiled. "I'm paying triple, Row. I've already found ten men."

I shrugged. "You don't have eleven, then." I leapt back to the dance and found Faith Corning.

Faith was no beauty, brothers, but she had a sweet pear of a widow's body and green, clever eyes—and she could dance! Already she wore four ribbons of love-pledge. "You've a light heart today, story-teller," she said. "I only wish your feet were light as well!"

I laughed. "Faith, how old are you? Forty?"

She threw her head back. "Forty-four!"

"I'd marry you today," I said, "if you would have me." I didn't know what I was saying, and Faith laughed so hard that I turned back and ran straight into Will Nettle. I embraced him. He looked worried.

"Michael," he said, "Lord Simon's been seen riding toward the square."

I paid no mind. The lord of the manor always came to festival.

Will said, "He wasn't due till evening." Then he shook his head, and before he could speak again we heard the lord's horse.

Simon De Burley was over-dressed, as though he'd woken early for the sunrise and had stayed in velvet overcoat and cap. His horse seemed to be made of the same velvet stuff. Both horse and rider stood in a gray steam. Brothers, here's the worst of it: No one took note of them. The dancers, the dogs rolled on, the pipers played and played. He rode into the center of the square and it was only when he raised his voice a third time that the field of folk stopped short and stared. They grumbled. Then, they listened.

De Burley ran his hand under his hat brim. "Good men," he said, "Our seed is being stolen by black crows. I need stout lads to scatter them."

There are no serfs in Gravesend, but more than half of the families are Lord Simon's tenants. They give their lord his share of harvest and work for him on the days set forth by custom. Whitsun was a holiday. The tenants gave their lord smug, thin, smiles and they shook their heads.

De Burley looked as if he'd dunked his face in flour. He opened his mouth to speak, seemed to change his mind, and turned his horse to go.

Before the horse broke in a walk, Rob stepped out. He grinned, and his sly, sallow face was beaming. "All right, men!" he called. "Off to scatter crows from the *Billing* field!" He turned on his heel and walked off, followed by ten nervous field hands. The line paraded past the horse, and our lord watched them, red around the neck. As they passed, he pricked the horse hard in the side and tore off at a run.

The square was dead still. The noon bell ran so suddenly that half jumped and half laughed.

Some one whispered: "They call his *son* an idiot!"

I heard another man. "It's his wedding's made him cocky. In less than a week, it is. When it's over the man'll have more land than a lord."

As for his bride, Jill Campe, she stood where Billing had stood, in her linen shift and yellow shawl, eyes turned up so not to meet the seeking eyes of neighbors.

The piper played the first note, and Nettle's shoulders eased down. "Well," he said. "Only a cloudburst." He stared at the mound of round cheeses. The piper played a second, wandering note, and stopped again. We heard a horse—no, two horses, thundering toward the green.

The beggar hadn't lied; the horses were as big as that old oak, Magog, and their riders were like gods or trolls. One wore rough red and blue and a square white hat with a blue feather. The other wore no hat; his hair was cut so close he looked like a great, shorn sheep, though his eyes were more like the eyes of a wolf.

The first raised a long, broad knife. "Thomas Attwell!" he said. "Butcher of London!"

The second bowed a little, and he drew his hand across his forehead. His marvelous black horse reared back and snorted. We wouldn't have blinked had fire sprung from its nostrils. He said, "There's news from Essex: the traitor-lords have fled to London, and their fellows, Gaunt and Hales, have sent your brothers lawyers with indictments. The people of Essex forced all lawyers to swear allegiance to the King and True Commons, and the Chief of Justice, Robert Bealway, swore on the Bible that he'd never conduct inquests against King Richard's men."

Attwell said, "Brother Harry and I also bring news from Kent."

The charm broke, and the crowd moved toward the Londoners in earnest wonder. One lad touched the horse, stopped short, and stared.

Attwell went on: "Abel Ker, a great patriot, had overthrown the Abbey in Erith, not a day's walk from this

square. The Abbot has fallen, and all the goods of the
abbey have been given to the poor. All the bound men
have been freed."

I felt sweat fall into my eyes until they overflowed.

"Now," Attwell said, looking each of us up and down,
his eyes stopping, I fancied, longer than they had to on my
face. "Now they're selling the abbot's sheep at a farthing a
piece and burning his papers and scattering his pack of
monks."

Harry stroked his horse's mane. "Their heads, my
brothers, have been separated from their bodies." He
smiled. "We're here to find more to join us. We call on
you to swear allegiance to the King and the True Commons."

Each turned to a neighbor, and I don't know what my
neighbor felt but I felt my maw turn and play like the
summer sun.

The boy who'd touched the horse called: "I'll swear."

Attwell nodded him up and five younger lads followed.
The rest of us hung back and watched the mounted men
and new recruits.

They gave us one more look, with scant hope. Then
Attwell said, "At least give your sons weapons."

Hugh the smith, who carried his straw hammer in his
hands, said, "They're welcome to anything in the shop. I
only wish . . ." Attwell waited, but Hugh didn't finish.

When the company left, the garlands seemed to wilt
and the cheese smelled spoiled.

"Erith," someone said. "Not a day's walk. I have a
cousin there."

"Abel Ker," said a woman. "Who's Abel Ker?"

"I'll go when they go after Hales or Gaunt, or . . ." An
old man stopped short. "I'm too old to go."

Slowly, slowly, the square emptied. I looked back and
met Jenny's eyes. She held Joe's limp hand and I knew
what she was thinking.

She said, "Hugh's gone. I don't suppose . . ."

"No," I said, "the mime won't go on, but it makes no
difference, really, Jenny."

We both stared low, at the gray grass scattered over

with ribbons that used to be yellow. We two stood there with two others: Joe and old Jill Campe. Jill's eyes were still turned up, set on the sky.

She said, "I've lived a long time, and only once do I remember people scattering like this, looking at neighbors with such faces. Thirty years ago, it came, and they say it was sin that brought it. Some swelled till they burst black. Some spat blood. We prayed, and it passed, but it came again. We prayed, and it came again, and I think the devil sent it to make us forget there's sense in praying."

Jenny stood, then. She freed Joe's hand and drew herself to Jill Campe's side. "I know," she said. "I watched my sisters die."

The woman shook, and didn't look at Jenny. "Death doesn't stop there. First he takes away everyone you love and then he takes away the rest. It's like a poison shrivelled this land at the roots." Her thin grey hair came out of its ribbons and her round, blunt face was striped with tears. "Oh Robert Billing," she said, suddenly fierce, "At times like this the world turns upside down full soon enough without your help!"

8 . Death Meets Three Sisters

A king had three daughters and each was so wise and beautiful that their suitors were blinded by them, as by the sun, and no man was able to choose between them. Therefore, they lived in a tower in great loneliness, watching each man climb the long staircase, see them, and leave confounded.

The sisters loved each other very much, and each was glad that she had the other two for company, but they were also anxious to see the wide world. Each couldn't help but wish she outshined her sisters, and would be taken from the tower to a fine place across the sea where she could rule as queen.

Then came the great plague, and many died. Cities were emptied and villages were abandoned. Rich folk fled to walled castles, but Death found them there. Abbots locked themselves in their chambers, but Death had a key to every lock and found all who evaded him. The three sisters lived far away from all cities, and their tower was high. They didn't hear about the plague. They knew that fewer suitors came to call, and that made them unhappy, for they thought the world had given them up for lost. Therefore, they were very glad when they heard the door open and they saw Death.

"We greet you," said the eldest, "and we are happy to see such a fine looking man in our chamber for we were afraid that the world had forsaken us."

"Look, sister," said the youngest, "He must be a great knight." For he walked with dignity and power.

Death asked, "Do you not know me?"

"No," said the middle sister, "for we have been here all alone for a long time, and here we'll stay save for the one you choose."

Death looked at them and said, "I choose the eldest."

The eldest said, "Bless you, sir, for you are a great soul to have chosen where all have failed to choose." Death took the eldest by the hand and they left the tower together.

The middle and the youngest sister were very happy, for they knew that they'd be traveling to their sister's wedding. The days passed, and no news of the wedding came. They wondered over this, and they were certain that their sister would have sent them word, but as the months went on they began to forget about their elder sister, and they wondered if another suitor would come.

Indeed, one afternoon, the door opened and they saw Death again.

"We are very glad to see you," said the middle sister, "for we would like news of our sister."

"Sister," said the youngest, "he has grown more powerful yet." Death was taller now, and dressed as befits a king, in silk and gold.

"Do you not know me?" Death asked.

"We know you for our sister's lord," the middle sister said.

"I have grown strong and need two wives," said Death. He held his hand out to the middle sister. "You will come with me."

The middle sister rose, in great joy, and Death took her by the hand and led her from the tower.

Now the youngest sister was alone. She was happy for her sisters, but she dreaded the days to come. She missed her sisters' company, and she became sad and thoughtful. She began to remember a time when the sisters weren't alone in the tower, when musicians played in the courtyard and fine ladies and lords came to call. Then, she would lean out of the tower window and call her sisters' names.

One day, the door opened, and she saw Death. He wore a jeweled mantle and a high, bright crown and she knew he ruled the world.

"I need another wife," he said. "You shall come with me."

"Gladly," said the youngest, "for it is very lonely

here."

He led her out of the tower and she saw that the
world had become dark and strange, and that kings and
emperors had been overthrown and Death sat in their
place. She knew that, not long ago, she would have wept
at the world she saw, for it wasn't a world that would
marvel at her beauty. Now she didn't care, for her heart
had grown dry and her beauty was dust. She was not
unhappy, for she knew that she would have her sisters for
company, and that she would see the fine ladies and lords
at the court of Death.

9. Trouble at Home

For all we cared, it might as well be winter as Whitmonday. Still, most held to custom—most didn't labor. Nor did most sleep. At least I know I didn't. I'd spent the night drinking thin ale from a bowl and drawing circles round the rim till the clay played a note. By dawn, I had a crick in my hand and a sense of danger, thin and dark as ale.

More worn than drunk, I left Jenny asleep and blundered toward the Thames. The morning warped, like thin wood riding water. My neighbors played at idleness, but holiday had warped as well, riding something deeper. Two old men sat in a clearing by woodside, tossing dice, with hatchet faces. A pack of gossips lolled and beat the Erith news like laundry. I saw a few men bearing their weed hooks on their shoulders, off to work, all custom broken. I wanted to lose Abel Ker and letters and monks' heads on poles, but when custom was gone, what was left us, brothers? Ah, there was the sweet air, the strong smell of grass bitten through by turned soil, the low corn. That should have been enough, I know. It should have been.

I passed the watermill. The wheel was bright and turning, and I set my mind to all the Whitsun wishes, and my own: to keep faith when put to the test again. I thought of windmills, then, and grinding wheat. Then I walked off, with hope I'd leave such memories with the mill. The three fields lay southeast, wheat, barley, fallow. I crossed toward them. A lad stood vigil, the lone laborer, chasing doves away.

"Ah—!" he shouted. He was nought but a green bean waving a stick. "Go eat on the lord's fields! Hey—"

"Let me by!"

Someone pushed past, frantic, breaking through the

grain. It was Will Nettle. He bounded toward the road, toward me; his face was whey and his fair hair was stiff with sweat and—I grew white—blood! I blocked his way and caught him by the shoulders.

"Billing . . ." He was heaving, short of breath. "Let go! I have to catch them!"

"What about Billing?" My stomach dropped. "Was it—"

"They were wearing leather armor and they rode . . ." He pointed south, toward the manor house, and he turned to run and turned again, helpless. "They didn't even let him take his slippers." And crumpled in his hand were Billing's long, pale shoes.

"De Burley," I said.

"Lord Simon said Rob was his serf, Michael. He . . ." He raised the shoes by the toe. "I'd come by to settle the wedding cider. One struck me hard, but I'm all right." He put his hand on the dry blood and smiled weakly.

"And they took him off?"

"They're probably scared of the men from Erith." Will shook his head and turned south. The road was broken with hard riding; Billing's trail was clear. I saw the lad, watching us now, heedless of the birds. They ought to be afraid, I thought. The thought was like a thunderbolt; it knocked me off my feet. I steadied myself. "There hasn't been a bound man in Gravesend since our grandfather's time."

Will looked at me, eyes narrow. "Yes, but—"

"We'll call a meeting."

Again, he stared. "On Whitmonday?"

I paced, and felt my hands meet behind my back, kneading as they hadn't in three years. "We'll gather at Saint Mary's, in the square. I'll ring the bell."

Again, Will was awe-dumb. "But they're at the manor, Michael. I saw them—"

I set a hard pace—Will struggled behind, huffing. "Spread the word, Nettle!" I called. Then I broke away. I ran.

I don't know who I told or even what I said, brothers. You might say I was taken by a devil. If I'd stopped and wondered where the running led me I would have shut myself in a cellar until the fever passed. As it was, I only felt the dark power that fills you when you run, fast, toward or away from something. I didn't come to myself till I was up in the bell tower, arm-thick rope wound round two straining hands, pulled up, down, up, till bell was ringing me: ALARM! ALARM!

The green filled. There were men still in their Whitsun white, women bound in ribbon. Their blunt faces were frozen; the alarm rang, always, for two reasons only: the death of a king, the coming of plague. I found myself facing the neighbors I'd called to alarm, and my own alarm had passed, leaving me dumb.

I stood by the church door, and faced the basin of clear holy water. I saw my long face, twitching like a rabbit's. The parson, Father Wells, approached and took my hand.

"Michael, my son, what—"

I found my voice. "They've taken Billing."

I met deep silence. One man asked, "Who? The Essexmen?"

Another looked like he would strike him. "Brother—no, the lord. Our lord."

I spoke on; I told them what Will had told me. My voice wandered, but I knew my craft and soon drew them in.

At last, an old weaver, Ted, said "We'll make up a petition. We've bargained with Lord Simon before."

A young woman called, "Aye! Before the lawyers came. When we had a king—not a king's uncle!"

"What does a lord care for the likes of us? He can pick us like corn cockles if he pleases!" An old tanner spat. "He dances to the tune of merchants and lawyers—"

"The king would play a different tune!"

My neighbors talked at once, babbling so hot and swift that I waved for order for a quarter hour with no luck. Then Nettle pushed up, his head patched now. He still held Billing's shoes.

He said, "Well, we can talk, but what about Rob?" His voice was pained, not Nettle's voice at all. "If we're here we ought to do more than talk."

There was a long, shamed silence. I broke in and
asked who'd help me draw a charter. Six, Parson Wells
among them, joined me cautiously, as though I was a
stranger.

We trooped back to my cottage, and left the crowd to
wander. One young man wept. "Oh, I wish I'd gone last
night! It's come to this, hasn't it? For the fools who stay
behind!" His wife cursed my back as I turned my edgy
half-dozen away.

I'd near forgotten Jenny. She sat in the big, empty
room, with her lame leg up, and met my eyes. She bowed
her head. "Well then," she said. "I'll be off."

She struggled up and the six men who filled our front
room edged back as she passed into the bower. I asked
them to remain; I followed.

She threw herself back on her straw and gazed
through a gap in the thatch; the sunlight sprinkled on her
face like pox. I sat by her feet and told her about Billing.

"Ah," she said. "For the sake of a friend."

I looked at her in despair. "Jenny, I don't think I have
a choice."

"Oh, you have a choice," she said, her voice still as
Saint Mary's basin, and her face as empty.

"So I'm to leave Billing at the manor? So I'm to
abandon a friend?"

"So you're to abandon your sister," Jenny said, "because she didn't play the tiler's daughter."

I threw up my hands. "Well, I've come to find some
sheepskin. I can't stay."

"Is that what it would take? Watching the clerk lift the
skirt? Call in one of your friends!" She sat up, then. Her
eyes were bright; the dull voice quickened. "We'll run the
mime through now. Get a hammer!"

I looked back; had they heard? No, I could still hear
them chatter. Jenny sat up and pointed to the cabinet.

"Get your bloody parchment!"

I shrugged, searched the cabinet and found an ancient
strip covered with Alf's figures. It would do. I left Jenny
and pushed a long bench into the front hall to seat the six.
I drew a piece of charred wood from the grate for

scribbling.

They muttered, turned the paper round and guessed at figures. They seemed reluctant to begin. Ted Weaver broke in: "I'm the veteran here, and I know one thing: It ought to be in the name of the King."

I wrote that down. The parson spoke.

"And you must remind our lord that Billing has always been a good Christian."

Martin Cater, a man I'd never said more than two words to in my life, watched my hand suspiciously. "Where did you learn to write?"

"A priest," I said, not looking up.

Martin said, "What priest?"

"John Ball."

I could almost feel the hairs on the back of his neck rise. "They say there was a strange time in your past, some wandering friar, some trouble, but if you'd told me that before today I never would have believed you. I don't know whether to turn you over to the law or shake your hand."

The rest stared at me. I'd never known how many in Gravesend had heard Ball's name.

Another stranger, one of Billing's field hands, sputtered: "Right before Might."

"Skill before Will," I said. We both turned red. I'd never known another soul in Gravesend had received a letter.

The petition wrote itself. There were some quarrels over precedents in custom, as no lord had claimed a free man as his serf in Gravesend in our lifetimes. "Our Lord," I wrote, "Protector, vassal of King Richard, we commend your soul to heaven and appeal to you as brother Christians." We'd completed it in less than an hour, and we returned to the church to set a fair copy on clean parchment.

The rest of Gravesend heard it from the church steps, though they listened less than cheered. A quarter of the crowd had armed themselves. They'd seized their axes, rakes and scythes and now they held them high, waved them like death, and pounded Mary's green till it drowned out the words of our petition.

I called: "Now we choose three to bring the charter to the manor."

"Why don't we all go?" Tess Drew called. "It worked in Essex!"

"Because this isn't Essex." Ted Weaver frowned, and wagged a finger at the wimpled wife as though she were a child. "I'll go. I've bargained with Lord Simon De Burley before. He knows me. Besides—you'll need a steady head."

"Hey—" a plowman called. "How about old Billing's son?"

Joe was sought, and lifted, like a sack of meal, on two men's shoulders. He smiled a little, dazzled by the view. His fuzzy eyes brought on boredom like a sickness, and after a short spell, they set him down.

"Will Nettle ought to go! He's been wounded and ought to have compensation." I knew the voice of one of his apprentices.

Will stepped forward, and looked at me miserably. I seized his shoulder, and pretended not to understand his pleading eyes. "That's two," I said. "And I'm the third." The neighbors cheered, then, and they cleared a path and urged us forward. The noise, the heat, were dizzying, and for a moment I stumbled between Weaver and shivering Nettle without knowing where we were bound.

The manor lay less than three miles south, across open country. The wooly green hills smelled of clover. After a time even Will's spirit rose. He pointed to a road he'd taken from Dover and named a string of good inns on the way. We chattered about everything but the petition in our hands. We took turns bearing it, so our damp fingers wouldn't stain the clean parchment. We paused at a tavern of some fame, The Ram's Head, and it took pleading to keep Nettle from settling there for the rest of the afternoon. By the time we reached the manor gate, it was early evening.

The manor was surrounded by a low, stone wall, and the gate was a scant five hands high. I wondered if De Burley was a dwarf; it's hard to tell when a man's mounted.

"Sweet Saint Thomas," Nettle said, putting his hand to his mouth, close to chewing the charter. "Look at the ironwork! I haven't seen the likes of that since I left Dover!" The grill on the gate had been worked in knobbly circles. It seemed a poor match for honest ivy.

The gate opened. A guard stepped out. He was an older man with the sort of face you see on veterans of the French war, red and hard. He wore armor, and a low helmet. Nettle touched his bandage and looked at his feet.

I tapped him on the shoulder and I whispered: "We have every right to be here."

The guard scratched a pocked chin and frowned. "Where are the rest of you?"

Weaver spoke first. "We're here to see our lord, Simon De Burley. We'd like to speak to him concerning a misunderstanding with the freeborn Robert Billing."

"That's no news," the guard said. "Where's the mob following you?"

"We've come in peace, out of respect and loyalty, according to custom—"

"I know you, Weaver," The guard said, "but who are your friends?" Weaver introduced us, and the guard frowned. "Well, I know the upstart from this morning, and if I try hard enough I'll probably place the tall straw-head with the smirk on his face."

"You could find ill to say about Christ Himself," I said. "But the fact is that we carry no weapons and that things will go better for Simon De Burley if he sees us now."

Weaver gave me a look like poison. The guard left us waiting and closed the gate.

"Poor Rob," Nettle whispered. "Less than a week from the wedding."

Weaver was still fuming. "As if anything could go better with a knight, with a lord." He raised his arm; we could just see the turret of a watchtower. It was dusk now, and a light burned in the narrow window. "Watching for more of us, likely," Weaver said.

The guard returned. "Sir Simon will speak to you now."

A younger guard moved us through, and led us down a white stone path. The house was big as a church, and the door perched on a set of narrow stairs. The young guard stood and waited for us to pass, maybe to make sure we didn't stumble. He didn't look like a veteran of much of anything. His helmet was pushed back, and he scratched a line of short, curled hair. We waited by an archway, and he presented us.

Nettle gave Ted Weaver the petition, and rubbed his hands together. Weaver stepped into the manor first. The front door led straight into the lord's hall. It was a broad, high drafty place, though a hearth as high as two men roared across the room. We stood close for warmth.

De Burley looked warm enough. He sat in hearth-glow, at the far end of a little table with two retainers. He didn't look up when we were annouced. The three were gaming— I think you'd call the game backgammon. A man wearing a red turban twice the size of his dome moved a piece up and dropped it like a coal. Burley wore the same soiled velvets he'd worn Whitsunday. He nodded gently, raised his head. "I know one of you."

Ted Weaver bowed. "My lord, we've come . . ."

"Oh, I know why you've come," said De Burley. "And as usual, I'm willing to make a settlement."

Ted close to bellowed with relief, and Nettle squeezed my hand. As for me, I felt a seed of regret that I couldn't understand and couldn't crush.

"Our petition," Ted said. With ceremony, he broke the wax drop that served as seal and opened the white charter.

"Hmph . . ." De Burley pushed his chair aside and rose. The two retainers looked up once, and went back to their backgammon. "Never mind the petition. I have some charters of my own." He walked to the far side of the hearth and opened a small trunk. Now, off the horse and standing, I saw he was no dwarf, yet as small a man as I had ever seen. He worked the lock apart. It took some time. He had trouble with the key and he cursed till the dark lid belched once and popped open. He took out a small, iron box and drew us closer. We looked at one another and approached. "Now," he said, opening the second box, "Billing has been in my debt for some time. His grandfather was never legally out of my family's service."

And that's when he unrolled the seven charters, each stamped with so many scaley seals it looked a lizard.

Nettle whispered to me: "Read them."

I stepped forward and stretched out my hand. Burley turned white when he saw I could read. He rolled the charters up and set them in the box.

"Here's the long and short of it," he said. "Billing has three hundred pounds that are mine, and when he pays them, he's a free man." He coughed. "That's the settlement."

Nettle said, "Sir, he doesn't have—"

"Well, then he lied to you!" De Burley slammed the trunk lid down. "Bad example, he is, getting beyond his station . . . plague's made you think you rule England . . . causing all the trouble up north!"

Nettle and I looked at each other. I was living on my sowing wages till Lammas, and my garden harvest was a loss. Nettle's heavy earning time was autumn. Between us, we could have raised a little less than half a pound.

"My Lord," said Nettle, "Sir, Billing is my friend. Could I please see him? Just to let his son and the woman he's to marry know he's all right?"

"I fear that's impossible," said De Burley. He turned toward the hearth. "He's in Rochester."

"Rochester!" Nettle and I said at once. Weaver didn't speak. He stared at the floor, the charter dangling in his hand.

"And Aaron's off to see him, aren't you boy?" He turned to the dark young guard the way a master turns to a dog. "Off to the castle. There was some danger, we thought, from the Essex mob."

Weaver straightened. "Sir, this man is a Christian and of good repute and he ought not be ruined forever."

Burley nodded toward Aaron. "That's fine. Now you'll be kept quiet for a while, yes?" The older guard crossed in and we were caught between two spears.

Young Aaron caught Will and Ted by the arm and the

older guard seized mine. We were led past the bored retainers, down a set of stairs.

I'd been in prison before, and was twice as scared as the others. Will and Ted weren't handled gently, but my old guard dug his fingers deep into my arm—he seemed to like it. He poked me forward with his horny knee, straight out the door, into the twilight.

We were led toward a little hedged house. The old guard pressed me against the wall and worked the door open with his free hand. He threw me in with such force that I fell against a shelf of jars and sent them spinning.

Will and Ted followed. Once we got our bearings we smelled ale dross and malt barley and we knew we'd been thrown in the manor brewing house. The door closed, and the room was pitch. I heard the old guard's voice.

"He's a smart one, catching the ringleaders."

There was a mutter—maybe the other guard. We heard one walk away. My eyes found themselves. I saw Nettle and Weaver straining off the top of a cask. I shook my head.

The door opened again, and the young guard stepped in. Will and Ted froze with their hands on the lid. He didn't question them. He stood and stared. Moonlight streamed through the broad door behind him, and he was black from top to toe. It's not a fine thing, brothers, strange eyes on you when you're helpless. Still, he had some charity. He bowed his head and pushed the blunt end of his spear through dust and rushes as like he was ashamed. I thought he'd been set there to guard the ale, but soon he let us be and locked the door.

I asked Ted for the charter, and used it, pointedly, to blow my nose.

Nettle and Weaver emptied jars of spice and heather till the air was sick with the sweet stink. They ladled out the ale. I tried to start a fire with Weaver's flint, and I worried the crumpled charter and at last set the two men to twisting rushes so I could milk some warmth out of them. The smoke was worse than the cold, and it wasn't long before we stamped that sorry fire out, but not before I saw something worth seeing.

The place the spear had played was clear of rushes now, and the hard earth had been crossed and recrossed round a firm scratch like a post. With some wit, scratches could be sails, the figure, a windmill.

I blinked out the last smoke and sighed low. I slept. It would be my last night of sleep for a long time.

10 . Trouble Everywhere

My brothers, have you spent a night on bare ground? Scribe, you've seen hardship certainly, for you've a tonsured pate and you're dressed like a monk. And Mayor, you were born common, they say, and earned your bread as a fish monger. Well, I'm a man who likes a little straw beneath me when I sleep, and the brewing house floor was bare. Hedge roots gathered in a knot between my shoulders. I slept uneasily and woke with a line of sunlight in my face.

Will Nettle and Ted Weaver were still sleeping. They'd sorted out a bed from hempen linen used to strain the ale. I watched them with envy and at last turned my cunning to the weak lock on the door. Light seeped though long seams in the walls, and the brewing house was so flimsy I thought: three shoulders will crack it like an egg.

Will turned and yawned. "Michael, could you empty a nut jar? It'll do for a mug."

I rolled my eyes, but I found his jar. Then, inspired, I cracked the clay butt on the floor. Acorns scattered and the crash woke Weaver. He sat up and raised his eyebrows. "Oh, Row . . . what now?"

I swept the shards together, selected the sharpest, bent by the door, and worried the lock.

"It's no use, Row," I heard Ted say. "I tried that last night, after you nodded off, with one of the jars you shattered coming in."

"Being thrown in, you mean, Weaver," I said bitterly. I tossed the useless shard with the others and leaned against the wall.

Ted crossed his long, thick legs and leaned back deep into his straining linen. "That old guard's always been sour," he said. "Still, there was a time he used to like me." Light entered clear now, and I saw the dusty jars of nutmeg and heather, the bushels of malt barley and the kegs of ale, the low table, the cauldrons. The roof was so low we couldn't have stood straight up if we'd willed it. This gave us a fine reason to keep sitting.

Nettle the brewer was at ease. He eyed the room with a craftsman's interest. After a while, he said, "I guess we ought to be scared."

By what must have been late morning by the slant of light, we were sitting by the far wall with our backs to the shelves, talking and pretending we could leave when we liked.

Ted's great, gray eyebrows beetled low; he drank his round slowly. "It used to be different," he said, "when I came here ten years back, in King Edward's time." He told us, then, of his old, noble journey, the pony he rode, the two lads who followed with a banner, his honorable greeting at the gate. "It meant something then, to be Lord Simon's tenant. We had a claim on him, as much as he on us."

I asked him why he'd made the last trip, and he brightened, hot to tell the tale.

"Back when you were off wandering," he said, "we built a fine bathhouse by the Thames. We worked all winter, gathering stone and lumber, journeying to Newcastle for sea coal so we could fill whole rooms with steam. We had a great festival when we were done, in early spring, plowing time, and two old widows were taken on as bathhouse keepers. A fortnight after it opened, a man came."

I said, "Weaver, I don't remember any bathhouse." He shot me a look that said he wouldn't stand for interruption. I took my turn with the jar of ale.

"This man was a lawyer," Weaver said, "and he had a charter proving the bathhouse belonged to Lord Simon and his retainers. We had Parson Wells read it, but the words were all strange and he didn't understand more than half of it. And your brother, Alf, Michael—this is just before he left for London—he could read, but he just read it through and threw up his hands and said he didn't want to touch

the matter. Then Martin Carter said that the river bank was
common land. The lawyer asked him for paper proving as
much, and Martin thumped his chest and acted like a fool.
The lawyer, well, he was from London."

Then Ted talked for a long time about the lawyer
himself, his sober cloak all lined with silver fur, his tall hat
tied by a black ribbon.

"It was hard to talk a man like that down, Row. He
said we brought the Newcastle sea coal with our lord's
wagon, and cut timber from part of the lord's forest, and
when we disagreed, he asked for paper and we had none."

We'd emptied the first jar, and Nettle rose to fill it
fresh. He'd listened to the story with the same, dumb,
eager face he wore when I told tales.

"Well, we thought, and the Parson looked at the
village rolls, and then we made up a petition. No one,"
Ted added, "thought it proper to sound an alarm." He
smiled harshly and went on. "I presented it because I
spoke well, and I was greeted with warmth, and the Lord,
a young man then, took me in and treated me as a father
treats a son. He fed me capon and we talked over the
petition and came to complete agreement."

Then I remembered that a bathhouse lay two miles
west. None spoke of it.

"He would keep on the widows, the proper thing for a
Christian man to do. He would allow us to keep fishing
rights near the house. You should have seen him going at
the lawyer like a dog to a cat." Weaver whacked his knee
and snorted. "The lawyer said, 'You're giving way!' and he
wanted to take everything, but Sir Simon wouldn't hear of
it. Oh no! He said, 'These people are my children!'—that's
what he said!"

Weaver went on: there was the meal, a meal he'd
never see the like of again, cloves and saffron, red and
white wine, the lord's sister, who let him commend her to
God as if he were lord himself. He chattered, gay and free,
and I felt miserable. Nettle looked now at me, now at
Weaver. He shrugged.

"Well," he said at last, "Times have changed."

Ted nodded, and he shook the jar. "And I say it's

because we don't have a proper King."

This was news to Nettle. "Richard's a proper King, even if he is only fourteen."

"But it's his uncle, John, who rules. The man surrounds himself with lawyers, robbers like Rob Hales—he's cause of everything that's wrong with England! He's overturned the true order of things—worse than the Plague!" Ted drank and snarled. *"He's* the plague, truth be known, he and his kind! It's John of Gaunt that's causing all the trouble in Essex! His stooges like Hales who tax the people into going against their natures. True lords like Sir Simon suffer for it!"

I closed my eyes and sank into the hemp. "Careful, friend, or you'll be calling those men traitors, like the butchers from London."

"And why not!" Ted slammed the jar down so hard that it cracked. "It's Gaunt we ought to turn on—not the lords who love their King."

I said, "Good Richard — Bad John. It sounds like something out of Robin Hood."

Nettle brightened at the prospect of a tale. I complied and sat up, malty hands on knees, to tell the tale of the death of King John.

"It's said that John took Richard's rightful place on the throne, and he ruled like the devil himself, making paupers of his people and a waste of green England. One day, he was housed at a monastery, and he asked a good monk the price of a loaf. The monk answered: 'One penny,' and John swore he'd raise the price twelve-fold. That night, the monk took pity on the poor and poisoned King John's supper. He was dead by morning."

Ted sat up and said, "Gaunt always did care more for gold than grain. It would be well, I think, if our John was poisoned during the night." His voice held a new note that made me shiver.

After another hour, the door opened. A page in blue stockings, with a face like a weasel, said, "Go on home, then. Out with you."

Ted looked glum. Likely, we weren't as dangerous as they'd thought.

Nettle secreted a jar of ale in his hand and we were shown through the manor's back way. We had to circle round the wall to reach the road again, and when we saw the iron gate we knew the failure of our mission as though for the first time.

Whatever fellowship we'd felt back in the brewery vanished. The early afternoon sky was bright, heavy, cold, like metal. Our journey would be brief, and there would be sorrow at journey's end. Each seemed to walk alone. I heard Nettle weeping, or it might have been Ted Weaver. First we passed the fallow fields, and then the fields of straw. Then we passed the green corn, a croft once held in common. We saw the greenwood, common once, cleared now and filled with Simon's sheep. At the Ram's Head, Ted turned.

He said, "You think . . . we ought to go to Rochester?"

I bowed my head. "Useless," I said. I'd seen Rochester Castle.

We walked on, and I thought of Billing clearly. I'd been so caught fast in my charters and alarms that a vision of him, bound and hungry, hadn't found itself. I knew, at once, that the same picture never left Will Nettle. I glanced at him as we passed the empty Kings Arms. He tilted the jar of ale to his lips, blinking often.

We'd dreaded meeting neighbors on the street, but streets were empty. We thought they'd gathered on the church green, waiting, and we steadied our hearts and readied ourselves, walking to Saint Mary's; we met no one. That seemed right: to enter that bright, empty square, to stand like dolts with our arms flapping, at last to knock at the church door like strangers.

A beggar answered. He yawned; he must have camped there for the night. His great deep eyes stared out like mushrooms. He gnawed bread and said nothing.

Will stared. "What happened, brother? Has every soul in Gravesend died?"

He looked at his bread. "They're at the crossroads with Abel Ker," he said. "They're off to Rochester Castle."

11. The Siege of Rochester

"You're as good as your word," Ker said to me. "I like that."

I still didn't like him, though he was hoodless now, and warmer towards me.

"You've made a good start here," he said. We stood on a high, coned hill, overlooking crossroads. Below were what I guess Ker would call troops. Men and women, still in Whitsun white, waved longbows and torn ale stakes sharpened into pikes. One old man sat alone, sewing the final colors on a standard of a crown. Children dove in and out like flying fish, trailing bright flags. High, on raised thrones, sat Lord and Lady of the Whitsun Ale, robed in their white and playing with their lamb.

Ker went on: "You made a good start, but you got it wrong, of course. I might have done the same thing, the first time. You learn." He laughed dryly. "Fight for the sake of a friend. Well, you could have fought and you may die yet. Ha! Threatening De Burley's guard with no one behind you but a cowardly brewer and a weaver who think's he's back in King Edward's time. Jack the Giantkiller!"

I shivered, though the sun was beating hard. "Have you ever been to France, to war?"

Ker shook his head. "Might go eventually," he said. "I hear there's money in it if you're canny."

I wished for one true soldier, then, to turn us from this madness. My neighbors clustered close, and swore allegiance to the King in loving, sing-song voices, the oath they dared not swear the day before. Essex men, Ker's men, led them, and those Essex warriors were everywhere. They raised loud, quavering cries, pushed giddy dancers into even lines, and tried to turn the Whitson Ale into an army.

Ker swore me in himself. "Repeat," he said, face twitching, gleeful, a man with a fat fish in a net. "I swear full loyalty and love and service to Richard, my King, and the True Commons."

I swore. I had no quarrel with Richard, though then he seemed as distant from this trouble as the moon. I tried not to look at Ker, who talked of love and loyalty and whose eyes traveled over my neighbors as I'd seen grocer's eyes travel onions.

He paced. "We should be on the road by now. Damn them!"

I said, "It's a short way to Rochester."

He spat. "You've walked farther, so I hear."

I felt fight rise like bile, but I kept dumb. Ker turned and pointed. "You — woman!" he called. "Leave those children home!"

He'd addressed Faith. Her son and daughter held her soiled white skirt and stared at Ker with desperate, weary eyes. Faith puffed out like a toad. "Leave me be, devil! I'll take them where I please!"

Ker straightened, and stamped down toward her. Gently: "Woman, can't you see they're tired? They'll only hold us back."

Faith snarled. "Well, I'll drag them in my dung cart if I have to." Both children bowed their heads and groaned.

"It's over ten miles—" Ker began.

I broke in. "She'll keep up!"

Faith waved. "Michael!" She held young Mary high to wave as well. "Hey, I want to march with you! Not with this nutcracker from Essex!"

"Then march behind him," Ker said, "As long as we march soon." He broke through the crowd and called his Essexmen. "Get them ready—do you hear? We've waited long enough!"

Nettle pushed by with his apprentices. The boys were bare-backed, burnt to peeling, sweating hard. They dragged two kegs of ale in a cart. Nettle bounded up the hill slope and smacked me on the shoulder. "Well, here's a chance to make up some bad business, eh? All of Gravesend here, and walking till they're blessed dry!" The two lads looked at one another and rolled their eyes. One called up:

"Will, sir, I'm not going."

Will turned sharply. "And why not?"

He frowned. "Well, it's dangerous, sir. We're laying siege to a castle."

Will shrugged, and let the boy run home. He smiled and threw up his hands. "What do you think of that?"

We walked down together, and Will and his lone apprentice shared the burden of the cart. Nettle peeled off his shirt, and as I passed he called: "Where's Jenny?"

I hadn't stopped in since I'd returned from the manor. "She wouldn't want to come," I said.

He shrugged and heaved the cart forward. "I could have carried her. Another stone or two's weight wouldn't have made a difference." The young apprentice gave me a conspirator's look, and smiled.

Six strong men gave their weapons to their mates and set their shoulders to the Lord and Lady's thrones. Ker pleaded, but they would not leave the gilt oak chairs behind, or let the white shoes touch the earth. They rose: the Lady closed her eyes and held the throne-arms tight, as her perch wobbled like a ship riding a wave. The Lord looked seasick. Then they sat straight, with a bright dignity. The Lady stroked the lamb curled on her lap. I stood by an Essexman, a yard behind. There was no question that the thrones would lead. We gathered our packs, and the march began.

The thrones set a slow pace. Ker's company of Essexmen had no qualms about passing, and soon we lagged a mile behind. The Essexman behind me, stunted, broad, maybe ten years my senior, asked if I was armed. I shook my head and he gave me a little dagger.

"A leader's weapon," he said. He carried a yew longbow. "They say Wat Tyler wears a dagger." I thought of Hugh, who nearly spoke the part of Tyler and who walked far behind, weighted by the burden of half the tooled iron in his smithy. I didn't want to lead. Behind, where followers walked, the mood was robin-blithe, and I heard two pipe tunes and pounding tabors.

"I've never been to Rochester," a man called. "Ah—what a Whitsuntide!"

There was agreement, and a lad called: "Let's have a song!"

"Robin Hood!" a man cried, voice hot to sing.

"I feel like Robin Hood," another said, "or would if I had less to carry. As it is, I can't feel anything."

"Oh, you'll feel something soon enough. Likely a pike through your guts!"

"Some Whittuesday!"

"How about Robin Hood and the Merry Men of Gravesend?"

The man from Essex turned to me. "Hey, Jack."

I turned. "My name's Michael." I'd never met the man before.

"Well, isn't Jack your name? I'd swear your name is Jack," he said. "I'm just wondering—could we hear a tale?"

"Tell your own tales." I was shaken.

"All right then." His eyes wandered back to the road. "I'd just heard you tell tales, when I was young."

I kept walking.

"Now what Robin Hood would do," someone said, "is he'd disguise himself as pardoner, hear Sir Simon's confession, and blackmail Billing out of him by threatening to post it on the Rochester Cathedral door!"

"Ah, we're all sinners," a woman said.

That stilled the chatter for a while. It was just as well. The path grew steep; they needed all their breath for walking. The six men gave in at last, and left the thrones at a fork in the road. Ker was right. I soon warmed to walking, even when the road turned stone and root and heatstroke, but I wondered at the sudden staying power of my neighbors. I watched the Lady help the Lord over a rut in the road. Two stout men struggled with Will's ale cart. They lumbered over hill after green, evil, hill and praise stuck in my throat for fear the Essexman would call me Jack again.

We stopped for a rest at a willow-rimmed creek that ran into Rochester's river. We were nearly there; Ker's company had likely reached town. Nettle drew ale for a sun-dried circle, and gave away two droughts for every one he sold for pence. I wandered off to dip my hood in water, and I caught sight of Dopey Joe.

I wondered if he'd followed or been taken. Just then, he was alone, staring at his dolt's face in the creek. I don't think Joe knew about his father; I don't even know if he knew himself away from Gravesend. I crouched beside him and held out a piece of bread.

"Joe," I said, "why don't you sit over in the shade?"

He took the bread and sucked the crust; his eyes turned up and settled on my own.

I said, "Your father would want me taking care of you."

He turned his small wit back to the bread, and I shrugged. I guess I felt some envy, some disgust. I left him, dipped my hood so that it filled like a cup, and shook it till the water strained out through the weave. I set it on my head and walked back, dripping.

Two neighbors stopped me. "Is there a long way, yet?"

I shook my head and sprinkled them with water. My head felt cool and clear. It's a neat trick, Mayor, if you're ever out at noon.

They asked: "What will we find in Rochester?"

I shook my head again. They badgered me, but I broke free and trotted off for fear I'd start in worrying myself. I called my troop back to the road.

The last few miles were walked in silence; I think they'd begun to be afraid. I turned back once. Their Whitsun garb was sweat-soaked, and the yellow ribbons ran. Faith pushed on, and her son Art pulled his share of the cart where little Mary curled asleep. I knew, then, that Gravesend had likely stayed awake waiting for us to return from the manor.

We moved at the pace of the lamb the Lady led by a frayed, yellow ribbon. The road was easy now, a stripe across clay country's dark green meadow. Still I near called for us to stop and rest again. We might have halted on the edge of Rochester's own commons, but we were forced on. A woman bounded over, rolling down like a red bolder.

"Brothers!" she called. "Brothers! Sisters!" She seized
the first she came to, Hugh, by the shoulders and kissed
him on both cheeks. He stood, swaying a little, baffled,
blithe enough. She wiped her wet hands on a butcher's
apron and set her red hat on her wimpled head. "We've
worried after you for hours!"

I was pressed forward and she took my hand and
pulled me off, walking backwards faster than we'd walked
forwards.

"The others arrived long ago," she said. She waved
her arm out, over lush, cropped meadow, toward the city
wall. "Abel Ker has gathered companies of the Great
Society and they're prepared to lay siege."

Her bounding walk forced us to follow at a trot. The
Lady slung her lamb over her shoulder, and men with
heavy pikes and scythes shrugged them back, and all
listened, trotting, to news wilder than we could have
dreamed. She said the city had been mustering for our
coming since they'd heard of Billing's capture. She said that
men had come from far as Erith, and a scattered few from
distant Colchester.

"The city's yours, my friends." She'd turned round
now that she'd set the pace, and she threw her leaden arm
around my shoulder. She spoke with warmth: "Ker
marched his company through the city gate. You'll do the
same." She bowed and introduced herself as Joan, the
butcher's wife. "We've slaughtered enough to feast a
hundred thousand tonight!"

Hugh piped up. "Well, there's a piece of luck! She'll
slaughter the Whitsun lamb!"

The wall was close now, and the sun on stone had
turned it brown and humble, like baked bread. I looked
now at the city wall, now at Joan's bloodshot face, and I
shook myself. "Have you freed Billing?"

She sobered. "He's in the castle keep—along with the
troops, that is, the troops still loyal . . ." Her eyes went
narrow and she whispered, "They can't hold enough of
their own men to protect more than the castle keep. The
rest have joined us!"

We reached the gate—it was flung wide, hinge broader

than two hands forced crooked. We stepped through and pushed into a narrow street stuffed with wild strangers. I looked for Joan and couldn't find her. We poked between two leaning rows of gray shops and taverns, inns with six-foot ale-posts crossing like thatch, broad trade signs hung eye level. Twenty sweet and sour smells met our white smocks and melted them. A baker with a green feather in his cap passed out white cakes. An alewife bellowed from her tavern roof: "Drink to Billing's health! Drink to the health of Abel Ker! Of Wat Tyler!"

I caught sight of a banner crafted like a windmill, sails turning. Will and Skill, I thought. Then I remembered the guard at the manor brewery; De Burley had said he'd be in Rochester. I looked for him, but the street was full of renegade guards and it was hard enough to find my own neighbors. I strugged to remember the man's name and called it once: "Aaron!"

Nettle was on the roof now, shouting at the alewife. Faith was knotting a torn end of our crown standard. I caught sight of Ted Weaver, heading down the thin slope of an alley that led to the castle wall. I felt alone and flustered, anxious to meet even Abel Ker.

Well, brothers, I got my wish. I saw him on a brown stone by the town hall. He'd cupped his hands and he was calling for order, again and again. His voice was flat, but it carried well. After a while, he had the crowd's eyes on him.

He said, "We've come for Robert Billing, a free and loyal subject of King Richard!"

At once he was drowned out by cheering. I couldn't help but be moved, as they cheered for my own friend. Ker cut right in and went on.

"The traitors are in the tower keep. And tonight, tomorrow, for as long as it takes, we will lay siege."

The roar came up again. I eased back on my heels and looked down, toward the castle. Later, I learned it had been new-mortared, to hold fast against Frenchmen. The walls were fresh-patched, yellow, grained with white, like cheese. Dry ditches lay all round it, and the great north drawbridge was raised high. We'd have to cross the ditch and hack our way through the raised gate. Once crossed and entered, we'd be in the court; there we would have to take the castle keep. All hushed, and I turned and saw Joan the butcher's wife leading a thing, like a bound beast, on a chain.

It was wider than two hay carts, made of black, smooth wood, and its crossbeam balanced a mighty spoon with a deep, round bowl, and tied back with a length of cord so black it might well have been braided in hell. Ker pointed and beamed.

"Brothers—a mangon!" He told us that the mangon had been captured, at great risk, from the castle itself.

We looked at each other. One old man started to laugh. "So we take great pots of spoiled gruel and fling them at the castle?"

"Stones!" Abel shouted, roaring over the weak laughter. "We throw stones, things on fire!"

A few moved toward the mangon, slack-jawed, staring. One man took his tiling hammer and hit it soundly on the cable. It quivered. All gasped and staggered back.

"No fear—it's empty!" Joan called. She put her hands on her hips and cheerfully told us what it might have done, had it been full. It took a while to know its power would face not us, but the castle wall. I turned and saw some dozen men and women loaded up with rope and lumber, set to bridge the castle ditch. I felt lightheaded; for the first time, victory seemed possible.

I wandered over; they worked like bridgesmiths born, and soon the knitted timber would be sound enough to hold the mangon. Already some had crossed the bones of bridge, working from the far end that hugged the castle wall. The drawbridge was raised tight, but certainly we'd break through before dawn. The keep was another tale; who knew how many guarded Billing?

Art, Faith's son, followed me. "Michael—" he called. "Don't go. Look!"

I turned in time to see a march, the last march of the Whitsuntide. Nettle led, bearing a heaped tray of roast lamb, and a long line followed, singing, piping, dancing something almost like the beggar's Morris dance. Then came the Lord and Lady, walking now, with bowed heads, scattering their garlands. Near at their heels, Rochester's butcher marched. He carried the lamb's head on a high pole.

The march was known to me—I'd seen it every year, save the years I'd been away from Gravesend. I couldn't understand the pricking in my shoulders and my neck. The lad pulled at my hand, frowning.

"Michael, you don't want to miss the lamb."

I shook my head. "Not just now, Art. Thanks."

He ran off to eat his share and left me at the far end of the bridge. My eyes passed over the long trail of broken garlands, and I tried to shrug my mood away. I pushed two workers back and crossed the half-built bridge which ended at the castle wall. I'd crossed worse bridges, and danger cleared my head.

Yet once I'd reached the wall, I saw that I'd taken the dare too lightly. I looked over my shoulder, and saw no bottom to the ditch. I thought of Jenny falling, light hair free, mouth open. What did I know? I hadn't been there. I felt not so much shame as a sudden wish to fall myself, land clean on my sound leg, and limp home. I clung to the wall. One man called from behind: "Are you steady, brother?"

I picked at mortar. "Steady as a stone." I flung a few stones back.

"Ah!" he called. I wish I'd had the nerve to turn around and meet his eyes; he sounded like a good man. "Tearing the castle apart with your bare hands, are you?"

"That I am!" I called back, tossing off a loose, light crust of rock and mortar.

Then I heard Abel Ker. "Very bold," he said.

"We could take it apart," I went on, "if there were enough of us."

Abel said, "There are never enough."

I looked back, then. The first man was gone, and I saw only Ker and his devilish machine. I jumped for the bridge and crossed, and I sat on the dry grass by the ditch's edge. Abel set Joan's stock of bacon fat alight, as the Mangon flung it toward the raised drawbridge. The sky

was dark now, and the flame was like water, but I was
unmoved. My head was full of a vision, of a hundred
thousand of us tearing a castle apart with our hands.

12 . The Fairy Garden

Once there was a little village by a river. The people were happy, and they kept a garden near the church. There, women grew vegetables, men fished, and the children climbed the big, old trees that grew along the water.

One day, a baron saw the garden, and he thought: "I've never seen a place so lovely, and so fit for a nobleman. My son can shoot harts in the shade and my daughters can float along the shaded river in a barge." He took three gold pieces and searched the village for the owner of the garden.

Now a young plowboy named Jack often fished in the river. The baron saw him sitting by the bank and asked, "Whose land is this?"

"It's mine," said Jack.

The baron was surprised, for Jack's clothes were all tatters, and he thought: "This boy is cheating his master." Still, he offered Jack gold for the land. Jack refused.

"This land is mine, but it isn't mine to sell," he said.

The baron frowned, and thought, "This little thief has lost his nerve." He rode on, and he found a weaver picking pears from a tree by the water. He asked the weaver, "Whose land is this?"

The weaver said, "It's mine."

The baron laughed, for the weaver had more hole than shoe and his hands were hard and streaked from the loom. He thought, "This man is cheating his master." Still he showed the weaver three gold pieces.

"This land is mine, but it isn't mine to sell," said the weaver. He gave the baron as many pears as he could carry, and sent him on his way.

Finally, he met an old woman digging turnips from a garden plot. He asked her, "Whose land is this?"

"It's mine," she said, "But I'm only keeping it for the fairies."

The baron laughed. "Well, the fairies have enough gold of their own. I shall build a fence around this garden, since none claim it, and my family shall confound the fairies." Laughing, he rode away.

He returned that afternoon with a dozen men. They set to building a wooden fence around the garden, and by evening it was done. They locked it with an iron lock and went home to sleep.

The next morning, the fence was gone.

The baron rode three times around the garden. The plowboy fished along the bank, the weaver picked his yellow pears, and the old woman dug turnips. All greeted him respectfully, but none could answer his questions.

That day, the baron set two dozen of his men to building a stone gate. It was as high as a tall man and was locked with two heavy bolts. The men worked till past their supper time, and the baron looked at the new fence with satisfaction.

The next morning, it had disappeared.

The baron threw up his hands in disgust. He brought fifty-three of his best men and they worked until midnight on an iron fence which overreached the trees. He sent fifty home and left three to guard the garden.

Two of them were so weary with their labor that they fell asleep. The third man dozed, but all at once he jumped and swore that he was dreaming.

A hundred in skirts and kerchiefs worked the fence apart with axes, hammers, and hands. They passed the parts along, all the while singing:

> Be you common—be you noble—
> Always be you wary!
> Two things you cannot confound:
> Thunderstorm and Fairy!

The guard tried to wake the others, but they slept on. He dashed through the village, and looked in every window. The women of the village were in their beds asleep.

When he returned, the fence and the singers were gone.

The baron rode through the next morning, and the guard told him of everything he'd seen. The baron shook his head and said, "No garden is worth this much trouble. Leave it to the fairies." He left the village and didn't return.

The village men returned the skirts and kerchiefs they had borrowed from their wives and sweethearts, and they enjoyed the garden for the rest of their lives.

13. A Victory

By dawn we'd blasted through the main gate, and we wheeled the mangon over the lumber bridge. Just as it reached the far end, a cable snapped. Wood showered down, and left the few score who'd passed before the mangon stranded in the court. The rest looked on, or plodded back to town for new lumber and cable.

I was among the stranded sixty, and like the rest, I turned full round and saw no castle keep. I saw the yellow walls, the yellow grass. The keep itself, like a charmed castle in a tale, had disappeared.

"Crosswall," I heard someone say.

The wall we'd taken for the keep itself only crossed the courtyard, and it would have to be passed, if we wanted to reach the keep, and Billing.

Ker tried to pelt that crosswall with fire and stone,but it was hard as earth's bones, and the mangon's fire barely scorched it. Five men poured the stones and fat and fire into the bowl. Two ropes formed the bridge now, and some spidered across, joining the new bridge builders, or circling south to the small gate that led straight to the keep.

A man with a wild, harsh face walked to the crosswall and kicked it. I asked him if he knew Rob Billing.

"Oh yes," he said, in a snap of a Rochester voice. "A great man, a man who defies traitors!"

Twice more that morning I asked strangers if they knew my friend. All claimed to know him well. One man died that day, loading the mangon. He spilled the flaming grease down his side, and he lay in the court, open wounds filling with straw. Faith cleaned his wounds with cold water, but it did little save turn the dust round him to grey mud. Ker stood by him; maybe he was a friend from Essex. He let Ker tip of cup of ale to his lips. He seemed a giant, so heavy, so tall, in so much pain. The foam ran down his beard. He looked up. "Who's Robert Billing?"

Ker whispered, "A free man."

He closed his eyes and Ker tended to the mangon himself. I saw Dopey Joe watch the bacon fat with glazed, round eyes.

Most were bored. Our mangon held less glamor in the clear day, and the crosswall let the fire roll off like surf. Half of our three score pushed the laboring bridge-menders aside and headed home. Not for the first time, I wished for a soldier, a man who could order spirit back into our sorry flesh. I thought of the old veteran at the manor. Then I thought of Aaron, and I froze.

I looked toward the keep turret. Aaron, whose family name I didn't know, was there. I knew it as I knew my own true name.

"Nettle!" I called. I waved and cried out, and at last he came.

He mopped his forehead. "What a business," he said.

I seized his arm. "Follow me."

He struggled, but I backed him to a corner and I told him what I'd seen, the windmill scratched out in the brewery dirt.

He shook his head. "I don't understand this windmill business."

I said, "There are mills in the letters! In Ball's letters!"

"John Ball?" Then, he looked frightened.

"The mill with the four sails! Will, Rob is safe!"

He was willing to know that much. His shoulders eased back, though his eyes still traveled up and down my face as if he didn't know it.

I went on. "We have to reach him."

He nodded. "I'll get Abel Ker."

"Damn Ker!" I turned back and glowered at Ker as he loaded his mangon. "He'd ruin everything. This is for us, Will."

His eyes narrowed. "Well, Michael," he said. "Pardon, but isn't it, you know . . ." He turned his eyes up and nibbled his lower lip till it was red. "Isn't it foolish for us to go in? De Burley knows us."

I grinned. "If we run into De Burley, we're dead anyway."

Will must have figured he was dreaming, then, or anyway he followed me just like you follow those dark folk in dreams. We passed through the courtyard unnoticed, and crossed the bridge, hurrying down a greener way, past young trees, toward the south. The south gate was scant four hands high; for the first time I knew that they kept gates small to keep troops from bounding through them in a hurry. This gate was just broad enough for two to pass at a time. The gate had been buried in ivy, but the small band gathered there had long since hacked the greenery away. All were strangers to me; none knew Billing. They didn't greet us; they were busy working at the iron and wood. Two men and a woman were digging under the gate; they hit raw stone. I watched them wedge their spades below, sigh, and lean, for a while, on the spade's blunt ends, mopping their foreheads, chatting. Then I turned east and saw a ditch.

"Hey there!" I called. The woman looked up. She was a little older than me, with clear eyes and strong, round arms. Her hair was pushed into a stiff, small cap, powdered over with earth. I took her under her arms and kissed her.

"Hey!" she called, laughing, struggling down. "You're younger than you look!"

Then I was off—I jumped into the ditch.

It wasn't as deep as the bridge-ditch. I landed on my side, rolled up, and blinked earth from my eyes. The sides of the ditch were loose and steep; that was fine for my purpose, less fine if that purpose failed. I stared up at the sun. Then I heard a shout and backed off.

Nettle fell harder, almost on his spade. He rubbed his eyes and smiled in shame. I looked at him, amazed, a little angry.

"That was pretty foolish," I said.

"Well, I'd really meant to throw the spade, but I fell with it." He rubbed his elbow. "That's why I fell so hard."

We set our shoulders into digging. Will used the spade, and I used my hands. We'd meant to share the spade, but by the time my hands grew too cold to work properly we'd hit the wall, and in our joy, we forgot the bargain. Will delved and I burrowed, blind as moles.

It was past midday when we saw day's light. My arms were white, chilled through. I threw my head back and smelled grass, sun, stone. My eyes cleared, and I choked. There was the keep.

We splayed ourselves down in the short grass, and I looked up again and went dizzy with height, weight. My eyes followed the seams of the squared corners. There were windows everywhere, and in every window an armed man. I felt Nettle close by, pressing me forward. I closed my eyes for courage and I crawled.

We must have been marks as easy as white coneys, but we had no trouble. We hugged the wall and held our breath. I found a deep barred window, not twenty yards away. I brushed Nettle's shoulder and I rolled across the field; he overtook me. Together we crouched on either end. We dared not look in, for fear of being seen. We listened.

We heard this: "How far have they gotten?"

Then someone said, "They're up to their necks in the crosswall. By the devil, this is getting tiresome."

The first man said, "Things have been going well."

I ground my cheek into hot stone and shivered with the weight of those words. Then we heard this:

"Well, I've got the keys, save one. The lord's swallowed the key to the south gate, I bargain. Come supper, we'll be out with Billing."

I called down, soft at first. Then I pressed my face between the iron bars and bellowed: "We've made it through! Let us in! Let us in!"

I heard a man step up; I was face to face with my guard. "Aaron Stone," he said. "We've met before."

Will crowded next to me. "Where's Rob Billing?"

Slowly, they drew Rob Billing to the window. Rob's lean face caught the light, and his eyes filled with tears.

Aaron went on. "We parted company with Lord Simon last night, brother." He turned a key and opened the barred window out so suddenly that it caught Nettle on the nose. "Our work here's almost done, but the lord's got the key to the south gate in his belly."

A lad, fifteen maybe, stuck his head out. "Are you one of the men from Essex?"

"He must be," said another. "Look how dirty he is."

Will said, "I'm a brewer by trade." Then he reached in and helped Billing out. Rob shook in Nettle's black arms like a babe. He was half-naked, crawling with lice. Will stroked him. "Tomorrow's the wedding, Rob. Jill's waiting." Then, he turned to me. "Michael, we're going home."

I felt a hard hand on my back. "Where are you going, now?" Aaron asked.

The lad called, "I hear they're off to Maidstone, to see the tiler!"

"Some folks will go on, I guess," said Nettle. "But some folks have had enough." He whispered to Billing. "Go out—see them. They'll want to see you." His voice was his own again; he might as well have been back at the King's Arms.

Aaron Stone said, "I'll go with you. Chances are there's been some trouble out front." He looked back. "De Burley's shivering somewhere there, but you've made a clear way for us and we won't bother with him." He turned to me. "I'm at your service."

Nettle crooked a free arm round my shoulder. "At someone else's service, friend. He's going back to Gravesend."

Stone smiled, and looked at me hard. "Is he, now?"

Rob looked through me. "You can't miss the wedding." He laughed weakly.

Aaron led us down our mole hole by the south gate. Billing seemed blithe and calm but he never let go of Will's hand. The busy laborers looked up and dropped their hammers. Between their wide eyes and the pounding sun I felt a ghost. Then I called, "We've freed Billing!"

They made a ring around us, and pushed closer. First one pointed to Aaron and called, "That's not Billing!" Someone whispered in his ear. The woman I'd kissed jumped, kissed me again, and ducked. Before I found her, I was on a pair of shoulders.

They came like a cloudburst, dozens, hundreds. I

looked back and saw Billing bobbing on shoulders, face dull green. I liked it—I'd not seen the wide world shoulder high since I was a lad riding my brother Alf's back. The warm heads, smelling of sour sweat and sunlight, dust kicked up by dancing feet, the great line weaving in a dance behind us—it made me drunk. I let the bliss take hold and settle deep; it would be my last chance before I returned to Gravesend. Nettle rode shoulders as well, though he tried to climb down. I waved to him and laughed.

"We're heroes, Will!"

"I'm tired," he said.

We settled just beyond the patched bridge, and I was forced to tell the story twice. On second telling, I began to feel uneasy. They were looking at me hard, with recognition.

Then, I saw Abel Ker. He stumbled down, arms crooked round two men's shoulders. His chest was burnt black, and his face was as grey as sand.

Someone whispered, "It happened two hours ago—mangon fell sideways. The prisoner's son fared worse."

So Joe was dead. I didn't look at Billing.

The same voice added, "He wanted to see you."

I sat still, as Ker was set, stiff with pain, beside me. "Hello, hero," he said. "Hello, Jack."

I tried not to back off; all eyes were on us. "My name-"

"You don't like me, Jack," Ker said, "but you're very like me. You don't fit." He didn't seem to speak to me, but rather to the crowd. "You'd like to live a quiet life, but discontent is in your blood. You'll die like me, Jack Straw."

He drew them in to carry him away. I couldn't move. The Essexman who'd marched beside me and who'd given me my dagger shouted: "That's it! Jack Straw!"

I said nothing.

"Jack Straw who traveled with John Ball and put straw in his hair and spoke when Ball couldn't! Jack for Jack the Giantkiller and Straw because you pushed a plow, you used to say!" He started toward me as Ker moved away. His eyes were bright, his bad teeth gleaming. "Jack Straw!"

"Go away!" I bellowed, though I knew it did no good.

"You said you were a black sheep from a gentry family

of Culpepper, or you were a priest, or you were a miller, and all the while we knew that you were only seventeen or less! You've been in jail three times!"

I put my head in my hands. The crowd moved closer.

"And when Ball disappeared for the last time you disappeared as well!"

I was in the center of a crowd that longed to stare at my bowed, broken face and know it. I couldn't raise it. I'd been found out and I could never live a quiet life again.

If I had looked, I might have seen Ker die. I knew the last meeting had strained the last life out of him, and I knew that he'd courted death to keep me out of Gravesend. I could have wrung my hatred tight, like hemp, or cut it with a knife. The crowd asked me where I'd been, if I'd heard from Ball. Would I come to Canterbury to free Ball? They were going to Maidstone. Would I lead them?

I looked up. Nettle had had his hand on my shoulder for a quarter of an hour and I hadn't felt it. Billing stood close by, face frozen. His were the first words I'd heard properly since Ker's.

"I'm going home," he said. "What ought I tell Jenny?"

I said, "Tell her I'm sorry."

Then he said, "Ought I have the wedding, with Joe dead?" Then, "Would you come?"

"And bring full force down on Gravesend? Oh, they'd love to get Jack Straw." My own voice sounded raw, altered, as though three years of friendship hadn't been.

"Please, Mike . . ." Nettle said.

"Call me Jack," I said. "That's my name."

He cleared his throat. "Please don't think we'd tell anyone. Don't think you can't go back home."

"Of course I can't," I said. "Not now."

He looked at me with new, hard, earnest eyes. "Do you want to go back?"

"No," I answered, easily, and it was true.

I'd come to Rochester for the sake of a friend, but I'd go on for the sake of myself, the self I'd hoped to leave behind and which had followed me and taken me by the throat. Brothers, Jack Straw is a mean bastard, a liar, an actor. He's no man's brother and no man's friend. Could I redeem him, as I'd wished at Whitsun? No, not Jack Straw, who'd betrayed John Ball in the end, the last time he'd been sent to prison.

Nettle said, "I'll stay with you, Jack."

"I don't want you, Will."

"You do," he said, "but you don't know it."

The crowd lost interest when they saw I wasn't going to tell tales of old adventures. Was I coming with them? They took that for granted. Only Nettle stood by me, hand on my shoulder still. I couldn't feel it, yet if he'd taken it away I would have crumbled.

"I'm your friend," Will Nettle said.

"Yes," I said. "I know."

TWO

1. Wat Tyler

They tell me the traitors fled north, to your London, Mayor. I led my weary troop of strangers south. There was no true direction then—no place to run. I'm not sure what became of Rochester. I piece together naught but a high blaze, a stack of smoking parchment, the mangon rolling down an alley like a loose beast. The smell of smoke might have been a tonic days before, but my heart was elsewhere, and I remember only blinking ash out of my eyes and wanting to sleep.

There was no rest that night; all mustered to walk fast and far. Dusk settled in near midnight, and when God's light failed they sparked their own. They packed and sang round fires that turned Rochester sky a blooming rose. These folk were armed. If Gravesend had turned pitchforks to pikes, these men held pikes in earnest. There were many bows among them, and broad axes. The faces were axe-sharp; they'd seen death now, for all the victory. Where were my neighbors? Some followed Billing home, and some stayed on. The few who stayed didn't know how to treat me, and I kept clear of them. I bartered a good belt for a suit of dark green and a cloak. The tailor's wife sold my Whitsun white to a rag pedlar for a farthing, and with that thin coin in my purse I left Rochester. I walked with men who knew the road to Maidstone better than Jack Straw, but they pressed me to lead them, as they knew my name.

It was a sweet road, over quilted crofts, and we walked at a high pace, twice the pace of Whittuesday. The distance was near even, maybe longer, but we reached Maidstone by high noon. The air was cool, and wind blew through a cluster of pear trees. My new tunic smelled of sweat, ash and pear, a sound, strong scent. I might have liked the walk for its own sake, abreast of good walkers on a long, bright road. Instead, I felt a stirring horror, and my maw churned like a full pot on a fire.

My company was Kentish, but I knew no more than twenty faces. A standard bearer clung on like a bramble; I couldn't shake him free. He was a tall lug who carried his broad, blue standard like a barge lofting a sail. Wind would force him forward and he feared to pass me, so he'd scramble back and lose his bearings. Sometimes he'd fail, and knock me forward with him. When wind was low, he'd ease his pained grip on the standard post and try to get me talking.

He began: "In Maidstone, we meet Wat Tyler." I didn't turn round to look at him, and he thought it worth repeating.

At last, I said, "I've heard of him." Hugh was with us yet, and he still carried his straw hammer. "The man with the daughter."

"A Brother of the Fellowship of the Great Society," he said. "He's an old soldier, beloved by the King."

"Many men have been to France, " I said. The high wind in the standard forced us far ahead of the troop, and I stopped short by a crossroad, uncertain of the way. I turned round. The standard bearer tilted his blue banner west, grinning like a dolt. The standard was worked through with yellow nettle thread—a hammer poised for hammering. I turned back, and trod down the broad west road.

I thought, an old soldier will be handy. I was no leader, and the troop of three hundred I led from Rochester had three hundred things to say about where we would go from Maidstone. There were veterans among them, but none seemed to take trouble in hand. I might have set them blazing with a tale or two, but truth told, I was full up with my own story, and moped on like a sheepdog leading three hundred testy sheep, like a sheepdog with no shepherd.

And like a dottling dog I tramped down Watling Road, a Roman Highway, with no mind to danger. The hedge might have been stuffed with Gaunt's spies and armed men, but we walked in bright noon, weapons slack on our shoulders or clean packed away. The sun made me giddy and my hood made me hot. I mused and moped, and plodded in my own grey fog. Nettle fell in beside me.

"Jack." He stumbled over the name. "Billing married yesterday."

"You can still turn back," I said.

Nettle kept pace. I wondered if he knew I led the company. "I hope Rob got the cider I left him . . . the day he was taken." When I didn't answer, he fell back into the Gravesend troop, under their standard of the crown.

We reached Maidstone by their market's closing; the sheep in their fenced croft bleated a chorus; I fancy it was the first time they'd met a flock of men. Bells tolled; we'd been sighted long before. We entered the town square, and hawkers pushed their fruit and wool and plovers' eggs in our faces. All Saints was dressed with Whitsun flowers; that near brought tears. Gravesend ran for the taverns. I turned to call them back, but then I shrugged. What else would I have them do?

I pulled my hood off and stuffed my shoes and stockings inside, swinging the weight back on my shoulder like a rucksack. The town cobbles had baked all day, but my red toes drank the air like water, and I stood, alone, in the square, and rubbed life back into my feet. It was a fair, neat square, new timbered, black and white, the roofs red shingled. A bridge arched the Medway and a new, pale castle stood a distance off, ringed round with trees. I sighed and started toward a tavern of my own. Then I found Nettle, walking off with Aaron Stone. They prattled, all cheer and fellowship, their arms crooked round each other. Will saw me and waved. I crossed to join him. Then I heard my name. "Straw!" I turned; a girl was calling. "Jack Straw!" She waved me over. I came, and Nettle followed.

"You'll be eating with us," she said.

"With who?"

"Tyler."

I frowned. "I have to see to my company."

"And that's why you have to meet with Wat Tyler," she said. "Come with me." Her voice was low and rough.

I liked her. Will stood by my side.

He whispered, "Should I come with you?"

"Well . . ." I faltered, kicking a loose cobble. "I think he wants to talk to me, you know . . . as a leader."

Will nodded, slow. "I understand."

Aaron came up behind him and whacked him on the back. "Come on, Will. Compare some pudding ale with Maidstone brewers."

The two walked off, and I eyed them. Before I had time to regret my words the girl was at my shoulder. "My father's expecting you."

"You're the tiler's daughter?" She didn't look fourteen, brothers. She couldn't have been fourteen. If she was fourteen, I was fourteen. She was short, but round and full all over, like a strawberry, and her black hair was free and treacle-thick.

She nodded. "You've heard the tale, then?" She looked bored. "Heaven knows how it ran up north. Was I too young to walk? Did the cleric have me legs-up in the bushes? Did I stand like a dope till my father flew down from high Heaven?" She took my arm. "Enough—you're hungry." The way she said it, brothers, if I hadn't been I ought to be. It was an order. She pulled me down a narrow alley where the cobbles buckled, rimmed on all ends with leaning inns and taverns, signs plastered with arrows, chickens, sheep. You might remember—I'd been in Maidstone before. I remembered the poor lads I'd met the day I'd turned Jack Straw. The town seemed to gleam now, to prosper like a corn-fed cow. Where were the beggars hiding? Kate turned a corner and stopped at a low house with a red tiled roof.

"Father!" she called. "I caught him!"

"Very good, Kate. Very good!" The voice went clear to my stomach, like a drum. She opened the door and I saw Wat Tyler.

He was squat, not over five feet tall, but broad and solid, like the stump end of a gospel oak. His armor was all rough and dense, like bark. He wore a helmet, but his hard, shy face seemed misplaced on that body, like a head on a chopping block. His stubby hands were on his lap, and an ugly little pug-dog played at his feet.

"I've been wanting to meet you," he said.

At once, I knew I'd wanted to meet him as well. I said, "We're in sore need of a soldier."

He rose, moaning, as if the hearth had baked him like a kiln. "First things first, Jack. Pour all strong drink into the river. Exile all thieves. You'll be left with honest, sober men—more you can't ask for."

"Will you two be wanting supper right away?" Kate asked him.

He shook his head. "I'll be showing Jack the letter."

She stared at him. "How far can he be trusted?"

"He's gotten one himself, Katie, dear." Wat opened a box by his chair, a plain oak box with a hinged lid, and he drew a folded letter onto the oak table. "Never could read," he said to me. "I know it by heart."

He gave me Ball's letter.

> Jakke Carter prayes yowe alle that ye
> make a gode ende of that ye haue
> begunnen and doth wele and ay bettur and
> bettur for at the even men heryth the day.
> For if the ende be wele than is alle wele.
> Lat Peres the Plowman my brother duelle at
> home and dyghte us corne and I will go with
> yowe and helpe that y may to dyght youre
> mete and youre drynke, and ye none fayle;
> lokke that Hobbe robbyoure be wele chastysed
> for lesyng of youre grace for ye have gret
> nede to take God with yowe in alle youre dedes.
> For now is tyme to be war.

"I've done as he advised," Wat said. "It's clear as day —We've set a store of bread and meat, found good plowmen who'll stay in Maidstone to tend to mowing while we're gone. Ball's a practical man."

I caught my breath at that, brothers, but kept dumb and gave Wat the letter. He set it in the oaken box with care.

"He's sent instructions to all ends of Kent and Essex.

Knows the country well. I heard him preach, once," he
said, "In Colchester, when I was young, before they took
away his parsonage."

Despite myself, I smiled. "You never heard *me*," I
said.

Kate said, "I did." I was aware of her for the first
time, standing behind Wat with her shoulders back, her
deep eyes on me. She turned and left me to Tyler.

"I was at war at the time," he said, "Fighting for the
King. I'm anxious to fight for the King again."

I heard a note in his voice that stirred me like the
Morris Dance, a note I'd heard in Weaver's voice when he
spoke in the brewery. I looked at him, hard. "Have you
met the King?"

"No, but I'm going to." He leaned back in his chair.
The room was dark, warm, seeped in bread and bacon, and
Wat's eyes looked out from that homey haze, bright and
certain. "Jack," he said, "we're going to have to talk about
where we go from Maidstone."

"To Canterbury," I said. "To free John Ball."

"No, after that. You understand, there's been talk of
marching to London."

I might have laughed then. "There's always talk."

"Chapters of the Fellowship have worked in London.
We have friends there."

What could I say then? "That's impossible. Half the
lords who fled are in London. All the men we've railed
against, Hales and Gaunt—"

"All the more reason—"

"All the more reason that it will be our undoing, our
downfall—"

"Or the turning point." Across what seemed a length
of miles, he set a hard, broad hand on my shoulder. The
arm was heavy. "If we're victorious in London, if we clear
out the traitors, the King will have his kingdom back. We
have to meet with Richard."

I sighed. "Tyler, he won't meet with us."

"We're fighting for him." Wat sat back and eyed the
low, rough ceiling. "Think on the letter, Jack. Ball says at
the evening, men hear the day. What more evening than

these times, when traitors rule? We'll raise a blaze and turn the dark to a King's day, heaven's morning."

I found myself muttering about Heaven and Earth, about them being one, and Tyler pushed in close to listen.

"You worked with him once," he said.

I said, "I did, once."

"And you shall again." At last, he seemed to ease away from talk of London. "First things first, Jack. We free Ball. Then we talk."

He called Kate in and she bore a pot of hot bacon and toasted cheese and filled two pint-high corken cups with ale. She swung her dark hair back, tipping the great jug, easing it down. Later, she filled our plates with oats, currants and apples. Through that heavy supper, Wat made me tell the tale of Rochester, of Ker's death, of doings in Erith and Dartford. Once, he asked me of my life with Ball, but he stopped when he saw the look on my face. I liked to hear him talk of the King. It gave me heart.

2 . Remembering Ball

Mayor, brother scribe, see your Jack a tall fair boy gone thin and white with too much walking and too little bread. I'm seventeen. I stand on the outskirts of a field of folk—say one five score and fifty. The town is Rye, a hill town flanked by walls, castle and sea. There's the smell of salt baked in the sun, though it's midwinter. Ball's preaching by a windmill near the river. I'm counting the crowd under my breath, keeping watch.

"Things won't go well in England until all goods are held in common!" he called, thin arms out, beard up like a beak. "This is a rich trade town, yet I've seen you sleeping all curled up for the cold like slaves, while your long bows lie beside you, bows you'd never use against your masters!"

"Preacher," someone called, "there's such a thing as loyalty!"

"To God," John Ball said. "To God and to yourselves!"

I felt a known, bright shiver up my back, and I turned round to see the mayor's long sleeves dragging toward Ball's circle. I walked to the agreed upon position, and raised my broad hat high.

I dove into the reeds. I'd picked the spot that morning; it served well. I packed my face with mud, stuck dry weeds in my hair, peeked out, and smiled at myself in the quick river. My teeth were white and widely spaced and I filled those gaps with more reeds till I looked like a bad harvest. I heard the mayor's voice:

"And all who listen to Ball are breaking the law as well and are subject . . ."

An instant more—I dipped my dirty frozen hat in the water and took a drink to clear my throat and head. Then I looked up. The crowd was thin. Ball told me to act if more than a third lost heart, and half were heading up the hill.

I jumped up, closed my eyes, and ran.

I felt folks jostle, knock me with their shoulders, heard them call their neighbors back to see. I opened my eyes. Ball was gone and I stood in his place, by the windmill, wheezing through my reeds.

"Help me!" I called. "Oh—help!" I twisted my voice up into the voice of a young lord.

They pushed in. A little girl called, "You have straw in your mouth."

I shook my head. "I was born that way, young miss. Oh—by all that's holy! Such misfortune! I'm the black sheep of a gentry family of Culpepper because I wasn't born with a gold spoon in my mouth, but with a mouth full of straw!" Then I tossed my head, and sang:

> Oh, a man must take what's left by law
> But only a mule can live on Straw!

"Ah—," an old man shouted. "That's Ball's idiot, Jack Straw! He's just smeared a little dirt on his face."

"I may be an idiot," I called, "but I'm no traitor!"

"Oh, aren't you now, working with a heretic," the man called, "A man who's been in jail and who isn't even a Christian!"

I paid him no mind and went on. "I'm no traitor, you understand. My poppa, the rich lord of Culpepper, he locked me in the pig trough in the kitchen and he said, Jack, don't eat my meat pies or drink my sweet ale while I'm gone." I stared off, for a time, eyes traveling over the easy, placid faces of my people. "I was very hungry," I said. "My poppa, he was out hunting the fallow deer with the King and it was no supper for poor Jack." Then, I smiled. A few bits of wet straw shed to the ground. "Ought I eat the pies?"

The grownups didn't care, or not yet, but the children were of two opinions. Half called "No!" and likely hoped I'd starve to death. The other half said yes, and I spread a muddy hand out and addressed them.

"Well, I didn't want to be a traitor. I wanted to be loyal to the man who helps me live and who gives me meat and beer and shelter. That was a problem, eh?" I stared through dirt-clogged eyes, up toward the hill. "I thought, Jack, who are you to argue with the one who keeps you going?"

"Right you are, Jack!" someone called. "The old way's the best way!"

My voice was low. "And so I ate the pies."

"You shouldn't have done that, Jack," the little girl said.

"But isn't it right that I be true to the man who protects me and feeds me and clothes me? And tell me, young maid, who does that?—I do! Who baked the pies? Me—Jack!" I took up a corner of my soiled, patched smock. "Who wove this so well? Me—Jack!" I frowned, and then my eyes turned sharp. "I'd be both fool and traitor to do such a generous soul wrong. Now, Lord Culpepper, he just locked me in a dark trough."

The girl nodded. At least I'd reached the ones who found truth in a tale.

"And now my father's after me with a broomstick, and I need HELP!" My eyes snapped wild again, and I wiggled my fingers through the air, dashing back through the warm, wool-clad crowd. I felt a few friendly hands on my back. I'd had better luck, and worse. I wished they hadn't linked my name with Ball's. Still, a few women dared to follow me and give me bread.

As for Ball, he looked at me and said, "Wash your face."

I shrugged. "Father, it's warmer when it's dirty."

"Tonight, we sleep by a fire," he said.

He'd said that the night before, and we'd ended up on frozen earth, wrapped in his cloak. I was doubtful, but I walked to the river and cleaned the mud from my face. I picked straw from my hair and unrolled my broad hat. It was frozen through, and wearing it did more harm than good, but I pulled it on to dry it and I started back. An old woman stopped me.

"You'll be needing a place to stay," she said.

I felt too grateful and abashed to speak, but I took her hand.

"You two do no harm," she said, "and winter is winter to those who are Christian and those who aren't." Then, she set her thick, warm shawl over my shoulders. "A law that makes hospitality a crime is the devil's law."

She led me to her house and sent me back for Ball.

The woman lived in a lean, clean room wedged between a cobbler's workshop and a smithy. The smithy turned the west wall toast-warm, and a high hearth blazed east so fierce that a chair yards away was hot to touch. Her young daughter brought in food, hot as well, and plentiful. There was pease porridge, fish and good rye bread. Ball talked about salvation, Heaven and Earth, Adam and Eve, and the old woman nodded, as though he hummed a tune she didn't care for but was too polite to cut short. Then he took out his pipe. That was better.

"Play something merry," I said.

The fire must have cleaned some of the vinegar out of him. He set his lips and warbled out a dance tune. I nodded toward the quiet maid and caught her round the waist. We danced a circle round the room. The woman watched us, smiling, as though she was thinking, yes, that's what having company is. As for the maid, she was a middling dancer, warm through, as if she'd spent whole years by that high fire. The notion made me giddy. Our feet swept rushes, acorn husks, clean straw. Woolen stockings hung in rows over the table. Garlic, pork and onions hung across the ceiling. That room seemed the brightest, warmest place on earth. I threw my head back, and sang with the pipe.

> Robin Hood and Little John
> They met at hot midday—oh
> At odd ends of a riverbank
> Each blocked the other's way—oh
> The bridge it was a narrow one
> And there their fellowship begun.
> Oh Robin Bold and Little John—

John Ball stopped piping. "Time for your lesson."

I glowered, and kept my arm crooked round the warm girl's waist. She wilted as Ball set the pipe on his stiff knee and rose to get his book.

"If you miss a day," he said, "you fall a week behind. You know that."

I turned to the old woman and her daughter, and said, "I'm learning to read Latin. Parson Ball is training me for the priesthood."

The girl smiled and tried to look impressed. The old woman merely nodded and cleared the table. They took the stockings away as well, and the room became an ordinary room.

They left us to ourselves, and we sat by the fire, close enough to chew the coal. It was our first night by a hearth in three months, and the old woman had spread Ball's bench thick with wool blankets, but he didn't give these wonders a second look. I took a dark red rug and bundled as John Ball opened the Bible.

"The Book of Luke," he said.

I said, "Father, are we going to stay in Rye for a while?"

He shook his head at once. "We're going to Essex."

I shivered, for we'd just come from the north. "They'll only put us in jail again, and people are so poor there. I hate begging bread from them."

"All the more reason why they need us," Ball said. "The poor are our neighbors." His voice turned flat, and I knew he spoke Long Will's words, from the book about the plowman. "Besides," he added, "you've spent a night in jail. You'll spend another."

"It may be more than a night," I said, almost against my will.

"Jack," he said. He looked up at last, then, and his eyes were cold. "Jack, you're falling under worldly influences. You're not willing to sacrifice."

I turned back to the book. Ball had found the Latin Bible, and we were cribbing it to Kent's English. His old English translation had been taken when they'd caught us in Colchester and Ball thought we could work Latin into

English better than the half - dolt Lollards anyway. He worked me through the gospels at a devilish pace. I took to the task like a pig to mud and Ball was often pleased with me. He wasn't pleased that night. I stumbled often.

"You're afraid, aren't you," he said at last.

I said nothing.

"I used to be afraid. Then they did everything to me that they could do. Twice, I spent well over a year in prison. They took away my priesthood, then my Christianity all together, and it took all of that taking to teach me that such things aren't theirs to take." He scratched himself. "I'm still a priest, and still a Christian, in spite of thieves. They can take what they can take, but—" He broke off and bowed his head.

I came up behind him; the room was still warm, and I took his head on my lap and deloused him in front of the hearth. Even in winter they flourished. I pitied him, yet I confess that some rebellious bottom of me preferred to feel the warmth of the hearth and the thrill of my own voice singing. Pity was too world-weary a feeling for a boy of seventeen. No one had told me this, yet I sensed it. I also knew those feelings were disloyal, and I stared at the coals and baked my face until they went away.

"Up north, tomorrow, then," I said at last.

He shifted his head and gave me a look of love that warmed me through. He rose and climbed on the hard bench. "Good night, son."

I rolled the rug around me and faced the hearth. "Good night, father." I looked at the Bible, the clear scribe's script, and above it Ball's English and my own. What did that careful scribe know of warm women? No less than I would. If I followed John Ball, pity would have to do for love, or women's love. I closed the book, and set my head on its cover, sleeping in fits, waking often to rake the hearth. I managed to keep the room warm till morning.

3. An Armed Man

Supper, quiet, and trusting company had eased my heart. We sat back on chairs as squat, solid and reliable as Wat Tyler. Wat's dog butted an ugly head against his knee. Wat scraped the last of his drippings with a crust, and sighed.

"Jack," he said, "we have a long day ahead, a long walk, then a longer walk. My daughter has prepared a bed for you. I suggest you use it." It was less suggestion then flat order, and it made me see the soldier in him. I wanted to rise, then, take his hand, beg him to make sense of the three hundred who squatted in Maidstone.

"What was it like in France," I asked. I felt like a lad begging for a tale. He didn't take the question in that spirit. He smiled, uneasy. I shrugged. "I had two brothers there. We lost them." I didn't have the nerve to add they'd likely deserted.

"Where did you serve? What's your family name—" He stopped short. "Oh, no need to tell me that. I'm sorry, son." He set an elbow on either side of the greasy table-top and set his blunt chin in his hands. "The crossing's clearest to me now, Jack, thinking back on it. The crossing from Dover, it was, back before King Edward died, before his grandson Richard took the throne. That was when the Black Prince lived, when there seemed a chance that John of Gaunt would come to naught."

He reached back for a full pitcher of ale, and filled both our cork cups till the foam ran down. He stared into the ale's thin, parting head, and I eyed my own. It mirrored the hall, the fire-light.

"I was twenty-eight," he said. "I had a trade, a wife, a daughter. Edward called himself King of France and I was one of those called to defend his crown. I'd heard that men could make their fortunes at war, and I set off to Dover to serve myself more than to serve my King. They taught me how to use a crossbow." He stretched an arm back. "Awful thing, a crossbow. Filled you with awe."

Crossbows had been banned by the church; they had strong springs and strips of plaited leather and they drove arrows through armor easily as paper. For all the church's orders Wat assured me that the boat had been packed with crossbows.

"Whether we used them or not," he said. "And they taught us to use them." He stared into his cup again. "It works changes in you, a weapon like that. A longbow is part of your flesh, Jack. You oil her, tend her, even talk to her when it suits you. Then they give you this crossbow with stresses and catches and a force that beats your own, and all at once you're not a man—you're a soldier. No wonder the mercenaries loved them."

"You met mercenaries?" Brothers, I admit that I'd hoped he could find a few and bargain for their service. Wat spat.

"How could I help but meet those bastards! The vermin of the war, they were. Didn't care about the King. Wouldn't fight other mercenaries. Talked about the looting they'd do when the battles weren't on, and when they were. I had to bunk with them on the crossing, and they were a hard, sour bunch. I climbed on deck to get away from them. They turned me sicker than the sea."

Wat gave his knee a whack and the dog hopped up neat as a cat and panted. Wat scratched him round the head.

"That got me thinking—why was I bound for France? Because I was conscripted? I loved my King, and the mercenaries made me see it. I thought of the King surrounded by the spies bought by his own son, John, just as I was surrounded by that lot."

I raised my cup and drained it. "Poor Edward," I said. "Rest his soul."

"I thought about the way his closest friends betrayed him, like the mercenaries who'd sell him for a shilling. The others teased me, told me Edward would have no use for poor men like Wat Tyler, but I swore myself to his service on that ship, surrounded by his enemies. It gave me spirit."

Kate came in, yawned, settled on a stool. "My father's going on about his friend, the King?"

"Richard's grandpa," Wat said softly. "Same foes, same friends." He looked down, cheerless, scratching round the clown face of his dog. "Ah . . . Pug," he whispered. "They laugh, but if they have a heart, they listen."

Kate filled my cup again. It was thin ale, and it grants no pardon, brothers, for what followed. I felt the words slip out and I knew better than to stop them. "Let's drink to Richard, then!"

Wat raised his head. "Bless you, son, let's drink." Kate filled his cup, though she didn't fill her own.

I thought, I'm drinking to plain fellowship, but I hadn't said fellowship. The toast came from my heart. Wat set his Pug on the floor and he waddled over, sniffing.

"Kate," Wat said, "show Jack his bed, and don't let him keep you by asking for a tale."

Kate nodded, and we rose together. She led me through a tiny, smoking kitchen, toward a ladder. She stopped there, and looked up. Her round, strong face reminded me of Pug's, and I couldn't help but feel a simple fondness for her, as I'd felt for food and ale and fire. "There in the loft," she said, and she turned back toward me, lowering her voice. "You do well to humor him," she said. "He'll be useful to you."

I frowned. "I'm not humoring him."

She ran a weary hand through her black hair. "You're a nice lad, Jack, nicer than Kate Tyler." She stood straight, smiling bitterly. "My mother was nice," she said, "but not nice enough, I think. Ask him about her some time."

I could have asked Kate then; she would have told me. It was a blow; I'd wanted to like her. Better silence that would salvage some of my good feeling than a tale to leave me puzzled. I'd lost enough sleep. I nodded a good night, and mounted the ladder to bed.

I fell asleep at once, and I would have slept well had I

not dreamed. It was a dream that went past fancy, a dream I ran through till I woke more weary than I'd been the night before.

I ran across broad fields I knew, Gravesend fields and Dartford fields, past cottages of neighbors, along rivers, and I ran with a companion. I knew the man was Ball, or thought I knew; I hadn't stopped thinking of Ball since I'd left Rochester. I didn't know why we were running, and I tossed possibilities to him. He tossed them back like apples. There were armed men chasing us, trying to pike our heads on poles; there were lawyers trying to lock us in a magic jail in Heaven; there were women—I thought of Jenny, of Kate, of the woman I'd kissed—trying to get a straight answer out of us. Then, suddenly, it didn't matter whether Ball was my companion for I had countless companions. They streamed behind me till the old road broke at our heels and I thought: no one's chasing me; they're following me to get to the source of the music.

For there was music playing. Relief pressed down so hard it hurt. I knew the place now. I was in Gravesend, running to hear the piper. The piper would be Ball. I would say what I'd said then. I'd invite Ball to dinner, and I'd go with him.

Would I go with him? Here was a chance to live my life again, not to set my hand between his own, not to set the trust I'd betrayed, not to break the faith—not to touch it. It would be like rising before finishing a tale; they'd hate me for it.

"Bide Lady Bide!" a boy called.

"No, Robin Hood and Little John!"

Then, something new: "I am your leader—follow me!"

We reached the noon-bright Gravesend crossroad, and the breath was knocked out of me, for someone else piped on Ball's tuneless pipe—a child. He was the cleanest babe I'd ever seen; the pipe and tune didn't belong to him, and didn't soil his clean, red mouth. Then we all bowed, for the boy was the King.

I woke with a start. Sun slanted through a gap in the tiles straight into my eyes. It was the morning before Trinity Sunday. I thanked God for my dream, and crossed the loft to peer through the crack. I watched the clear sky through my weary, dazzled eyes. Again, I thanked God.

4. Little Goldengrain

An honest plowman lived with his wife in a little house. They were poor, but very happy save for one thing: they had no child. The wife would often burst into tears and cry:

"Ah—if we had a child it would turn the very grain to gold."

Soon after she gave birth to a little girl with golden hair. She called her little Goldengrain.

Goldengrain grew up to be beautiful. She worked very hard in the fields and gathered the wheat into sheaves for her father and mother. They came to thank her, and they were amazed, for the sheaf of wheat she held against her shoulder had turned to gold.

"Ah—little Goldengrain," her father said, "We shall not be poor anymore." He took the golden wheat and bought a cozy house and hired laborers to work for him. Goldengrain never worked again, and she grew white and soft, like a lady. The family lived in great joy, until, one day, Goldengrain's gentle mother died.

The father mourned for a long time, but life goes on and he had to take another wife. He married a handsome haughty woman who scorned him because he used to push a plow and scorned little Goldengrain because she used to work in the field. She spent the rest of the poor father's money quickly. One day, the chest which had held the golden wheat was empty.

"Wife," the father said to her, "I am afraid I shall have to work in the fields again, for you have gone through all of our gold."

"There must be a place where you can get more of it," she said, "and you are keeping it from me."

"You are my wife and I can keep nothing from you,"
the father said. "Little Goldengrain, whom you dislike so
much, gathered wheat, and when it touched her shoulder it
turned into gold."

"You fool!" his wife cried. "Why don't you send her
out again?"

"Ah, it wearies my heart to see such a beauty
working," said the father.

"Beauty or no, she is a low, common, girl and ought
to work if it does us good." And she ran to Goldengrain's
room and pulled her downstairs by her golden hair. She set
a sickle in her hand and said:

> Gather Gather Gather
> Little Goldengrain
> So your good stepmother
> Can have gold again.

Little Goldengrain walked, sadly, to the field with her
father's laborers, and cut grain. She returned to her stepmother with an arm full of gold. The woman was pleased,
and she sent Goldengrain back to her room and stored the
gold in the chest.

The next day, she thought, "The gold in the chest will
last a year, maybe two. Why not have the girl gather
enough gold to last ten years?"

She ran up and pulled her stepdaughter down the
stairs, calling:

> Gather Gather Gather
> Little Goldengrain
> So your good stepmother
> Can have gold again.

Little Goldengrain took the sickle and gathered five
sheaves of wheat. Her stepmother was happy, and she
filled her chest with pure, bright gold.

That night, the stepmother couldn't sleep. She walked
the length of the house and thought, "How poor a place
this is. How thin the walls are and how worn the

furniture. It is a peasant's house indeed, which suits my husband and his daughter, but I deserve better. I deserve a house as fine as a Queen's."

She woke poor, tired Goldengrain and said, "Cut and bind all the wheat in the field!"

> Gather Gather Gather
> Little Goldengrain
> So your good stepmother
> Can have gold again.

Goldengrain spent the rest of the night in the great field of her father, and in the morning, five hundred bundles of wheat lay at her stepmother's feet.

Goldengrain's father was unhappy, but he didn't want to go against the wishes of his wife. He gave the stepmother the gold to do with as she pleased, and after some thought, she conspired to buy all the fields of grain in the Kingdom. To all of these she sent poor tired Goldengrain. Soon, the stepmother had enough gold to last a thousand years, and wanted more. Soon, there wasn't enough wheat in the kingdom to make bread, and people began to go hungry.

One day, the King came riding through the country and he paused to watch a tired, thin girl cross a field. Her soft eyes were sad and her golden hair was tangled through with golden wheat. He dismounted and followed, drawn by her beauty and moved by her sorrow. He watched her open the door of a little hut, and there, among great chests of gold, a bloated, haughty woman sat. She laughed and cried:

> Gather Gather Gather
> Little Goldengrain
> So your good stepmother
> Can have gold again.

He watched in wonder as the girl began to cut the wheat. At her touch, the wheat turned to pure gold.

His heart turned over with love and pity, and he came

to the girl in secret and asked her to run away with him.

She said she would go gladly, but she didn't want to hurt her father, whom she loved well. He promised that he would give her father a great fortune for her sake, and so she climbed onto his horse and together they rode over wheat fields to his castle.

As they passed the gathered gold, the spell broke and it turned to honest wheat again. Soon, all had bread enough, and there was plenty of good bread at the wedding. All lived happily, save the stepmother, who was burnt for her crimes on a stake of twisted straw.

5. At the Fighting Cock

Wat had been up since dawn. He'd left bread and cold bacon on the table and I helped myself, setting my big feet up, throwing bacon rind to Pug. Pug was sow-sleek and saucy. An easy life had spoiled him. Most hounds I'd known were handy; they could shepherd or hunt coney. I hadn't seen Pug hunt but I'd bargain that a strong buck rabbit could have made short work of him. I did as Wat had done; I scratched a circle round his wrinkled head. He licked my fingers red and nuzzled close.

Kate passed, at work. I watched her for the pleasure of it, the moment by the loft's ladder forgotten. She crossed the room, turned a pan of hot gray water out the window, set it down again, stretched up on her two sound legs, and sighed. I thought: the clerk who dared peek under that skirt had more than a tiling hammer to contend with. Likely, Kate had kicked him in the head. The room was just as it should be—dry wood by the hearth, a line of forks and pots strung on the plaster wall, fresh rushes strewn, windows wide open. I stroked Pug's prune-nose and I dozed, my head filling with folly like a haze after a rain. I thought: this is my front hall, my dog, my table, my wife. Ah, Jack, I thought, you're falling under worldly influences. Yet fancy carried me and I thought: it's my wife there by the battered empty basin, wiping her hands on her blue skirt, wheat flour from a morning's baking in her hair.

Kate turned. "My father's outside," she said. "He's expecting you."

I sat back and scraped the last ring of fat with my last crust. "We'll be moving on today, likely, Kate," I said, smiling up at her as I fancied a husband might. "And you'll be marching with us?"

"No, not me," said Kate, and her face turned hard and secret, the face I'd seen the night before. "I've walked my share. I've walked the way from Colchester to Maidstone." She pointed to her boots: dark, scuffed, cracked boots that seemed a sorry end to those good legs. "I used to be a tireless walker, but not now."

"You never know when you're through walking," I said.

"You don't know, maybe," Kate said, turning toward the open window. "And you'd best find out where my father thinks the King will lead you. As for me, I hold with no leader. I stay put."

I sat on that thick, oaken stool, my mind set on my dream, on Richard's golden face. To turn from that face seemed as daft as turning from the sun. And in this mind I had no wish to hear her tale of walking. I wouldn't hear it for a while, and then against my will. I rose and found the door, and I leaned back, hand on the latch, just watching her take up a broom and sweep old rushes back to scatter new. I faltered there, wanting to kiss her, to say something that would make her think of me when I walked on. It took all my will to free the latch and stumble out alone.

So I was in the alley, off to find Wat Tyler. Pug followed, so close at my heels I near kicked him. I turned up and I met a broader way. The tavern street was deep in Maidstone folk packing bread, beans and cheese. Lads lay belly-down on the cobbles, sharpening cleavers. The black and white timber hung with new standards, fresh-dyed and dripping. Already some bore red hammers, blue crowns, white plows. Warblers wove through, warbling. The shingled roofs, the birds, were drenched in sunlight thick and sure as snow. I wandered down that road, Wat's dog between my feet. Then I saw a company of men, led by Wat Tyler.

Wat saw me. "Jack Straw!" he called. "You'll come with us!" He wore his armor, and a helmet which caught sun like a mirror.

I asked him what had been decided.

"Oh—" He waved toward the men. "They come from

every town and village. We're meeting at the Fighting Cock to talk of aims, roads, the like." He caught his yapping Pug in an arm and whacked me on the back. "Sleep well?"

"I did," I lied, bone-weary.

"Well, between the two of us, we'll get these troops on the road to Canterbury by supper." He crooked his thick arm round me. "Good men here. They need a little direction, but you've done well with them."

I shrank back. "I've done nothing."

"Ha! You've gotten them this far. We've had no looting, no stealing, I gather. That's more than many a good captain can do, Jack." He walked on, rubbing his nose thoughtfully, as if there weren't a score men behind us. "We'll have to make a list of traitors. Can't have them all in ten directions if we want to keep the King's favor."

I nodded. When he spoke of Richard I felt the face on me, and heard the pipe. "He'll favor us," I said. "But will his uncle John let him send word?"

"We'll hear from the King in Canterbury," Tyler said. "When we have a clear petition, he'll answer it."

We crossed the town square. The sky was clear as water. I wondered at it. We'd had fair days since Whitsunday, but this was no thin drought light; it was warm and full and smelled of growing. I'd never known a summer like it. Folks ate the warmth for breakfast. Ten women sat sewing up the ends of a new standard, and their needles and nettle-thread flew like raindrops. A lad ran up with dye, swinging the full bucket like a bell. More, every shop door was flung wide—bakers, tailors, weavers scattered their goods free as air. I understood why I could find no beggars in Maidstone. On order of Ball's letter all put their hearts into lending neighbors full strength for the road. A hungry soul can't march, can't fight, so every soul found bread. Who did they muster for? For Richard. My heart rose like a loaf. I turned to Tyler. "It's all in his name," I said.

Wat gave me a look of such heady love that I thought he'd scratch me round the head like Pug. He beamed. "Son," he said, "we've got spirit here—you see it!"

I nodded, light and giddy.

We walked down a narrow way. I looked for the ale-
post of the Fighting Cock, and found none. We passed
dark, greasy butt ends of butcher shops and bakeries till we
met a trickle of an alley roofed by leaning wattle walls. A
name was scraped onto its side: Joint Lane. It was more
like a crack, truth told, ten yards long, so low that even
squat Wat had to duck. We followed. I knew none of the
twenty men save two from Gravesend: Martin Carter and
Hugh Smith. They trailed without a greeting. The hollow
dribbled muck and stale ale, and it was so dark we knew
Wat only by the yapping of his Pug.

A redhead blocked the door; he looked like the en-
trance, dark, close and devil-ugly. He held a clumsy sword.
"With whom do you hold?"

"With King Richard and the True Commons," Wat
sighed. "Come on, Jessie. Save it for the fight ahead and
let a poor tiler through."

He shrugged. "Don't want to take any chances. I know
your face, but who's the kid with you?"

"Jack Straw," said Wat, "and that name ought to be
password enough."

His arm dropped. "Straw . . . sure." He blushed and
ran a sticky hand across his face. He smiled. "I should
have known you, Jack. I'd heard you speak once, when I
was a lad." He turned, unlatched the door, and called:
"They've come!" He led us through a short hall to a nook
that smelled of mold and barley.

We settled round a long, low table, and an ale wife
handed round clay cups filled with brown ale. The room
was stinking hot, and the wife steamed and sloshed and
gossiped and we didn't settle in until she'd gone. I looked
for Hugh and Martin. They huddled close, staring at Tyler
with edgy awe. Hugh pumped a stick of his broken straw
hammer up and down his back. Tyler himself sat at the far
end with Pug nestled on his lap. He held the highest cup
of ale with the bravest crown of foam. He'd sat me at his
right hand with such pomp that I felt abashed, and stared
at my high foam till it stared back. Wat set his helmet on
the table with a crack, licked a line of free foam from his
cup, and began:

"We're all here," he said, "because of what we hold in common. I've winnowed it to this, brothers: We'll have no King named John!"

The words took hold and at once all were Robin Hood foiling King John for Richard's sake. They stomped and whooped till the cups bounced and Wat raised a hand—they fell silent.

"We know a John who would be king has caused his friend, Hales, to tax us three times and push us back into bondage, against the will of our true Lord, Richard. And Richard calls us now, men. We'll answer the call, and take our trouble to our true Lord and our King!" He stopped and raised his own cup. "We'll have no King but Richard!"

They drummed cups till the table was a tabor. I felt my own hand rise, my own cup drum and toss ale up and down. I drank.

We settled in, each man a beacon of high fellowship, his around crooked round his neighbor, each save the man beside me. He strained forward and called: "What about the common land!"

A plowman at the odd end rose and called: "If law comes from the King, Richard knows we have right to commons! He'll save them!"

So came the first point of our first petition. I pressed char to brown paper and I scribbled.

"And rent! What about that man, that Rob Billing and the three hundred pounds! We need a fair price—fair and constant!"

"Four pence!" a thin man with a shock of white hair called. "Four pence an acre it was in King Edward's time!"

I wrote: "We ask a fair and constant rent of four pence an acre."

"Fishing rights! What more right do those Tomfools have to lay claim to own a river than a wind?"

"The King knows," Tyler said, calling order. "He knows, for he's the Common Law made flesh. We'll free him from the traitors and he'll see justice is done."

There were more tales than air in that dark room. One told of foiling tax clerks, one of sending rotten fish to the manor house, after the lord's lawyer took away common fishing rights—he'd claimed the fish was now the lord's. One told of waking to find the common garden enclosed, filled with the lord's sheep munching down careful rows of cabbages. Martin told the Gravesend tale of the bathhouse. I whittled clear points out of those wild tales, and scribbled them till the char was a nib, and my hand black.

Then Wat broke in. "We bring these points to Richard, yes, but better to free him from the evil traitors who make a slave of him. Hales, who bleeds us with his tax, Gaunt, who'd take his place as King—they must be pruned from Richard like foul branches from a healthy tree!"

"And the clerics," someone added.

The company pounded their cups to shards! Scribe, you'd have sprung clean out of your skin!

"Those robbers!" a man called. "Those anti-Christs!"

"The hardest masters, they are! For all their Christian talk!" a man called, a freed serf from Erith's abbey.

"They live like lords—like kings! And we'll have no King but Richard!"

That oath, which Wat had stamped new on our hearts, set those hearts beating. It took the biggest man in the room to silence us.

He rose, as broad as he was high, all of it hard and dark and sopping wet with sweat and ale. His hair was black as the table, and he raised a red, wet hand. "The greatest traitor in England," he said, "is Simon of Sudbury, the Archbishop of Canterbury."

His voice filled the room like darkness. We leaned in close to listen.

"Hear this tale," he began. "Pilgrims were walking to Canterbury, years back, when plague came to their village, to seek the shrine of Holy Thomas Becket. They crossed paths with Sudbury, who was London's bishop then, and he called them fools to hope for help from a Saint if God cared nothing for them. Well, Thomas of Aldon answered him. He said, 'My Lord, in the name of Becket my patron, I stake the satisfaction of my soul that you will close your life by a most terrible death.' " He looked around the room. "I am Thomas of Aldon. For this and other crimes, Sudbury deserves death."

Aldon's voice quivered like a sword striking a stone. We were still stones ourselves. I had my own reason to hate Sudbury, brothers, one you'll know by and by. Then Wat said, "Tomorrow, we'll be in Canterbury. There'll be time to contend with the bishop."

Someone said, "Captain, the bishop's chancellor. He lives in London."

I stopped scribbling. I felt Wat's eyes on me.

The list of traitors grew. Two men said nothing—Aldon and myself. One stranger from London called out so many names I left off listing them. Not one was known to me. They didn't seem good Saxon names, and I took them for Norman. What did I know of Flemmings, Lombards, then?

"Mainly," said Wat, "we have to seek out Gaunt, Hales and Sudbury."

They sang the three names softly, all together, like a prayer. Did they know that the three could only be found in London?

Four hours after we'd entered the room, we parted. Some found the back way, others, like your Jack Straw, wandered through the tavern's drinking hall. I blinked with even the dim light that slanted through the window, and I didn't see Will Nettle until we were nose to nose.

"So," he said. "How goes it with the leaders?"

I shrugged, and let him set me on a low bench by the door. The air reeked of bread and cheese and my maw yapped like Pug. Without a word, Will opened a sack on his lap and handed me the best part of a loaf.

"I expect they don't feed leaders," he said warmly. "Robin Hood lives off roots and poaching, eh? Well . . . Michael . . . I mean Jack . . . you look a wreck."

I sighed, and set down the gray mess of notes to free my hands for bread. I must have smeared char round my eyes—that alone makes the boldest man look haunted. "I didn't sleep last night."

"Nor did I." Will looked content and rested. "I stayed at this same tavern. Lots of women wanted to hear all about Rochester, wanted to bear my child . . . you know . . ." He wasn't certain if he could talk to Jack as easily as Michael. Aaron sat up. I hadn't noticed him before.

"You were with Tyler?" he asked. "Ah—he's a King's man."

"So am I," I said, knife-sharp, through bread.

"Ah, yes, but they say Tyler's met him." Aaron leaned back. He'd taken off his helmet and his hair stood like a hedge.

Had I met Richard when I'd dreamed? Well, Tyler hadn't—that I knew. I near told Stone as much, but I let matters rest. "I'll see you soon, Will," I said. "We leave at sundown."

Aaron Stone smiled, sly. "He'll be there, Captain. No fear. I'll keep him out of trouble."

Will leaned against that Stone as though they were old friends. I left the Fighting Cock uneasy.

It didn't help to walk into full noon heat. My weariness threw me against the door, and I watched strangers pass with loafs and steaming new-dyed flags and baskets. If any knew me, none spoke, and I searched for friends. When I saw Hugh and Martin I waved up a wind. They crossed toward me, heads low like oxen. I didn't like the look of them and I stepped back and hit my head on the doorpost.

Martin spoke first. "We'd like to know, sir, Jack . . . We'd like to know why you didn't tell us."

I rubbed my sore head. "Tell you what?"

"Who you were. Who you are . . ." He edged close, voice bitter. "Our chapter of the Fellowship has fumbled on for ten years. And for all we knew you'd gone off with a friar—but John Ball! Jack . . . if we'd known—"

"I wanted to protect my family," I said.

"And well they were protected. All dead or gone, and Jen a cripple."

"The plague was not my doing," I said.

Hugh spoke then, soft. He was not a cruel man, and he only barely said, "You could have stayed home."

"Now?" I froze. "By God's wounds, Hugh, you think I'd stay home now?"

"We meant then, when you left with Ball. Why didn't you have the stomach to stay and fight at home?" That was Martin, and his voice held no more pity for me than a beggar for a cat.

I didn't like the question. It was one of those ripe apples of a question that hangs in the air till you can smell it rotting.

Hugh set a hand on Martin's shoulder. "We took long enough to act ourselves. We could have mustered up enough to—"

"If he'd been with us, we could have kept our bathhouse." Carter said. "Why, we'd all heard of Straw! We waited for him, and he never came! Ball never came!" He turned to Hugh now and the two men faced each other. Carter was a head shorter than Hugh Smith, and he had to turn his red face up. He bellowed: "If we'd had Ball and Straw we wouldn't have let so much slip by!"

Hugh looked back, shrugged, and led Martin off toward the square.

I took root by the Fighting Cock's doorpost for a full hour. I sat when my legs held me no longer, straining to fashion the life I might have led had I stayed in Gravesend, the wife I might have taken, a small dark woman like Kate Tyler, maybe, my battle with the lawyer over the bathhouse. Maybe I'd have met Jenny as she journeyed home from Dartford Market, burdened with a heavy basket. I saw myself astride a borrowed pony, meeting her before she reached Will's ditch, trotting her home before supper. That night, she would dance with Nettle. I mused on just that way, making a good tale of it. Then Faith Corning passed.

I hadn't known she'd stayed on. She'd changed her Whitsun whites for a rough brown skirt and wool cokers, and she dragged her Art and Mary by the arm like poppets. She stopped and smiled.

"You're surprised to see me?" she asked.

I nodded and rose. "This is no place for mothers, Faith."

"Well, really, you'll be needing someone handy with the wounded, someone with sharp eyes. And children can go anywhere, like cats." She wrapped her arm around me and pulled me into the sunlight, toward the square. I heard music now, a lone pipe, the drum-beat of the men and women packing. "I've led many a harvest march. You think we have no place in this march, storyteller?"

Mary took my hand, and I looked at her soft face, too young yet to be a proper face. I said, "You knew Rob Billing, but you've no right to drag your son and daughter through to Canterbury and tell them it's a harvest march."

She stopped, then, and pulled Mary back. She said, "Neighbor," for she refused to call me Jack, "I'm here because I love my children, and because I've seen them hungry, and because maybe if you turn the world upside down something worth having will fall out of it—like bread. Why are you here?"

I faltered. "Because I love my King."

She tossed her head and started toward the square. Her children followed after, laughing at the birds and banners. She left me with her reasoning. She left me to my own.

6. I Earn Ball's Bread

It was the Lammas before Richard's reign began, the year the Black Prince died. Ball sat on a wet post, scratching his pate. It would have been a keener scene had it been winter, but it was summer, and we starved abathe in gentle sunlight. Two things made our work the harder: there was the place, the heart of Essex, there was the plague.

It was its third sweep in thirty years. The first time a village near Gravesend had been emptied, and I'd heard tales about mothers giving death their sons, or priests allowing men to die unshriven for fear death would take them as well. The second coming had been called the Children's Plague; it struck the young. Now plague had come again, and Ball and I would enter villages were bells were always tolling. There was a rank cloud over towns and a hale man might be in fever, hacking blood, and dead in three days time. Some grew black boils and spots, swelling until they burst into a stink of death.

Still, we were spared, though we followed the path of death like threshers, Ball said, following a scythe. Some thought we carried death with us, and barred their gates when we approached. Some listened to us only to walk off when we couldn't answer their bewildered questions.

As for Ball, he woke each dawn declaring that the end of the world had come and that God had spared him for a purpose. He grew hasty and forgetful, thinking I'd never seen the gospels and forcing me to turn the same Latin to English again and again.

"Now I want you to read me Matthew," he'd say.

"Oh, father, I can recite the book by heart, and I'm tired."

"You know you forget your lessons."

I'd go over each line doggedly. Once, I confess, I caught myself praying to Christ to take him away, and I choked, as if he'd heard me. I'd been with Ball for four years, and if he didn't know my own heart as well as he knew the inside of the threadbare sacks he strung around his middle it was my fault. My secrets burrowed deep till I was stuffed with them like straw.

"The plague is Judgement," he said. "It's God's way of choosing his elect!"

Once he said that to some Fobbing tradesmen, and they flew at him like mad dogs. I drove them back with a stick. They were weak and miserable, and even my feeble thrashing kept them off the parson. "You don't know, father," I said. "They have brothers, fathers, friends who've died."

"Things will go better for the poor when this is over," he said. "Lords die as well as bondsmen. It's God's equalizer." Then he'd laugh bitterly. That bitterness convinced me that he still had a soul, that he could still feel pain. I clung to that hard laughter with both hands.

"Father, let's go back to Kent," I'd say. "We're going round in circles. Folks here have heard us before, and they have harvest and other things on their minds."

"Ha!" he'd say. "You're worried about your family? Your father gave you to me, boy! I'm sure he's forgotten all about you by now."

John Ball pushed all things too far. It was as though he wanted me to wear thin and break, like his sorry string of purses. Even his thin beard had gone thinner with his tugging.

We were on the edge of Rochford. The sea looked black and a seagull stared Ball down. He turned to me. "Jack, you'll have to get us some supper."

I stared down at the town with distaste. It seemed hung black with clouds—plague fog! No, it was only rain. "You take shelter in those bushes," I said. "I'll try to beg us some bread."

He smiled. "That's my boy."

I plodded down the half-mile, feeling every step. The

fields had been reaped early, and the stubble stretched to eye's end, gray as stone. Ball was right—High Doom had come. It might take Domesday to bring Heaven down to Earth. A world of fire seemed likely, then, at least as likely as this Jack heading back with honest bread.

Rochford's streets were near empty. Two mourning women passed, talking. One held a basket.

I blocked her way. "Bit of bread for—"

"Get on with you." Her voice was soft and even, and it floated back like smoke as she walked on. They were the last I saw walking that night.

The whole town seemed a whisper, shuttered, ready for the storm. The long, ash-timbered houses lined the street like two gray walls. They might have hoped the rain would break the heat and ward off plague. I moved on, aimless and uneasy, watching my own shadow. I'd have to stop. I'd have to make an effort before I returned to John Ball empty-handed. I chose a random house and knocked.

"Who?" I didn't like the voice.

"A Christian!" I answered, trying to sound at once blithe and desperate.

The door opened a crack. "I don't know you." I saw a piece of a man's face. It was a dull face, without spirit.

"Do you have bread to spare?"

The door closed.

I shrugged and walked on. The first hard pellets of rain, no—hail, were falling. I put on my hat, through wear had made it sinister, and tried to summon up the nerve to try again.

Then I saw a bakery window. It was empty. The shop was closed and no doubt bread had been stored to be sold, day old, in the morning. I stood there longer than I'd meant to.

John Ball hated thieves. He said that they debased themselves by acting in secret. A hungry man had a right to bread and ought to say so in the open. If he took the bread in secret he acted in league with the Devil. Ball had many a hard argument against Hobb the Robber, but I could remember few of them that night.

I tried the door. It seemed locked at first, but it had

only swollen shut in the heat. A good pull, and it opened. I stood with the latch in my hand, hail pattering on the brim of my hat. My first thought was: how daft, to stand out in the hail. Of course, I didn't try to tell myself that was why I entered the bakery.

The dark room reeked of leavening. My first five steps brought down three stools and half a dozen pans. Then my eyes found themselves and I slipped into the kitchen. I found nothing, and I felt, to my credit, some relief. Then I saw a sack behind the kneading board. I looked up and around, stuck the sack under my arm, and picked my way through the front room, setting stools right and closing the door.

The door wouldn't close. It had grown too wide for its frame. I cursed it, but I let it be and started back again.

I hurried now, stuffing the sack under my smock to save the bread. My mind was full of hail and darkness and I barely knew where I was going. Where had I left Ball? I knew my feet would lead me there. Then, someone called:

"Hey—lad!"

I looked up. Someone had opened a window, some young man with a jug in his hand.

"You want some shelter? It's a hard night!"

"Thanks, no," I said. I walked on.

"You're mad," he called. "And ungrateful!" but he closed the window and I barely heard him for the hail.

I reached John Ball and found him huddled by the hedge. He had a sputtering, useless fire going. "I had a lucky night," I said. I showed him the bread.

He broke off an end and blessed it. "Come close to me," he said, "and we'll pray for these good Christians together."

God help me, I kept my heart from him and prayed.

7 . Encampment

Tyler led us through Kent like a swollen river, and like a flood we tossed our share of flotsam. Once we met a company of pilgrims astride fat, friendly horses. They were shaken at the sight of our two thousand, but they settled down when we told them we'd let them go if they would swear allegiance to Richard and the True Commons.

"Well, is that all?" A short, bold woman in a broad hat set her hands on her hips. "I was afraid you'd take all we owned, I dare say." She swung down, and the others followed.

They all mumbled and took the oath in off-key chorus, hands on purses. It made me glad of my own mates; I'd hate to travel any distance with that crew. Likely they couldn't have gone three miles on foot.

They lost us at a tavern near Stockbury, and we let them be and headed for the manor house to seek the lord's allegiance. The manor gate was open, but the lord was gone—none of the half-soused guards could help or hinder a search. We rattled through the empty hall where curtains had been wrenched from walls and bronze-worked doors pried clean. Wat pushed into the lord's solar, and found a chest of papers. Two dozen packed in round him; they were for burning every paper in the room. Wat piled my arms with parchment.

"Find the charters of bondage — that's what we're after," he said. The men behind me grumbled, hot for a bonfire.

Yet I found tinder enough to feed a high flame in the front court. We set our first camp by the Lord's fishpond, fishing, dancing, feeding paper in with toasting forks. There were charters forbidding poaching, walking across enclosed crofts, bound men marrying free women, working for a wage above the low, set rate. The convicts were in Sittingbourne jail, and Wat promised he'd lead us there at dawn.

Two men prowled the empty hall, and Tyler caught them with silver plates in their packs. He backed them almost into the fire and stared, like a dragon, into their eyes.

"Next time," he said, "you'll know better, won't you."

They nodded.

"Because next time I'll give the men orders to shoot."

They exchanged looks and gave the silver plates to Tyler. Wat turned and tossed them into the fish pond. They dimpled the water and were lost to mud and stone. He turned and caught my eye. "Chasten well Hobb the Robber!" he called. I turned back to the fire.

On Trinity Sunday, we opened our first prison. We marched in force to the weak gate of crossed iron, and Wat faced the guard, called him "Brother," and asked for the ring of keys. The guard eyed the wild, high forest of our pikes and sniffled like a babe lost in a wood. He pushed the key ring round and round his hand.

"In the name of the King," Wat Tyler said, "and the True Commons!" He stretched out a free hand; the other held his dagger. The young guard passed the sopping leather ring to Tyler.

At once we bounded for the doors. We shimmied down and found men packed so tight we had to pull them from their cells like turnips. They were more turnips than men, truth told, with tangled root-gray hair caked with a filth that smelled less sweet than earth. We'd meant to free the poachers only, but we didn't leave a soul behind. Half were naked. Ten lads collected breeches, cloaks and empty sacks and set to dressing them.

We spent the best part of the morning on the green, patching the worst wounds. One boy peeled the men a peck of apples, but most of them had lost their teeth. The few who had teeth nipped and gnawed and one poor soul lost the three teeth he had to apple-core. Soon the time had come for me to lead the men in the King's oath. One tall, bandy-legged lad, who'd spent a month in Sitting-bourne, came to me in secret.

"Speak plain," he said. "The King, what does he care about the likes of us? It was his law that put us in there." He blinked back, toward the prison. "Statute of Laborers they call it."

"That's not his law," I said. "It was set by Richard's enemies, against his will."

"Why would he will the lives of the likes of us one way or the other? He cares no more for us than his uncle, John." The lad frowned and glowered. I matched him.

"It looks like Sittingbourne hasn't broken you," I said. "That's fine. Would you like to give it more time, then?"

He scratched his head and stared.

"If you don't take the King's oath," I said, "we'll lock you up again."

"You can't do that!" He staggered back, death-white. "You—" He faltered. "You have the look of one who knows."

"Yes, I've been in prison," I said. "That's why I give you warning."

He nodded, and walked back to the others. The convicts huddled up and muttered, and when I shepherded them up the church steps, all swore.

Aaron armed the new recruits. Some were agile with longbows, not surprising in poachers. One small, sly man with more scar than face played tricks with a dagger. We had a long road before us, and by midday we'd restocked and we were ready to walk on. Two hundred, villagers and prisoners both, had joined us at Stockbury. They trooped behind a standard, a man's discarded, lousy prison shirt strung on a pole.

The earth itself changed as we wandered south. We left the clay country, the violets and daisies, and we entered the dense forest that lined the river Stour. We took the long road, for every mile added recruits to our company. In Faversham, we came upon two hundred in a church square, amassed for Trinity Sunday. The chapel door drowned in white roses. We settled in a clearing by the square, and the parson approached with caution. Were we the rebels?

Wat answered: "Father, we're no rebels. It's those we fight who are the rebels."

I pushed forward. "Look in the book of Luke, Father—Jesus asked for the freedom of captives, for the liberty of the oppressed." I quoted chapter and verse and he looked at me, that poor, confused, mild man, as though I were the Devil himself. "Today the scripture has been fulfilled in your hearing!"

The tenor bell rang three times for the Trinity, and there was such a shout as hadn't been heard in that village since the Conquest. Men, women, children, took up their garlands and joined us. The parson stayed put, and his parish flowed round him like water round a stone. He waved a little. We left Faversham flanked by a line of young maids with white roses in their hair.

We camped near Dunkirk, in sight of Canterbury gate, in a clearing by the main road ringed by apple trees. Every apple tree had its crow, and we gathered wood and water to their calls.

Dusk gathered round the leaves, and we turned our eyes to the first spark of the fire.

Someone sang, strong and low:

> Oh where are you going
> Said Milder to Malder.
> Oh we may not tell you
> Said Festle to Fose.
> We're off to the woods
> Said John the Red Nose.

Three joined:

> We're off to the woods
> Said John the Red Nose.

"Hey, Thomas," called a young girl, "that's a Christmas song!"

"It suits the night, love." I saw Thomas of Aldon at last. His broad, round arms were piled high with wood. He

stepped forward, threw three logs on the fire, and was lost
in a sky full of sparks. His low, quavering voice carried far.

> And how will you shoot her
> Said Milder to Malder.
> Oh we may not tell you
> Said Festle to Fose.
> With bows and with arrows
> Said John the Red Nose.

This time, two dozen joined the chorus:

> With bows and with arrows
> Said John the Red Nose.

> Oh that will not do
> Said Milder to Malder.
> Oh what will do then
> Said Festle to Fose.

> Big crossbows and cannons
> Said John the Red Nose
> Big crossbows and cannons
> Said John the Red Nose.

The song's strong melody drew the two thousand
voices together. Their faces were a blur of smoke, fleet ash,
and singing. I moved off to a smaller cooking fire where
Wat sat, toasting his toes. He looked at me, flushed and
happy.

"It's near unnatural, Jack. We move like the wind."

"They'll say we were possessed by demons." I sat
beside him, eyes full of the fire.

"Or angels," Wat said.

I toasted cheese and watched the new-freed prisoners
suck their sops and milk. I felt a fury and a peace I hadn't
felt save in the early days with Ball. My cheese caught fire;
I blew it down and chewed the smoking crust.

"I don't see how things could go better," Wat said,
"and after we get Ball we three will talk of London."

I shook my head. "We'd walk into their hands."

He sighed and sat up. "Now, son, we're already over two-thousand strong, and there are easily as many across the Thames in Essex, waiting to join us and meet the King."

"Tyler—" I began. He raised a hand.

"Let me finish. There are journeymen and apprentices and I don't know who else in London—at least three chapters of the Fellowship, all waiting, waiting. Whose hands would we walk into, then, if not the hands of brothers?"

Again, I shook my head. "I've seen their power, Tyler."

"Well, have you ever seen the likes of this?" He faced the main fire. It was cut to bits with wild dancing. Close behind, a second fire was burning. Aaron walked there, helping children knock old pikes and axes on whet stones till they sang. The edge of that far light hit spinning women, women gathering herbs, and a few, very few, asleep. "Son," Wat said, "if we want to keep what we have we need the blessing of the King."

"But London . . ." My voice trailed. Lords chose to flee to London for a reason. It was a lawyer's city. If blessing carried us forward it seemed a place where blessing could be blown away with one sweep of a parchment charter. More likely that the King would come to us than we could reach his London tower and live. I'd never been to London. I knew one man who had: my brother, Alf. He hadn't returned.

Wat started to speak, but stopped short. Will Nettle had crossed close enough to hear. He stumbled on a sack of cheese and mashed it. He looked at it, at me, uncertain. "I hope I'm not cutting you short, Captain Tyler," he said.

Wat shook his head. I was so glad to be spared more talk of London that I jumped up and cried: "How's the Gravesend company?"

"Homesick for Gravesend, but Hugh Smith has a voice to shake apples off the trees, and there's been a lot of singing round the fire."

I looked at Tyler; he'd shifted his feet close to the

blaze and turned his firm will to his toes. I rose. Nettle wrapped his arm around me and he walked me toward the road.

"Glad to get you back for a minute . . . Jack," Will said. "There's a decent house not half a mile from here. Think you can spare the time?"

I nodded, and we left camp. The night air was all haze, sweet and cool. It seemed a wonder to walk without thousands behind me. I felt a wet home-longing then, and I looked at Will and strained to see him as I had a week before. He bobbed along, saying this and that, saying too damned much about Aaron Stone.

"He's a married man," Will said. "That set me thinking about Jenny. Did you leave her with a neighbor?"

"She's by herself," I said. I added, "She's used to it."

Nettle frowned. "Herself? With her lame leg? Well, I expect you know best." We plodded on. The woodside piled high on either end of the long road, and we had naught to look at but each other. Nettle stopped by a turning, and said, "Well, I've decided, enough is enough. I'm going to ask your sister to marry me."

I snorted. "Why? You don't think I take proper care of her?"

He went on. "Oh, I know I did an awful thing to Jenny, snapping her leg back, but I meant well, and I think she forgives me."

"She forgave you long ago." His face was so doggy, his eyes so mild, that I choked back a giggle. "She doesn't give it a thought. I know I don't."

His jaw dropped. "But you . . . don't you . . ."

"You want me to snap *your* leg? Don't be a fool!" I sounded more like Jenny then I knew.

Will brightened and he seized my arm so hard it hurt. He pulled me, at a run. "By Sweet Saint Thomas, let's drink on it!" I struggled to keep steady. We reached the tavern in an instant, and Nettle dropped me like a sack of corn.

It was called The Pilgrim's Staff, and its ale-stake stretched a good nine feet, tied round with long gray rushes. It had at least five fires going; light spilled past its court onto the road. There was a sign over the door, a picture of a scruffy monk, the sort of monk who wouldn't think himself above a drink. Nettle pushed in, and I followed.

It was hard to find a seat and we crowded between two men from Dartford. The ale wife took her time drawing the draughts, listening to tale after tale.

She asked, "Didn't you loose thieves and murderers?"

"We don't abide that lot," a big, harsh, handsome man replied. "But they're sworn to serve Richard our King and we trust they've changed their ways."

"Ha! Trust!" She turned back to the empty cups.

"Maybe they'll turn their craft to killing traitors."

"There are plenty who'd call you a traitor." Her voice was playful, but the man sat up.

"If you were my size, you wouldn't have said that and stood there, so nice, pumping ale."

She yawned. "I said there were plenty. I didn't say I held with them."

Will struggled up and came back with two pints. He licked the foam and frowned. "Poor stuff."

Still, he tipped the pint up and drank to Jenny. "What if she won't have you?" I asked him.

Will couldn't hear about the racket. "What?"

I called, "I don't think she'll have you!"

But Will smiled. "We had a good year before the fall. I've never spoken of it, but she remembers it as well as I. You didn't see your sister when she bloomed, Michael. After your father died she tried to work his thirty acres on her own. She used my oxen. I'd watch her goad the pair, whistling, walking backwards with her skirt hiked up. I'd help her, for a tithe of brewing barley, since I've no land of my own, and she'd tell tales to those oxen till I plowed a crooked row, just listening. And after mass, she'd walk round Gravesend, talking about Heaven, with a pair of eyes so bright you'd swear she was in fever. I should have asked her then, but she was too young. Then, I found her there. I picked her up and she struggled like a cat, and she cried. I'd never seen her cry before."

"Well, Will, you broke her leg. She wouldn't laugh," I

said, smiling in secret through the ale.

"No—this was before. It was after I'd snapped it that she stopped crying."

I nodded. "If you're going to ask my sister to marry you you'd best know what you're in for. She's a puzzle."

Will spoke in a warm whisper, now. "I know her, though. And if she knew I'd take her with the leg, and with what made her cry in that ditch—"

I laughed in earnest. "I'd say the falling was enough to make a maid cry, Nettle."

Will sat up, rose red. "Well, you're right . . . Jack. But when a maid's alone, when she can't move. And she was bruised there—"

"From the leg," I said.

"True enough—but—" He stopped short and shook his head. "No, it's a muddle from my muddled brewer's head. Pay it no mind." He rubbed the edge of his cup and sat back.

Faith sat across the room with her children. Little Mary hopped on her bench, singing:

"We're going to Canta-berry! We're going to Canta-berry!"

Faith shook her head. "Dearie, save your spirit for the road." Then, she saw me. "This'll be my first time in the holy city, storyteller. I don't suppose it's yours."

I shook my head.

"You were there." She frowned, staring. "You were there with Parson Ball."

I nodded, uncomfortably.

Will said, "Want to finish my pint, Jack? This stuff is like paint."

Then a lad stuck his head through the door. He called, "Message from Captain Tyler! We're moving on!"

Folks rose without a grumble. The big man leaned over the cups and smiled at the alewife. "How about three kisses, love? For Trinity Sunday? Father, Son—"

"Out with you!" she cried, but she kissed him three times.

We walked back together, as night grayed into dawn. We didn't feel the sleepless night, the first of many. Faith's daughter trotted ahead.

"Momma!" she called. "What's Canta-berry?"

"It's a very holy place, Mary," Faith said. "You'd have to ask Jack Straw."

She didn't know a Jack Straw, so she hopped on toward the camp.

The great fire was ash, and many lesser fires were down to embers. The green clearing was trodden down to earth now. Joan the butcher's wife stomped out the last of the sparks, coughing in the smoke.

We moved again, gathering so suddenly you'd think we'd never left the road. Bread was passed back; its crust was burnt black, but it was white and soft within, a good loaf. Who'd brought it? Many loaves were thrown till they seemed to rain down from heaven. I marched between Wat and an armed man. We munched and scattered crumbs and our own silence drew us forward fast and blind as mist.

Then the gray sky turned white. The white turned blue, like snow. We saw the west gate, then. We saw the spires of Canterbury.

My heart froze. The west gate housed Sudbury's prison. In that tower I would find John Ball.

8. I Part With Ball

I'd only been to Canterbury once before, in John Ball's company. It was three years ago, and the thought of spires, of monks, of bells as big as churches tolling, stirs me now. Ball stood by me then and we covered our faces as we passed through the west gate. Despite failure, we were notorious.

"Son," he whispered, "this is a holy place. Step softly and we'll find a proper crowd to stir to action."

I wasn't happy, though we were in Kent. We hadn't entered Gravesend, and we'd passed through Maidstone only to find the peasants seven years older and seven years leaner. The square by the Cathedral gate was swarming—merchants passed pilgrims samples of new ale. The cobbles were sticky with the stuff and the smell near drove me mad.

"Here," Ball said, pausing at the thickest end of the crowd. "We'll set up shop here."

"No, Father," I said. "They'll only put us away again." We'd only gotten out of jail a month before, and I wasn't anxious to return. Ball seemed to be. "What good can you do locked away?"

"More good than we can do if we keep silent," he said, eyes bright.

I knew better than to answer back. "Let's sit and break bread and wait till the time is ripe."

Before he could argue I had him sitting with his back to the wall drinking water from my battered water skin and grinding his teeth on a crust I'd saved for a week.

"And look!" I said. "I've been keeping this for you." I took out a piece of cheese. It was gray, but sound. He looked at it as though the holy ghost had settled in his

hand. His face brought on a wave of resentful pity. I'd
stolen the cheese that morning, as I stole all our food now.

I watched him eat the cheese and wash it down with
the rest of the water.

I took the waterskin. "I'll fill that at the Stour," I said.
He nodded. I left him sitting there, his arms hugging his
long legs. The few hairs on his head had gone gray since
he'd called me to him seven years before. I left him and as
soon as he was out of sight I was at ease. A merchant
stopped me.

"Parson," he said. "Care to try a bit of ale?"

I shook my head.

"It's festival now, Father. You'd be supporting the holy
city of Saint Thomas." He held out a clay mug the color of
a robin's egg and the foam on top was thick and smelled
like bread and burning wood and all good things. At last, I
nodded. I half-expected him to turn into a devil and burst
into flame. Instead, he watched me drink. "It's very good,
eh?"

I told him that it was very good.

"You'd want to tell that to the folks at the Red Pony."

I shrugged and left him to refill the mug.

I stopped and peeked through the Cathedral gate. The
lawn was blue, and young clerks walked in pairs; one
paused and pointed east, toward faint, rising stars. I saw
Saint Augustine's abbey and wondered if I could have been
a monk. Some poor lads rise through ranks and become
abbots. I knelt by the river Stour and thrust the skin deep.
I would be Michael the Abbot—no Jack for me—in a rough
robe lined with fox fur, riding a fat pony followed by a
pack of greyhounds.

I stared at my face in the water; it was true—I had the
face of a parson, though it could hav‿ been the face of a
thief. It was a hard, long face with little bright eyes, a
deathly grim face I distrusted on sight. I couldn't claim it.
A wave of homesickness came on so I could hardly see the
river for the tears.

I stood, then, tried to shake it off, and turned back
toward the square.

But I'd come too late. Ball was on his feet, in the

center of a circle of ale-drinking clerics, merchants and guildsmen, crying: "The Spirit of the Lord is upon me, because He has annointed me to preach good news to the poor. He has sent me to proclaim release to the captives, and recovering of sight to the blind, to set at liberty those who are oppressed—"

I heard a cleric whisper, "That's John Ball."

"No it isn't," I said carefully. "John Ball's in jail."

He turned and my stomach dropped to my feet. "Who are you?"

"Oh, nobody."

"You're Jack Straw, John Ball's fool!"

"I'm nobody!" I said, raising my voice now. I hurried off, knowing it was too late.

"You can not serve two masters," I heard Ball say. The merchants moved off, ill at ease, and the square filled with our faithful, the poor, the tired, the bored. Some looked at him, almost, with my old love. "You can not serve your slavedriver and the God who lives as Holy Spirit in you. Heaven is a gift from God, and you must turn away Satan who will give you only Hell on Earth and look to your inner God who demands Heaven on Earth!"

I wanted to run. I thought about another month in jail where rats settled on my stomach and the air was full of the smell of John Ball. I saw a heavy man pass and the long-known sickly feeling spread up my back. I put straw in my hair.

He saw them too. "Blessed are you when men revile you and persecute you and utter all kinds of evil against you on my account—those are the words of Jesus Christ, my master, my only master, who bought our freedom with his blood—"

"John Ball." The name hung for a while.

Ball looked up. "This is a holy city," Ball said, "and you defile it with your wickedness."

"This man is no Christian. He's been warned not to speak here. All who listen to him are liable to prosecution by order of Simon Sudbury, Archbishop of Canterbury."

I looked up. The crowd was thin, now. I counted, heavily, under my breath.

Then I looked up again. They were taking a fighting
Ball away. He was calling, calling: "Jack—carry on!"

I closed my eyes and ran. I didn't admit, till my
pumping heart brought me down, that I'd run in the wrong
direction.

Now I lay, my whole world white. A shadow fell over
my face and I saw a guard leaning on a longbow and
smiling a hard, square smile. "Jack Straw, I'm to arrest
you." He leaned over. "Sudbury wants you excommunica-
ted, like your friend."

I started to shake, not a shiver, but a spastic shake
that nearly threw me in the river. I tried to say something
but my mouth wouldn't work right.

He knelt and looked at me closely. "You *are* Jack
Straw."

I think I shook my head.

He took off his helmet and filled it with water. He
hesitated. Then he set the rim to my lips and dribbled a
handful over my forehead. He looked at me for some time,
as if he was trying to decide if I was good to eat. "You
aren't stupid," he said. "Jack Straw's not your real name."

I turned on my side in the grass, waiting for him to
kill me.

He set the helmet on his head and plucked the
bowstring. "You get on home." He nodded, satisfied. "Get
on home and work for a living." Then he left me there. I
prayed for him to come back, to kill me. I turned and
watched the sun set over the west gate and Sudbury's new
prison. Where did Ball want me to go?

Then I knew it didn't matter where Ball wanted me to
go. I was going home. It was over. Brothers, I felt such
relief, and such deep shame. Stay on, I thought, betrayer.
Lie here until they come and kill you. Still I knew that I'd
get up and walk back home to Gravesend.

I did go home. For a while I told myself that's what
Ball would have wanted, but I confess that I never believed
it. I wondered how he'd get on without me, and was
startled by my own indifference.

I couldn't bring myself to stay on the main road, for

fear they'd followed. The walk home took near a fortnight.
I hadn't a penny and I didn't have the heart to beg or the
spirit to steal, so I lived on two days worth of bread.
Somewhere there, I found I'd carried the cribbed Bible. I
tried to barter it, I think, with no luck. Once, I found some
spoiled fish outside a market. A woman saw me stumble
once, and made me sit down.

"I can't bear to see a young man starve," she said.
She fed me toasted cheese and beer and bacon, and made
me sleep in a real bed with bolsters, though I told her I
was in a hurry.

I don't know the town—I can't remember. It wasn't far
from Maidstone; it might even have been a day away from
home. She babbled half the night, about her husband who
was off at war, and her little daughter. Then she looked at
me, hard.

"I know you," she said. "You speak at market
squares."

"No," I said. "That's not me."

"I could have sworn . . ." She shrugged and turned
down the covers. "Well if it isn't you it's someone who
looks very like you." She sighed. "Jack Straw. Jack for Jack
the Giantkiller. He made some of us feel like Giants,
sometimes, though I'm certain he came to a bad end."

She tucked me in, and I slept very well.

9. God's Brewery

They say God has a brewery in Heaven, and angels gather barley here on Earth. They come disguised as beggars or poor plowmen. They hire themselves as laborers to rich brewers by day and disappear by night, taking a tithe of barley with them. In return, the brewer gets a barrel of God's brew. Many a tavern has made its name on the ale brewed in Heaven, and most brewers are glad enough to lose a portion of their barley for a taste of Heaven's ale.

But once there was a brewer who didn't know the angels. He needed men to harvest and hired them at once, but he began to notice that a portion of the barley disappeared.

"I don't trust them," he thought. "They must be brewing their own ale on my barley." So he watched them closely.

One evening, he saw two of the angels, dressed like ragged peasants, walking out of town with full sacks on their backs. He resolved to follow them, and set off directly.

He kept a distance at first, but soon saw that they had taken a strange road. He kept closer for fear of losing his way, and at last they turned round, saw him, and laughed.

"Fool!" they cried. "You've followed us clean off the earth and into Heaven!"

He looked around and gasped, for he was ankle deep in cloud, and the two peasants had sprouted wings.

"Well, there's nothing for it but to show you God's brewery," said the first angel.

The brewer would rather have gone home, but he said nothing and he left himself entirely in their hands.

They took him to a great cauldron, bubbling brown and smelling nasty. "Here's where God brews trouble," the second angel said. "Stare in if you dare."

The brewer could do nothing but stare in, and there he saw himself following the two angels.

They came to a cauldron at its second stage of brewing. It was frothy, at a low boil, and smelled sweet. "This is where romance brews," the first angel said. The brewer looked in and saw his wife, young and handsome, crossing a summer field.

"This," said the first angel, "is where God brews a sanguine humor." The miller looked into the clear, calm cauldron, just at the right state for fermenting, and he saw his own, silly face.

The angels laughed merrily and showed him how trouble turned to romance and at last to sanguine humor which was poured through a sieve of birch twigs to ferment into God's beer.

The brewer thanked the angels and returned with a barrel. Ah—he thought, when this runs dry I'll turn to the secrets I've learned today and make my own beer quite as good at God's.

The brewer's fortune rose. Everyone came to his tavern to drink his wonderful ale. It caused humorous, romantic trouble, made the most stolid women tipsy and the most solemn men blithe dolts. His house became famous, and he hadn't a worry for he knew he could repeat the miracle of the ale.

At last, his supply ran low, and he set a deep cauldron above a fire.

Ah—he thought. What had been trouble? The two angels lounged nearby, and he remembered. "Here you are!" he cried, and he tossed them into the pot.

His wife ran in. "Darling!" she cried, "What makes you laugh so?"

"Here you are!" he cried, and he threw his wife into the pot—it frothed into romance.

It bubbled steadily, until the boil rolled down. He stared into the calm water and thought: Of course! "Here I am!" He jumped into the pot.

So did the brewer enter Heaven by another door, if at all, though few who drink God's ale can be kept beyond the gate.

10. High Mass

The west gate of the jail was high, and we thundered up a narrow spiral staircase. The steps were bent and broken. We had only a rope to grasp. My dagger nipped my leg. Most of our troop had gone straight on to Canterbury; only three were needed at the tower. Wat was with the others. I felt naked without him.

We stopped midway, at a barred passage. I was mute, always would be by a prison gate, but the man beside me boomed:

"Open in the name of Richard and the True Commons!"

The warden muttered. "I've been watching for you. No fuss." He scowled. "I took your oath not half an hour ago." His hair was sparse, his eyes spring onions. He fumbled for the key. "Go catch your Ball."

I found myself in a dark hall with a nib of a window by the ceiling. There were four cells there; three were empty. The fourth held Ball.

He didn't look up. The warden turned his key and called: "Hey, Jeremiah! You're a free man!"

He'd lost what hair he had, and his long legs were stretched out, gray and bare. I'd yet to see his face. His voice was thick. "I don't think I can get up."

My own voice found itself. "We've come to fetch you, Father."

"Jack?" He stirred. He looked up and I caught my breath. His face was water-gray, save for two red spots on his cheeks. His cell was speckled over with spit and blood. His eyes were ringed in blue.

I said, "Jesus Christ!"

"Oh, I know what you're thinking," the warden said.

"No, it's not plague or he would have been dead a year ago, and me with him. It's a wasting sickness. Spitting blood and coughing blood. Three years in prison and who's well? You've taken your sweet time, eh?"

Ball turned that awful face to me. "Why do you call me Father, Jack? I'm not your father."

The two beside me stumbled back, maybe in horror, maybe at a loss. Ball sat, his long, bruised gray face staring, his red cheeks stirring with a long, sour breath. I stammered.

"We're here now. I hope we're not too late." But as I said this, as I took his arm, I ached to run. I bested my worst self and helped him up. "We're to go to High Mass together. In the mother church."

"The only church I hold with is the church of the vessel of the Holy Spirit." He whacked his chest and coughed. His voice still held a flat, engaging note. He'd be all right. Then he showed a few teeth. "There've been some big doings, eh?"

"Yes," I said, almost yes, Father.

He let me prop him like a warped plank. "I can walk now, I think," he said. He looked at my two mates for the first time. "You are God's elect," he said to them.

They exchanged a look. They'd learn to like John Ball.

"How many more?" Ball asked me.

"Near four thousand." I watched his long jaw drop. "And some say we'll double that in Canterbury. This is Kent alone—we don't know how many rise over the river in Essex."

"And I've heard a name," he said. "Wat Tyler."

I nodded, and my own glee made me babble. "He's a wonder, parson! He's got us roaring, ready, strong—"

"And is he a Christian?"

Again, I nodded.

He frowned and looked at me hard. "I don't mean does he wear Christianity like a shirt. Where do his loyalties lie, Jack?"

"With the King," I said. I turned to the other men, who eyed us steadily. "As do mine."

"There's only one King," Ball said. "You know that."

I felt sweat trickle down my nose. The men stared at us like two of a kind. The warden chuckled. I needed air. Ball's swollen eyes were poking, testing. I took his arm and started down.

We stepped out into sunlight, and Ball wavered, blinking. "It's been three years . . ." He rubbed his eyes with his black sleeve. "I'm dazzled." I steadied him and let the others pass. The men turned back, but didn't stay to listen; I guess they trusted me for Tyler's sake.

"Parson." My voice was so faint that I feared he wouldn't hear me. "In a while you'll have to take an oath."

Ball stopped blinking; he looked at me. "Oath?"

"You'll have to swear allegiance to Richard and the True Commons."

He frowned; the old Ball was back now, entirely. "That's nonsense. I know my own allegiances."

"Parson." I raised my voice and pleaded. "They know you and they want to hear you but you have to . . . well . . . it's proof of good faith."

"I've always said that folks confused Kings." Ball bounded forward, hands working behind his back. "Now that all Comes of thinking there's a King for Heaven and a King for Earth, but Jesus made them one by calling common custom the Kingdom of God. Now the king of England may be the source of custom, but—"

"Please!" I seized his shoulder, shouting so they must have heard me back in Gravesend. "You have nothing against Richard and you have nothing against us!"

Ball answered through bared teeth. "I will swear allegiance only to God and his Elect."

"It comes to the same thing, doesn't it?"

He tugged what was left of his beard. "I take the oath if it is put into those words. Words are all."

I'd lost hope. I looked at his gray, stubborn face and walked on dumb until it came to me. We were in sight of the square. "Allegories!"

Ball paused. "I'm pleased you remember the word."

"The King and the True Commons—why can't they be an allegory for God and his Elect?"

"Principle," he muttered, but I knew he'd taken to the

notion, and at last, almost in Tyler's hearing, he said, "If it makes things easier . . ."

I nodded till I near lost balance.

Wat stamped toward us, helmet low, mail gleaming. He held out his big, hard hand. Ball took it. Ball was three heads higher than Tyler, and though both men were in their forties, Ball looked fifteen years the elder. Wat shook Ball's long hand with spirit. The two took a swift dislike to each other.

"Well now," said Wat. "Well, I heard you speak, Parson, in Colchester long ago."

"Did you?" Ball asked. "And did it influence your life, would you say?"

"I couldn't tell you if it did a thing for me, one way or the other."

"And yet you're here, aren't you?" I turned to Tyler. "That's what Ball wanted. For men to turn their longbows to their masters."

"Now that's the wrong way to put it, Jack," Wat said, not for the first time. "We fight for the King." He turned back to Ball. "Your letters have been a great help, Parson. Very practical."

Ball frowned. It wouldn't have shaken me if Ball's bare skull frowned. The two walked ahead, and we pushed into the square. There was talk of a great oath-taking, but most in Canterbury had been sworn in long ago. There was talk of a sermon—Ball's idea.

"First the High Mass," Tyler said. Three men set emptied carts up into a tottering platform. Wat climbed aloft, arms wagging to keep steady. The folk were drawn to the light on his armor, and they turned. He called: "We gather in an hour to bring doom on all traitors!" The broad square blurred with cheering, and Wat swam through waving arms and staffs and pikes and struck my shoulder, smiling. "A good lot," he said. "Honest tradesmen." He twisted his helmet free and scratched his head. "You haven't had breakfast yet."

Ball and I shook our heads.

He took each on an arm and led us south, past the Cathedral gate. Already a new man balanced the platform.

He was a clerk who fancied himself another Ball, railing against Simon Sudbury. Ball looked back once and spat a line of blood onto the cobbles.

We passed bakeries, fishmongers, butchers, cobblers, all doors flung wide, all goods burdening pecks and baskets. Drays dragged by fat mares drew a ton of salt meat to our camp, and a pack of dogs followed, drawn by the smell. Smiths trooped by, with quivers of cock-feathered arrows and new-strung longbows. Merchants barked and bellowed, hawking, but our company had light purses, and they sold naught. In the end, through fear or fellowship or both, they gave their best away.

We found a lone corner of the camp, by a steep gray stone near the Stour. Most of our company still wandered Canterbury proper, and they'd left the camp in haste. Our goods were scattered round a slope, edged by marsh reeds. Three wives cooked bacon on a grate; they looked up with greasy, eager faces. The smell turned me to stomach, and I filled my arms with pork and bread. Ball mashed a lump of bread, kneaded in his pink spit. He knew his prison maw too well to feed it meat. I found some boots and black stockings; I dressed him like a babe. Wat perched on a Stour stone, with a clean view of the square, reckoning up our number.

Wat turned, eyes glazed. "Jack," he said. "We have ten thousand."

Ball turned as well. "I think I could eat a piece of cheese, now."

I stumbled down the slope to get it. The smoking bacon fat on the grate turned air to wavering water, and I blinked and tried to find the sack of cheese. It was hard enough to see the three wives—smoke turned them to witch spirits. Smoke even turned the north wood quick, I thought, like a wild troop drifting toward me. Then I looked again. My eyes weren't fools. There was a company coming.

I froze with my hand on the colby cheese, thinking: The London traitors have acted at last—it's the end of us. I saw standards, long poles topped with small, dense burdens. Two men bore them, swinging them round so blithe that I felt they must be our own folk, bearing sacks of barley corn flour for standards. I settled then, and broke a hunk of cheese for breakfast, watching. They were full of spirit, less marching than dancing. Well, brothers, when my cheese was gone they'd danced in close enough for me to see that the poles held not corn, but severed heads.

They'd been ill hewn, and the long jog had poked one pole clean through an eye. That was the monk's head, a head with a tonsured pate gone brown in dry blood. The other head had bobbed hair, and the blood that tipped the yellow bangs was fresh enough to shine. No, brothers, I couldn't see their faces. They'd been stuck on a slant, so that their heads bowed. The necks had likely snapped.

The men who bore the heads were strangers. The folk who swung their staffs and pikes in concert were strangers. I tried to look past those free heads, and couldn't. I turned and hurried up to Wat's stone, choking back my breakfast.

Wat was sitting with his hands on his knees, facing the Stour. He looked up. "Do I hear something?"

I pointed, dumb.

Wat looked over his shoulder and jumped. "By God!" he shouted. He tumbled down and thrashed through reeds, crying: "You should have waited! You should have waited for the meeting!"

He blocked their way, and the men who bore the heads stood with the dripping burdens balanced on their shoulders, in plain terror of Tyler. One, a lad more at ease dancing than speaking, stammered. "Captain, these men . . . they're traitors to the King and people."

The other started in. "I'm holding what's left of a lawyer." He smiled, anxious, and shifted his pole forward. The head snapped back. The face—two bloody eyes, a flat nose, bad teeth, fair bobbed hair—was forced toward Tyler's face. Wat backed away.

"From here on, we do things properly!" His voice shook with terror or anger, and the bearers quaked. "We write our grievances. We give them to the King. He gives us leave to execute the traitors and we execute them!"

They nodded weakly. One asked, "Captain, what should we do with these?"

Wat said, "Throw them in the Stour, men. If any loved them, let them fish them out!"

Ah—then they whooped! They fought to get to the bank, to toss the heads high, raising a cry that froze even Wat Tyler's blood. He walked back toward me, muttering, "They must have hated them. They must have cause to hate them. The King would want such men dead . . ."

He crossed directly and slapped a steady hand on my shoulder. Ball looked up from his bread.

"We'll go to High Mass," Tyler said. "From here on, we announce our intentions."

I pulled Ball up and the three of us left camp. Many stayed by the riverside, straining toward the sinking heads. Wat pushed through to the square where a new orator wavered, railing against Hales and the tax.

He cried: "We pay our shilling and Gaunt builds his new house in London—his Savoy manor! How many girls like young Kate Tyler—"

Wat pushed the speaker off with one sweep of his arm. "All in order now!" he cried. "We're to attend High Mass!"

Wat stepped down and a path cleared for him. He took Ball on one arm, me on the other, as though he were warden, we the prisoners. The Cathedral gate was open.

We stepped in. Silence was so sudden and entire I thought I'd fainted. Everything was empty. I moved on, locked in Tyler's gliding arm. Even the troop behind us kept peace like a pact. We paused at the threshold. The red spots on Ball's cheeks were very bright. We entered the Cathedral.

I looked up—my head swam. The ceiling was too high to see. Windows tossed their stained light everywhere, on the stone floor, the walls, the tombs. My knees turned water, and it was only Tyler's arm that kept me standing. We pushed on, passed a tray of candles burning for the souls of the dead. The bishop sang High Mass from a point so far away I couldn't bear to think it part of the same room. His voice thundered and I fell like a man before a storm. My knees gave out. I took Tyler with me this time. He took Ball. The three of us knelt behind a row of monks.

Were they afraid? I don't think they knew who knelt with them. The back end of the Cathedral was thick with our folk. They pushed through the door, fingered the walls, played with the candle tallow. Yet soon they too were on their knees. There was no fear; there was prayer only.

Tyler whispered. "Now!"

I started; it was like a slap. "What?"

"We announce our intentions now!"

I started to say something, but Tyler stood and pulled me forward.

"Brothers!" he called. His voice outmatched the bishop's. The monks and pilgrims turned. "Brothers, we're here to tell you to elect a new Archbishop. Sudbury is a traitor. In a week, he'll be dead."

The nave seemed to crack like a nut, white mortar falling, folks wild for the door. I shuddered with fear and ire and sorrow. I searched for Ball, whom Sudbury had caught three years before. He struggled through whooping, wailing men and women; he bore a stool up by the legs, a mount for his own sermon. I searched for Tyler; he shook yet with the power of his words.

The bishop was gone. As for the monks, they huddled up together, waiting for a path to clear so they could return to the abbey. I guess they had no love for Sudbury. Maybe they had no love for God. I saw fear enough; they feared us more than God. I stood in the center of that overturned Cathedral, terrified.

11. John Ball's Sermon

Then there was Ball's sermon. He'd set his dark, high stool not five yards from Cathedral gate. Ball would preach many sermons in the days to come, but this first one, beginning in a fog of fear, ending in tireless walking, meant the most to me. Ball preached at sunset, after we'd left High Mass. I stood by Tyler, wrapped in his red arm.

"Old Sudbury's in London," Tyler said, "acting as Chancellor. We need to talk, Jack."

I kept an edgy eye on Ball. His stool was well crafted, dragon-legged, and polished to a bite save for a pale oval worn down by the bums of monks. Ball set his foot there now, leafing through a book; it must have been a stolen book, for Sudbury had taken his Piers Plowman long ago, and I had his lone Bible.

Tyler turned his helmet on his head and frowned. "What are you afraid of, Jack? It doesn't make sense, to stop here."

"And you think our ten thousand will walk the seventy miles?"

He turned to them. "They're not afraid."

I followed his eyes, watching men and women. They leaned on the gate like it was their own, whistling and sighing, drunk with the scene in the Cathedral. A tall lad found his way onto the platform, slapped his big hands on his head, and crowed: "Alas! Christ preserve us from these demons!" and he looked so like a daft monk that soon the whole of them were laughing till they choked. The up-turned, rosy faces were fearless indeed. I couldn't laugh. I muttered, "They don't know the danger. They can't see past their fun."

Wat shook his head. "You can't see past your fear."

He started to speak, but he stopped himself and drew his
dagger. It was the first time I'd seen the blade. It was
sleek, not a notch on it, but the handle had already worn
itself to the shape of his hand. He set it in his open palm
and stared at it, soon looking up with peaceful eyes.
"You're against going because you're scared of death, but I
wouldn't think you'd mind dying for the sake of the King."

I shrugged. "I'm not a soldier like you."

"Aye," he said, "but you've got a powerful soul, son,
and it's watching souls round it quicken to life, to action.
You see, but you're too frozen with a fear of doom to join
us." He set his hot hand on my arm. "There's more to—"

A lad broke in. "There's a messenger here! From
London!"

Wat stared past him, straightbacked. "Who from?"

The boy's lean face cracked in half with a smile so ripe
with joy it tears my heart to think of it today. "The King!"
he cried. "By Holy Thomas, Captain, the King!"

A horse kicked up a storm of dust; the messenger
dismounted. Wat ran and threw his arms round him. The
messenger turned white. He was three hands higher than
Tyler, and his bloodless face stared out from that embrace,
mouth twitching. He slapped the wrinkles out of his fawn
surcoat. Sweat stood on his cheeks like pebbles.

"Brother," said Wat. "You come from the King!"

He nodded, turning round once, doubling over like he
had a cramp. A thousand of our company had drawn a
close circle round the man and horse. The messenger
staggered back, and straightened.

"The King would like to know your purpose in
this . . ." He paused, and drew a handkerchief from his
fawn belt. He passed it over his brow. "In this matter."

"We wish to kill all traitors!" Wat said. "For love of
him, we would kill Sudbury, Hale and Richard's uncle John
of Gaunt!" He turned to our folk, to the thousands more
who pushed in till the square pressed them like curd.
"What message do we send the King?"

At once, they answered: "Kill all traitors!"

I felt sweat trickle down and fill my eyes till I saw the
tight bright place through tepid water. I saw the sun ride

all the bare and hooded heads, the soft bobbed hair of the messenger, the steam rising from the flank of his gray mare. I looked and thought: this is like a tale I might be telling, The Peasants and the Messenger, say, or How the Dandy was Pressed into Cheese. All it lacked was a sure ending, and that lack was sore. My sour, numb, storyteller's soul, maybe very like your soul, brother scribe, looked on with doubt and distance. Yet after that day, I was scribe no more.

I watched the messenger dismount and ride straight through the crowd. His horse was terror-mad, but harmed no one. A long troop followed him and called their greetings and good cheer.

A woman trailed a blue banner. "Give the King our love!"

"Tell him we'll have no king named John!" An old man wheezed, and shook his fist. "We're with him!"

"We're all sworn to his service!"

He must have had companions for a good five leagues. They waved pikes and bows and I doubt if he saw anything but a mad mob out for his blood.

These well-wishers left the square near empty. Few heard Ball's first sermon. Wat helped John Ball swear his oath, and Ball spoke the words back, and kept both small, bright eyes on me as if we shared a joke. A few folks greeted him; they'd heard him preach before. They were kind enough, but their words were wrapped in mistrust like sweet nuts in shells. I guess they thought a man who'd preached rebellion for twenty years and who sparked this rebellion from a cell had murky motives. He'd not sprung from empty air when needed, like Wat Tyler; he was tainted by time and failure. His sallow skin and blood-red cheeks summoned up more disgust then charity. I guess they feared they'd look like Ball before the month of June was over.

Ball spoke to them. "So, son," he said to a man with a pointed chin and a lot of stiff, fair hair. "Why are you here?"

"Taxes," he said, uneasy. "And just when I had enough set in to keep my family well through winter. Can't garden on the commons anymore."

"And so poverty shall always lead good men into God's camp," Ball said. He looked as though he'd pat the poor man on the head.

Then, Ball paused, and mounted the platform, laying his strange book on the stool. He had his back to the Cathedral, and he blinked west, toward a sunset just the color of his cheeks. The mayor, who'd sent Ball to prison three years earlier, sat among us that day. He'd stripped himself of any badge of office, and he bundled in coarse wool and sheepskin, like a peasant, but I couldn't forget his face.

I sat in a corner with my knees up, wondering what John Ball was thinking. How long had it been since he'd spoken without fear of prison? How long had it been since he'd spoken to an eager three thousand? If I'd seen Ball thus, three years ago, would I have left him? Well, my Whitsun wish found itself, I thought. I've saved him, set him here to speak his heart. For all the town turned upside down, cathedral bells rang Evensong. Ball looked up from his book and began.

"I've just been reading the holy gospel of Mark," he said. "I don't think most of you have heard the words of Jesus. Yet you know them far better than the false priests and bishops and archbishops because, by your will or not, you live like the apostles, without possessions. You are the people for whom Jesus spoke."

Here he looked at the mayor, and he smiled bitterly, but he didn't point him out. It wasn't that sort of sermon. He turned, instead, toward the fair-haired man and his fair wife and children. He went on.

"I have been reading and remembering one of the great miracles of Jesus. Jesus cured a man of paralysis. You may have seen that miracle staged by your fellows at Easter or Corpus Christi, with one soul lying stiff and a friend taking the part of Christ, healing him. Well, friends, you have seen that miracle performed in earnest today. Christ has also healed *you* of paralysis."

There was a mutter, more baffled than wary.

"I will recite the text for you," said Ball. Then, he

cleared his throat and gave me a look that said: correct me if I'm wrong—you know it as well as I.

We'd worked on the translation together. The bond between us was so sharp it hurt.

" 'And they came'," he said, " 'and brought Jesus a paralytic carried by four men. And when Jesus saw their faith, he said to the paralytic, "My son, your sins are forgiven." Some of the scribes were sitting there, questioning in their hearts, "Why does this man speak like this—it is heresy!" ' "

He stared out fiercely. They looked back with shy, open eyes.

Ball said, "It is heresy to cure paralysis. That is why they call me a heretic. You were paralyzed, and according to the holy words of Jesus, you had sinned. The scribes who make the law which binds you, clerks and treasurers, would have you lay dumb and numb while they strip you of all you've worked for, fought for. I say that this is their sin, and it is also yours, for you must listen to Christ and be paralyzed no more! To remain lying abed is to sin against Jesus and against his Father and against the Holy Spirit!" And with each word he whacked the big book on the stool. His eyes were wild.

We all were listening now.

" 'Jesus, knowing in his spirit that the scribes doubted him, said to them, "Why doubt? Which is easier, to say to the paralytic, 'Your sins are forgiven' or to say, 'Rise, take up your pallet and walk'?" ' " Ball took a breath. "Your sins are always forgiven! Always! You are poor and you have suffered. It is far harder to rise when commanded and claim the Heaven God has built for you on Earth!"

It was hard to tell where the words of Mark ended and the words of Ball began; all rolled out in that heavy, urgent voice. The words of the gospel were written in Ball's heart. His authority was there, inside him, and his own words were as holy as the words of Mark or Jesus. I thought: this is heresy, wonder, the mating of Heaven and Earth!

I puzzled, and I listened.

" 'Jesus said, "I say rise, take up your pallet and go

home," and the man rose at once, took up the pallet and went out before them all so that they were amazed and glorified God, saying "We never saw anything like this!" '
Now I say that we must rise and go! We must claim Heaven—claim Home. Not some Kentish cottage but the land, the goods, the wealth we've earned by being spawn of Eve and Adam! Can the Duke of Lancaster, old Gaunt, though he says he owns half of England, claim a better ancestry? Take up your pallet and go home!" His voice was a command, a soldier's voice. "Go to London, where your inheritance awaits!"

I looked at Wat, who had been sitting near. At the word "London", he jumped up, surprised but ready. "Hear this!" he called. "Hear the parson! We leave for London in an hour! Gather your things and prepare for a long march. We shall find peace and welcome at the end of it!"

Ball didn't hear him. "Rise from the pallet!" he said. "Rise from the stupor, from the dream! Rise and go home!"

Something in me broke. I thought: what's the difference between life and a tale told round a fire? A taleteller can step into a story, can choose it over numb, dumb life, can live it. I'd rise from my long stupor, sins forgiven, rise above law to a world where justice is done, rise to Heaven.

I felt doubt fall away like a suit of lousy clothing I'd long ached to leave behind. Relief blinded me. I wanted to weep. Yes, I'd fight for the King. I'd go to London. Victory was heard as certainly as day at evening. I wondered if I'd been the only one who'd melted so under John Ball's words. The whole world seemed altered, to hold a bright, deep, second world of possibility. So, I thought, this is what it's like to see clearly.

I walked toward the gate and found Ball sitting on the stool. My heart beat back for a moment, hard, and I clasped his hand.

"You've done it," I said, shy, for I felt I didn't know him. "We'd been walking a rut till we near buried ourselves, but we'll stop now." I'd meant that I'd been buried, but I was too abashed to say it.

Ball nodded, brushing off the book. "Are we starting off just now? May I rest a while?"

I took a corner of my soiled tunic to hold the book. He frowned.

"Just a hymnal. Touch it. Use it. Can you read, Jack?"

I blushed. "You should know."

"Out loud, I mean." He gathered his thin pouches and old cloak together. "I want you to recite the psalms tonight, out loud, while we're on the road." He didn't look at me, and he spoke in haste. "I need to rest, just now, but no one else must rest."

I looked at the cobbles. "I don't do much speaking, these days."

He spat a weak line of blood. "I want them to know psalms as well as they know those funny stories they tell at taverns. To confuse them with—" He looked up and smiled, weakly. "No. Not confuse."

I don't think I loved him more before or since. His hollow face was glass. His flickering cheeks were like low flames; they turned him lamp. One hand held his little purses loosely, the other pressed the great, worn, psalm book toward me. The fire had gone out and everywhere was sleepy, peaceful light. When he'd spoken I knew him as I hadn't. I remembered why I'd followed him.

He said, "Blessed be the Lord, who made Heaven and Earth."

We walked toward the Stour camp, arms linked. I was proud to be seen with Ball, proud to carry the psalm book under my arm. His name floated over the water, back again. We both knew they spoke of more than Ball. They spoke of Earth and Heaven, and of London.

12 . Tireless Walking

And even you, Lord Mayor, must have heard wild tales about the walk from Canterbury to Blackheath. We met the distance in a day and a half—seventy miles! Our troop grew greater at each turning in the road, and east, across the Thames, the Essexmen were mustering to meet us. Oh, there are just so many times a man can catch his breath and wonder, and we'd all passed that mark long ago. We knew ourselves heros as we marched the broad road, arms linked, fast and fearless. Thomas of Aldon's voice carried us forward like song:

> And how will you bring her home
> Said Milder to Malder.
> Oh we may not tell you
> Said Festle to Fose.
>
> On four strong men's shoulders
> Said John the Red Nose.
> On four strong men's shoulders
> Said John the Red Nose.

There were fifty among us who claimed to be Robin Hood. They joined us north of Canterbury. They were an odd lot, dressed all in green, bearing longbows as tall as themselves. They could have passed for brothers, with their hard brown faces and their hair bleached white with sun. They kept each to a company and didn't try to best each other at shooting. This was a relief to Wat, who'd feared we'd be held back while they aimed at tiny leaves on tree-tops.

I wove among the marchers, circling, turning, dancing

my old Straw dance while I sang out psalms:

> Hear a just cause, O Lord
>   attend to my cry!
> From you let my vindication come!
> Let my eyes see right!

"Ah, Jack, what's that about then?" A young plowman stomped ahead and tapped me on the shoulder with his spade. "My eyes see right?"

"You haven't heard the tale?" I gawked. "A great Norman Lord's eyes failed him once, and he promised to free his bound men if they'd give him their eyes." I took his spade and twirled it round, walking. "Well, he got a full ditch of good Saxon eyes, and said, 'You're free,' and they believed him, yet all the while they were in fetters." I poked the long spade toward the Kentish companies. "So we called ourselves free men, and all the while we saw the world no better than the blind earth we turned. But now we see right, and we set our spades to other purpose than turning clods of earth." I tossed the spade back to the man and danced away.

And I did worse than that with psalms, my brothers. For all I spoke, Maid Marion and Richard the Lionhearted lived in David's court and sang with him. I'd sing:

> Because the poor are despoiled
>   because the needy groan,
> I will now arise, says the Lord.
> The promises of the Lord are promises
>   that are pure.
> Silver refined in a furnace on the ground.
>   Purified seven times.

I'd sing it for the Lord of Earth and Heaven, a creature with Christ's mercy and sweet Richard's face.

Ball marched by Tyler. Tyler glowed and pumped along, fire-red. Ball's long legs soon warmed back to walking. He coughed and spat but he kept a good pace and the distance was no object to him. The two men disliked each other still, but Wat had been impressed by the sermon; he'd never spoken to Ball of London.

"He's no King's man," Wat said to me, "but he's useful."

"Ball's a King's man," I said, laughing, though I didn't think to tell Tyler which King. They were all one.

"I can't make head nor hind of him," Wat admitted. "Still, his words are clear enough."

We didn't stop to sleep. We walked through a night full and loving as a cat. A woman led, a torch in her hand. She had a clear voice that held the tune by a hair. Her skirt was hiked high for walking.

> And how will you cut her up
> Said Milder to Malder.
> Oh we may not tell you
> Said Festle to Fose.
>
> With knives and with forks
> Said John the Red Nose.
> With knives and with forks
> Said John the Red Nose.
>
> Oh that will not do
> Said Milder to Malder.
> Oh what will do then
> Said Festle to Fose.
>
> Big hatchets and cleavers
> Said John the Red Nose.
> Big hatchets and cleavers
> Said John the Red Nose.

Will Nettle caught my arm. At first I didn't know him. He looked an age older. His blue tunic was open and even in the cool night the dye ran with sweat. He said, "Do you think we'll be stopping in Gravesend?"

I frowned. His voice felt like a drizzle. "It's doubtful," I said. "No one's tired."

He puffed to keep my pace and spoke in bursts. "I

thought you'd be wanting to see Jenny."

I shrugged. "Why would I want to see Jenny?"

He spoke up, then. "Jack, I may die in London. For all this good fun we may all die there. You have the power—" His voice trailed and he pulled me to a halt and held my eyes with his own. "Just once, I'd like to speak my mind to her."

I looked at my friend. His face, for all the trouble, was at bottom the same face he wore in Gravesend. The glamor hadn't touched him. I said, "You want to stay in Gravesend?"

"Ah, no Jack. You think I'd abandon you now?" He pushed his hair back and he bowed his head. I was glad he didn't meet my eyes again.

I hurried on and pushed ahead like a hound loosed from a chain, my Straw tricks wild again, yapping out my psalms:

For he who avenges blood is mindful of them.
He does not forget the cry of the afflicted!

Ball and Tyler walked a pace apart, behind the high, hot torch. They set me between them, and I strode front and center, following only that lone, singing woman. Her thin legs caught the torch blaze like a fairy's.

I spoke without thinking. "When do you fancy we'll reach Gravesend?"

"By midday, Corpus Christi, at this pace," Wat answered, "if we don't sleep."

"Oh, I was going to ask after that Bible." Ball turned, face absent. "Perhaps you could fetch it."

At once, I felt a wave of horror. I'd have to face Jenny.

Wat frowned, and pulled his helmet low. "I don't think it worth a stop. We have the hymnal."

"We would do well to travel with a Bible." Ball spoke half to himself, but Tyler listened and he shrugged.

"Oh, if you don't take long with it, I guess we could sit and rub our feet. Still, so close to the end of the road . . ." He muttered to himself, and walked on.

The sun rose to our backs, and we reached Maidstone by late morning. The whole town filled the square to greet us. We had to stop if only to push through the hundred who bore baskets and banners. Two women bore a proud new standard, Adam delving, Eve with spindle. Kate Tyler stood among them, some ways off, and she swung a basket full to overflowing, warm with bread and sour with cheese. Her hair was twisted back, and her face was round and white like a moon or a cheese. All marveled to see the famed Tyler's daughter. Tyler met his dog and begged forgiveness. I wandered alone to a pear orchard by the edge of open country. It was our land now, won by faith and tireless walking. The road ahead was light and long and beautiful.

I stood, delight whistling straight up from my toes. But no—it wasn't from my toes at all. I turned and saw Kate Tyler.

She'd passed her basket back, I guess. Her hands were free. I took one of those hands, which smelled of bread, and pressed it to my lips.

She said, "You're changed."

I slipped my arm around her waist and laughed. "Did you know me so well, Kate, that you can mark a difference?"

Her eyes were her father's: steady, dark. She kept them on my own light, hectic eyes until I blinked. She said, "Jack, Straw burns to nought in fire."

I might have puzzled on the riddle once, but now I caught her and I kissed her. Brothers, she matched me, warm and steady. One round arm pulled me low until we kissed behind the milkweed. We weren't at it long—we couldn't be. We heard the first of the troop drawing near. Kate sat up, picked a string of gray twig from her hair, and closed her eyes.

We were dumb. Odd, after we'd kissed I found it hard to look at Kate. I knew I hadn't wronged her, yet I felt I'd wronged someone, broken some oath I hadn't even known I'd made. I thought: you'd best look your fill now, before you leave. She knelt, parted the weeds with her hands, and her face was lost to me. She spoke at last. "The banner's

there," she said. "We started spinning it the day you freed
Rob Billing. It's finer work than we could have done in a
year's time. It seems a shame to see it out in wet and
dry."

I cupped her shoulders, drew her back. "The weather's
kept dry and fine." She faced me now, hands on her
knees, skirt spread round her like a puddle. I hesitated, but
I said, "Come with us, Kate."

She bowed her head.

I took it in my hands and raised it, and I kissed her
round, soft nose. "Ah, you think a little fire will burn this
Straw to ashes, then?"

Kate said, "I was talking about my father."

"Ah! I understand now!" I whacked my hand on my
knee. "—BAMM! Tiling hammer through the head!"

Kate whacked her own hand on my mouth. "Hush,
Jack." She rubbed her head with her free hand and
frowned. "I told you, I've done my share of walking."

"And so you'll be warmed to it, Kate," I said. "We'll
warm each other."

She shook her head so hard her hair flew back, and
when she looked at me again, her eyes were fire. "Jack
Straw!" she whispered, "I walked from Colchester to Maidstone to search for my own father, who'd left my mother
when I was a babe."

I sat up. "Why did he leave you mother?"

Kate answered me. "Because he was afraid."

I eased back, laughing. "You father could no more be
afraid than you could be a maiden, Kate."

Kate rose. She stumbled back, blinking, as though I'd
slapped her.

I stood, myself, and laughed. "Your mother told a tale.
Wat Tyler? Break faith because he's afraid? Afraid of what?
Is your mother a witch, then? Come here and give your
friend a kiss goodbye."

"I'd sooner kiss a snake," Kate said. "Go back to my
father, go back to the traitor—who thinks he can cover his
traitor's tracks in fire!"

That's how I left her then, up to shoulder in milkweed, hair in black strings, bold eyes inside out. I thought

as little of her as a hound a flea, for she'd called Wat a
traitor. I shrugged her off so easily that by the time I'd
reached my own folk I had no wish to look back.

I passed Ball, and he turned and eyed me. "Did I see
you with a woman, in the wood?"

I nodded. "Tyler's daughter," I said. "She's a fool, like
all women."

Ball nodded, tugged his cloak a little closer round him,
and strode past me like a heron. I crossed straight to Tyler.
He marched, the sunlight dancing on his helmet, his
daughter's eyes all bliss and freedom in his face. I thought:
I won't let any shadow fall on this day or this journey.
More likely Kate was traitor than her father. More likely
she had tumbled with the clerk than Wat would break a
marriage oath for fear.

I don't know the pace we walked. We seemed to walk
like mortals; maybe the road itself had turned fairy, or
maybe, I thought, walking, this is what it's like to understand, to walk in tales: if you know how the world works
it works for you, and miles become feet and your feet are
set on legs a mile long.

I told my tales, though they were pale, now, only
muddled tries at telling our own story. The Robins sang
and bragged. Ball was silent, but that was Ball. Wat
beamed at all who crossed his path. Pug followed us for
three miles. He turned back when we forded a stream. Wat
said it was just as well.

Night came again; why did we never tire? Wat Tyler
held the torch, then, and led the singing. He was tone deaf
but his voice was drowned by fifteen thousand voices:

> Oh how will you cook her
> Said Milder to Malder.
> Oh we may not tell you
> Said Festle to Fose.
>
> With pots and with pans
> Said John the Red Nose.
> With pots and with pans
> Said John the Red Nose.

I heard a high laugh, turned, and saw Faith Corning. She held her sleeping Mary in her arms. Art was awake, singing, waving a pointed stick. Faith was weary of him, and she swatted the stick down.

"You'll take out an eye with that, I swear!"

"More than an eye, mother!" Art grinned, and his voice was lower than it had been the day before, but he kept the stick down. Faith shook her head, caught my eye, and frowned.

"What will we find in London? Has Jack Straw ever been to London?"

"No, Faith," I said. "Not even Jack Straw has been there."

"Your brother's there, isn't he?" She closed her eyes, straining to remember Alfred. "Will he meet us?"

I shook my head, and thought of him. He'd be twenty-seven now, a long-john like me, though pitch dark. He'd be a merchant, if the wind had blown his way, and I didn't think he'd like us.

Faith looked grim. "It isn't meet to break with family."

I laughed. "Ah, have you heard the tale of the squirrel whose brother sold the family's pelts for nuts?" Still, I didn't like the smell of the conversation. We were on the edge of Gravesend.

We arrived at Corpus Christi dawn. The sun caught on the Thames, the river that passed through the village and would flow, like us, to London. I'd thought Gravesend would greet us like Maidstone, but no more than half a dozen met us by the King's Arms, and their hands were empty. They seemed anxious only for their neighbors, and none seemed to know me. In truth, the town seemed to hold more pigs than people, and I wondered if my neighbors hadn't turned to belled, sly pigs to confound me. I sniffed the air; it didn't smell like home, but like chalk, sheep dung, mold and timber. I froze, nose high, and then I knew: it was the first time I'd entered Gravesend as a stranger, as Jack Straw.

Ball looked at Tyler. Tyler frowned and turned. "We'll stop here for a while and get our bearings."

The company turned sour; they saw what I saw, a

gloomy river village that promised no gain. "We have our bearings!" someone called.

"Ball doesn't have his bloody Bible," Wat muttered. He called: "An order's an order!"

The men and women milled through Gravesend, stomping through the empty streets where pigs and loose hens roamed. Staring down the Thames, they packed the wharf till it groaned. I walked south, down a gray, hard trail, past sheep and flint-walled ferrymen's cottages. I had to strain to find the place familiar, and the more I knew for home the more my new bliss drained away, the more I felt Mike Row. And worse, when I found the right road I'd have to meet Jenny.

"HA!"

Grabbed from behind! It was Will Nettle, and I'd never seen him happier. He took both of my hands and kissed them. I snarled. "You scared me, you bastard!"

Will backed off, laughing, jigging round me like a May Fool. "Ah, bless you, by Saint Mary, I commend your soul to Heaven! I was sure you hadn't spoken, but you had!" He took my hands again, his gray eyes at once wet and blazing. "This means life itself to me!"

He pulled me to the right road, walking a clean sweep up hills, down hills that all looked strange to me. Then we passed something, a hoe left gardenside to rust, my hoe, my garden. Recognition spread like paint. We reached the door and I'd lost what sure wit I had. I hugged the threshhold, frozen.

"Well," said Will. "Open it!"

I pushed the door ajar, and blinked with smoke. The stink rose next, like rotten mutton. Then I heard breathing. I blinked and strained and staggered toward the sound. I made Jenny out, barely. She sat with her leg on the trestle table, staring at the dead grate.

"I'm back," I said.

"Yes, you said that before." Her voice had thinned. She was thinner too; she must have lost a stone's weight in a week. "And has your Whitsun wish come true, brother? Have you been put to test and not betrayed one you love well?"

I looked back toward the door that seemed a mile away, for Will. I couldn't see him.

Jenny went on. "Word has it you're off to London. Give my love to Alf. He always cared for me." I heard her fumble. She drew the shutter open. She looked back at me with a face that near matched Ball's, death white, hollow, grubby, the face of a babe left to starve and smother in the mud. She saw herself in my face, and she smiled. "No charity this time, brother. Lord Simon's threatened them; no good feeding Jack Straw's sister."

I said, "How ought I take that, Jenny? Ought I take a toasting fork and poke it through my gut?"

She yawned. "Going to London comes down to the same thing, I think. You'll die there and go to Heaven."

The last spark of my own joy drove me on. "Jenny— it's true though. Heaven's here."

"Here?" She gestured round the smokey, rotten room. "Was it worth Joe Billing's life to even try to turn a place like this to Heaven?"

I turned. "Well, I'm here on an errand." I pushed past, to the bower for the Bible, and heard Nettle stumble in behind me.

Leaving that hall was like leaving hell. The bower stunk the worse, but it didn't have Jenny. I nosed through the oak cabinet and found the Bible. Ball's letter fluttered out. I wondered if I ought to read it, see if I could decode the words now, like Tyler, but I let it lie. We'd gleaned whatever wisdom we could from them. I thought: Will's asking Jen to marry him. I turned the big book to the psalms, granting him time. We'd never set an English crib above them, and my Latin was gone, but Christ knows by that time I didn't need a book before me to know psalms. I whispered:

> I lift my eyes to the hills.
> From whence comes my help?
> My help is in the name of the Lord
> who made Heaven and Earth!

I thought about Heaven and Earth, about loyalty, oaths and fear. Then I could grind those hard, dark stones no more, and I stepped back into the front hall. Nettle had gone. Jenny hadn't moved.

"Well," she said. She sat up.

"I'll be back."

"No," Jenny said. "You'll stay right here." She brushed her stray, pale hair out of her eyes and said, "You'll keep your bargain—you said you'd stay if I played tiler's daughter." She stretched, and her white sleeve was caught up in a yellow ribbon. "Well, if Nettle's guessed it, you might know. The part's my own, Michael."

I couldn't take my eyes from that ribbon. "Jenny—you haven't said Will could take you!"

She laughed in earnest. "And for all this time I thought you'd wanted him to take me!"

"Not against your will, Jenny," I said.

"Against my will? No, Michael, the men in the ditch were the ones who had me against my will. But there was no man with a hammer then." She looked down and coughed. "Will is a good man, and what I said made him happy. He treated me well, while you were gone, and if I can't love him, he deserves some solace. He had the sense to tell me that he didn't care if I was no maid."

I looked at the lame leg, slung over the table like a white sausage, and up from there to the brown skirt, the narrow shoulders, the loose, dirty hair. I looked at everything but Jenny's face. She went on:

"And then it came to me, the old bargain. You said you'd stay. You said you'd keep the bargain. Now I've done my part of it." She turned the yellow ribbon round and round till her sleeve twisted like a screw. We both knew that I wouldn't stay.

I said, "That was a game, Jenny."

"And what you're doing now is grander than a game." She nodded. "It must be worth the world, since I can't go."

I fumbled. Then I said, "Even if I hadn't followed Ball, it would have happened."

But she shook her head. I felt horror—then fury.

"You blame it on me, always! If I had stayed, if I had stayed! And what if bloody Alf had stayed!" I paced the room, and kicked up rotten rushes till it took a stout heart to shout through the stink. "You say you played Kate Tyler! I've met Kate Tyler now!" I'd forgotten that I didn't like Kate Tyler anymore. At once she seemed a queen who could have jumped out of a ditch as deep as hell and killed her tax clerk before he touched her. "If I'd stayed you'd be as bad or worse! And you'll be none the worse for me leaving again!"

She looked back without blinking. "No worse? Well, what am I brother? I'm not made of straw." She turned back to her grate. "Goodbye, Michael."

I left her there and walked off with my Bible.

I reached the King's Arms less Straw or Row than some red, storming creature. Will was there; he'd filled a few carts with the last of his ale.

"So I go hungry later. Ah—Heaven and Earth are one, Parson Ball. You're right!" He spoke so earnestly—words melted down like sunshine. Ball didn't hear. He took my Bible and was lost to all save the apostles. We started west, toward Blackheath, my companions drinking, laughing, trailing carts burdened with Nettle's leaking casks of ale.

I kept as far from Nettle as I could, and I walked my wild anger into Watling Road until it lost itself in the hard earth. Yet all the while the troop around me stayed blithe, tipsy, loving. In that manner, we reached Blackheath. It was a wet evening. Were we weary? I was sick at heart, but even I had no thought of sleep. We sat in that broad, damp clearing three leagues from London, straining to make out the lights at the top of the tower. Some wondered if we'd walk those final miles and cross the bridge, but I don't think a soul doubted in earnest. Not that night.

Closer, and coming toward us, were thirty thousand more from Essex. That night, we camped, told tales, and waited for word on London.

13 . Corpus Christi

Blackheath was broad enough to hold our fifty thousand. Essex pondered our tales and told their own. More than once, I fancied I saw the old, dancing beggar, but many danced that day. Yet more spoke, and we heard many tales of the attack on Rob Hale's Essex manor.

An old wife hugged herself, laughing. "Why, you should have seen us throw the curtains to the bound men. They set them on the grass and let the dogs hump bitches on pure cloth of gold! Ha! He'll find nought but a shell when he returns!"

"No worry," someone called. "He shan't return!"

They bounded toward old friends and strangers both. Some found kin who'd turned outlaw and fled to the greenwood. The air was thick and warm, the sun a clot in rain clouds, but it would be a while before the storm began, and all there had stood worse than rain.

Ten lads pitched tents to keep food dry. Our shrinking stock of bread was set under tarred canvas. They'd tacked torn standards up into a tent for Tyler, and red and green bloomed vivid as the sky turned grey. Wat hadn't used the tent. He walked round, kindling fires, heaving hewn logs up for storage, talking to the Essex captains.

I tried to force Ball into the tent for a nap, but he stood like a tent post, hot on preaching his next sermon. He'd made a full half-dozen on the road.

"It's Corpus Christi, Jack," he said sharply. He tugged his beard and his deep eyes traveled the thousands with suspicion. "Why aren't they at prayer?"

I near dragged him to bed by his long legs, but Art Corning pushed in. He'd been on watch, and he'd run the quarter mile like a rabbit. "A man on horseback!" he said.

"Oh—Jack! I think he's from the King!"

I asked "Alone?"

He nodded. "We have to tell Captain Tyler!" He seized my arm and pulled me through the Kentish company. Tyler was circled by tall men heaped high with wood.

Art spoke, and Tyler nodded. "Ah . . ." He smiled at his men. "The King answers." He scratched his neck. "That man at Canterbury did his work. By God, we've earned the right to meet him now. I'm sure we'll meet him, Jack."

He flung his arm around young Art, who blushed and squirmed and smiled. He wrapped the second round my waist, and walked us to the tent. The man and mount were waiting.

I'd figured on another edgy dandy with bobbed hair, but this man was at ease. He wore a long, brown coat, and his brown hat was plain as toast, but his horse was treasure enough. Its brown coat caught light like the Thames. He told us that his name was Alderman John Horn, messenger from the King.

He stayed amount, and spoke: "I bring you this message, from Richard. He begs you, for his sake, to return to your homes."

Wat looked at John Horn for a long while, measuring. Horn looked him in the eye; his own eyes were clear gray and powerful. I couldn't help but like him.

"We wish to meet with the King," said Tyler. "He has been misled by traitors. Tell him to come to Blackheath."

"That is your message?" Horn frowned.

"And we have a petition." Wat looked at me. I drew out the fair copy. Horn dismounted and led his horse forward by the rein. He asked to see the charter. I hesitated, but I gave it to him. His eyes passed over the page, and I knew he could read. He was a while with it. Wat watched him carefully. Horn looked up.

"You realize all of these men are in the Tower of London with the King?"

If Horn's news cracked Wat's faith he didn't show it. "We're Richard's army," he said, "and he'll know it when he sees what we've done for his sake. He'll hand the traitors over."

Horn went on. "John of Gaunt's in Scotland."

"No doubt . . ." Tyler's voice wavered now. "No doubt
mustering an army against his young nephew."

Horn shook his head. "These demands—"

"It's a petition," Wat said, straightening. "We're free
folk, and we ask for what is ours, our common land, an
end to the reign of lawyers, and fair rent."

"I see." Horn rolled the parchment round, and set it
in his saddle-bag with respect. Horn made to mount again.
Tyler stepped forward, and layed a hand on his shoulder.

"Horn," he said, "You'll swear allegiance to King
Richard and the True Commons."

Horn's calm began to waver. "I'm the King's servant.
And Alderman to the city of London."

"Then there ought to be no conflict," Tyler said.

Horn tried to turn the horse, but Tyler took the reins.
"I'd consider such an oath to be insulting," said John
Horn.

"Ah — but needed," Tyler said, "if you're to see
Richard alive."

Horn steadied himself by his mighty horse. At last, he
said, "I'll swear." And he swore, brothers, in a voice that
gained strength as he spoke. Then Tyler gave his horse's
head a gentle cuff and shook Horn's hand.

"Wait," said Wat. He turned and called Hugh Smith
and Martin Carter over. "These men will go with you to
contact London brothers of our Fellowship."

Horn looked at Tyler. "I pity you," he said.

"Don't," said Tyler. "And don't pity yourself. You're
one of us now, Horn. Pity only Richard, and serve him."

Horn had no answer. He mounted and started west,
Hugh and Martin at a trot on either side. Our folk watched
the three men, dazzled and heartened. They shouted good
cheer, but they couldn't follow far; we lay too close to
London.

And they were testy now; the gray light spread like
dirty water, and fires were cheerless without night. Some
from Essex knew Jack Straw, and they whistled me over,
hungry for a tale. Only the gray tales came to me: Death

and his three wives, the man who ate his son and threw
the bones under the table, the maid who flayed the skin of
a charmed deer, in truth her brother. For despair, there are
psalms enough:

> Let not the flood sweep over me
> or the deep swallow me up
> or the pit close its mouth over me

"What do you mean, Jack?" they'd ask. "Tell us what
you mean!"

I'd blink and ponder and I'd say, "You'll have to ask
David the Jew who sang it first." I'd stand by myself,
puzzling at the Thames as it flowed under London bridge,
and sing:

> What I did not steal
> Must I now restore?

Worse yet, I faced Will Nettle. He sat gossiping with
Aaron Stone, drinking his ale, stringing longbows. He
waved me over three times. I played blind and he called:
"Over here, brother!" I played deaf, and he ran up and
tackled me and then I played no more. His ale breath alone
was dizzy stuff, and I had the whole of him on me,
heaving with good humor. "Ha! Brother!" He gathered me
in his round, warm arms. "I like that better than the new
name I have to call you. Will brother do, then?"

I shrugged and tried to struggle off. He'd have none of
it.

"Ah—" he said, forcing me down by Aaron. "But sit
beside me and let's talk like old times." He sat himself,
and leaned back on his arm, sighing. "You know, that's
what I'd wished for at Whitsun—for her to take me. Ah, I
hoped you wished with care, brother!"

I muttered something about keeping faith. Will leaned
in close to hear more, but Aaron broke in and sniggered.

"If I'd wished I think I'd have done no better than to
wish for such a fortnight. Fair weather and fine company!"

I shot up, straight and strained as a reed, and I cried:

"You're a pair of slobbering fools! Here on holiday! Drinking, looting—"

Aaron edged off, then, but Nettle moved close, staring out with wonder and concern. "Looting? Well, I do drink, brother, but I'm steady."

"It's not that." My voice went wrong, and I turned so I wouldn't see him. "Will, why are you here?"

Will didn't answer.

I bowed my head. My eyes traveled the length of Blackheath, marked every crack and tuft of yellow grass. "If you're here for my sake, Will, go home."

I heard Aaron mutter, "It's a little late in the day, I'd bargain."

"Go home and try to marry Jenny. You could have saved her back then, stopped them. You saw her lying there, broken. You did nothing. Nothing but break more."

I felt a hand under my chin. Will turned my face, roughly, and he looked into my strange eyes as though they held my sister.

I said, "You saw her that same day, and you did nothing."

That should have snapped the friendship, neatly and forever.

But no, Nettle's round eyes fluttered and he staggered. "I did nothing. You're right. I let her cry, and I saw blood, but I thought it was from the fall. I thought it was something I could fix, and I didn't stop to guess. I should have known. I should have found the man who did it. No — I let him go . . . or them go . . . I . . ." His eyes sharpened and hung on my pale, wooden face like hooks. He said, "She told you. You can't forgive me now."

I turned and walked away. I looked back once, and saw him in Stone's arms, quaking and sobbing. I passed my woe along, then, like a tale.

Yet other tales were told at Blackheath. Ten men and women from Colchester had covered a hill with tarp. They'd started through a Corpus Christi cycle, formed for a finer, moving stage and a smaller circle. Now the mount was an island, near lost in flags and standards. Babes sat on their mother's shoulders, pointing, poking. Mugs of ale,

I guess the last of Nettle's, were passed round, and a loaf of bread piked on a pole bobbed from end to end till it was nibbled to the wood.

They'd reached the Fall, and they'd get no further than Isaac's binding before sunset. The man who played the woman, Eve, wore a white mantle—who knows where he got it? The serpent, Lucifer, held one of the apples the lad had peeled for toothless convicts days before. The apple had gone brown as dung, but it served well enough. The man who spoke the part of Eve smoothed back a horse-hair wig and greeted the serpent:

> Eve: If I ate the apple, I would
>   be to blame!
> From joy our Lord would us expel:
> We should die and be put out with shame,
> In joy of paradise never more to dwell—
>
> Serpent: Of this apple, if you will bite,
> Even as God is, so shall you be.
> Wise of cunning as I you plight,
> Like unto God in all degree.
> Sun and Moon and stars bright,
> Fish and fowl, both sand and sea,
> All things shall be in your power;
> You shall be God's peer.
> Take this apple in your hand
> And to bite thereof you're fond.
> Take another to your husband—

The serpent was thrown backward by John Ball. He pushed next to Eve, and sent the wrinkled apple flying into the Thames.

"Hear me!" he called, and his voice rang and pleaded. "Hear me out!" He was blinking and a drool of blood caught in his beard. "Hear me out before you leave paradise!"

The sea of folk seemed eager to listen. I guess they thought it was part of Adam's Fall.

John Ball strained forward, clutching for the few hairs

he had lost long years ago. He said, "The serpent—oh children—the serpent is the King!"

Silence was broken by a single, chilling gasp. Half the folk thought it was a joke; the others thought they'd heard wrong. Ball's face was red all through now, and his eyes were dark and flapping, like two crows.

"You've heard the rhyme—we all have—'When Adam delved and Eve span, who was then the Gentleman'!"

Some smiled then. Eve stepped forward with a drop spindle, and the man who took the part of Adam moved in with a spade. Ball paid them no mind; he was turning his mill now, grinding out his thin, strong grain.

"In Eden we have power over ourselves, and when we bargain with Lucifer we bargain for a different kind of power. Who bought our souls with Lordship? Who but the serpent? Who but the King?"

Adam and Eve exchanged a look and turned away. The serpent returned with a second apple, and tried to speak, but Ball pushed him back with a wild, determined arm.

"Who but Richard? Who but the King? Oh take what we have! It's ours, for we're no Gentlemen! We need no blessing!" Ball walked across that mount and back again. The crowd began to thin out, scatter. "We need nothing but the spirit of God in our hearts!" he cried. "Richard can't give us that! Richard can give us only Lordship— He'll betray us!"

I felt a strange old shiver spreading up my back, and I turned to see Tyler, hand on dagger, charging toward the mount like thunder. I wanted to run to Ball, yet, by God, oh brothers, I stood and watched Wat take Ball under his waving, wild arms and I saw him whisper in his red ear harshly. That didn't stop John Ball. He railed on. It wasn't till three men joined Tyler that the parson stopped fighting and began to cough.

Ball coughed and spat right on the feet of the men who held him. They backed off. Tyler didn't need them now. Ball was too busy coughing, shaking, spitting, to preach on.

Night came at once; the sky turned glassy blue. The

walk caught our company then; they slept, at last, under
the starless sky. Wat snatched my arm, and pulled me to
Ball. Ball was through coughing now, and his face was
empty and terrible.

"See he keeps quiet," Tyler said.

Ball looked up, and the fluttering eyes had folded their
wings. I felt my own eyes glaze with fear. Ball asked, "Will
you keep me quiet, Jack?"

I did not answer, all the while knowing my chance
had passed again, that I'd betrayed John Ball again, and
would again, and ever would, for all the Whitsun wishes in
the world. I took my good belt-bartered cloak and wrapped
it round Ball's shoulders. I couldn't be his son, or his good
servant, yet I could nod my head as though I loved him
still.

14 . The Barge

The next morning stunk with ill omens. The first rain fell and a quarter of our bread was spoiled. Even Tyler was uneasy.

"Tell them a tale," he said in haste. "Do something. Get their bloody minds off London."

We'd figured we would march in, as we'd marched everywhere, but Wat was uncertain. We had the Thames to contend with now. Would London Bridge be raised against us? We waited, and we didn't know if we'd enter the city on Tuesday, Wednesday or no day. Folks hopped pebbles on the water, and they talked of mowing and sheep shearing, a bad sign. Some whittled tinder into weapons. I sat in a circle of crouching, wet companions and told tales with feigned spirit. I fooled no one.

"Why no tales of London, Straw?" a tall man called, spitting out the words like tar. "I think that dark place we see from this hellish heath's a fairy city! I think all the lawyers only say they come from London! I think they come from Hell!"

"No, this Jack Straw's got a merchant brother there," a woman called. She snorted, rolling on her heels. "Or so they say. More likely Straw's from London himself, and he's a devil!"

I started in, helpless. "You want a tale about a devil? You want to hear about the Miller and the Devil? The Devil and his Confessor? Well, once the Devil felt he'd been too long without confession, so he searched the whole of the world for a friar who'd shrive him—"

I went on. It did no good. All eyes saw nothing but the city and all ears heard nothing but the silence.

Even the Robin Hoods were losing heart. Ten disappeared. The two score who remained shot arrows up at naught till many ran for cover. Wat was worse than any; his eyes never left the road. Ball sat in the tent, no will to rise and preach again. I found myself without a friend. Once, I sought Faith Corning. She sat sharpening her teeth on brick-hard bread; we'd little bread to spare now, and if we camped on the heath much longer we'd have none. Faith gnawed and sucked and looked up.

"Is the storyteller weary of walking?"

"Walking and telling stories, Faith," I said. "How are your children?"

"They're trying their hand at fishing," she said. "Nothing else to do." She loosed her hood and let her gray hair down. "Have you seen Will Nettle? He looks like a ghost."

I shook my head. The dull, gray heath seemed thick with ghosts.

Three men who'd been bathing dashed past, shaking off water like three dogs. "The barge!" they cried. "The barge!"

Faith waved, laughing. "Well, my children caught a big fish! It must be the King himself!"

I turned back and saw Wat rushing toward them in full armor. "Tell me! Tell me, Sam." He seized the tallest by the shoulders. "Is he alone?"

Sam shook his head. "Some men say they know two on the craft, two lords: Salisbury, Warwick. The rest are strangers."

Wat found me and pressed me forward. We pushed to the bank. Our thousands overtook us and they filled the narrow strip of bank a quarter mile deep. Some floundered in the water, wading out to see. Wat cried: "Get back!" He threshed through them like long corn, and cleared some twenty yards between our company and the Thames. I stood foremost among them, holding the boldest back with long splayed arms. Wat stood lone in that clearing. He bared his head and threw his shoulders back, at strict attention. We watched the barge.

It skirted the water, a sail full of the low storm breeze, a purple sail. Slow rows of oars pressed forward to a drum beat, faint yet. The ship's stem turned, and a gilt prow nosed south, toward us. The wind pressed the barge to our bank, and the oars tried to turn it north again. But then, drums stilled. Oars rose. Adrift, the barge approached.

A curtained canopy ran poop to bow. One end draped back, caught in a gold ring. It fluttered, and the breeze filled with a scent like wine and lavender. The dark within that canopy was dense as char, and we could see no more than a few spade beards, high black collars. We saw no King. Yet then, the closed end of the curtain parted. We saw his face.

It was a boy's face, soft and covered with gold down. It was the face of Richard in my dream. He stared out, like a stricken hart. His light eyes caught my own, and flashed toward Tyler. He called, then. His voice didn't carry far.

"Men," he said. "Go back to your homes."

Wat paused, and slowly, burdened by his armor, he lowered himself on one knee. I followed. Soon we all knelt.

Wat spoke. "For your sake, we shall not."

There was a pause. The others had caught Richard back, and he strained toward us, sunlight pale on that shy, curious face. He called: "What would you have me do?"

Wat Tyler answered: "We would have you come aland and we would show you what we lack." Wat's fuzzy head was bowed, and he held out his empty hands. "We would have you give up all the traitors to us."

Richard called: "Men, I've seen your list, and I can not accept the demand. Several of those men are with me on this boat."

There was a stir behind me; our folk shouted, pushing forward. Wat jumped up and waved an arm in fury. They settled back. "Sire," Wat said, "I would speak to you now, if I might."

A man on Richard's left came to light now, an old man with a long face and a forked pepper-grey beard. He set three fingers on King Richard's shoulder and he spoke. "Sirs!" he called. "You are not in such order nor array that the King ought to speak to you!" He pushed Richard back and drew the curtain.

The drums began again. Straining against the wind the poop moved round and the barge rowed away.

Wat didn't move. Our company mumbled, brushed their shirts and breeches, and some called to the barge. "Bless you, Richard! We're with you!" I edged up, and put a hand on Wat's shoulder. He flinched.

"He's gone now," I said.

Wat looked at me. His face and eyes were full, as if he'd been knighted. "He's with us," he said softly. "He would have come ashore."

"I know." I tried to lead him back to camp, but he'd not budge. His eyes kept to the fighting purple sail.

"We'll come to him, for they won't let him come to us, Jack. If only . . ." He turned toward London.

I nodded.

"If we could just be sure the bridge would be down and the gate would be open . . ."

He bowed his head, and started back to camp.

I felt Richard there still, like the smell of smoke. I'd seen his face, and it had been pitiful, wonderful, the Richard in my dream. It had been a wild face, full of hope. He was a King, and capable of love, loyalty, dignity. He was a youth of fourteen, and could be taught compassion. I'd seen his face and knew they'd not yet owned his soul!

Oh brothers, Mayor, scribe, there was such joy then! My own heart grew the larger just to hold it. Only myself and Tyler knew the truth; we'd been close enough to read his face, to read our victory in it!

The clouds grew porridge dense, and a new drizzle fell. We sat in the tent. Wat waited. He wasn't anxious now. I found myself keeping by him, just to know there was another soul who'd seen Richard.

Ball hadn't seen the barge, and didn't ask about it. He'd aged another ten years since we'd reached the heath, and I began to wonder if life out of jail was bad for his health. A woman forced food on him, but he coughed each morsel up coated in blood.

Wat turned to Ball and snorted. "Why, what a state our new archbishop's in today!" The notion tickled him, as any notion would have, then. "Ha! How would you like that, Parson? Archbishop Ball!"

Ball spat again. "I would sooner dig a hole in the

ground and bury myself alive."

"Don't worry, Ball." Wat sat back, nodding with the rain. "You'll get to preach yourself dumb in London."

"I'll get to die there as well," said Ball.

"Oh no!" I looked at him with the warmth that a blithe man feels for everyone. "That you won't do. You'll get Heaven on Earth, just as you always wished."

Then, slowly, John Ball rose. He braced his legs a pace apart and shook bloody crumbs from his gown. "You'll bargain it out!" His voice was powerful. "You'll bargain Heaven out of your own hands!"

"Ha! Listen to old prophet Ball, the ball-less prophet!" Wat was having fun. "Maybe out of *your* hands. Your time is over, Ball, the time of waiting. You wrote it once yourself, Ball—Now is Time!"

Ball leaned against the tent-post and gestured toward the door, backed by a wall of dirty rain. "*They* have to build Heaven, not Richard."

I turned to Ball, all charity. "You're a forerunner, Parson, like John the Baptist."

"—who ended up with his head separated from his body." Ball didn't go on; that was fine with me.

We heard a splash, then, and the sound of hooves. Horn looked through the sloppy fold of our tent.

"Wat Tyler?"

"Horn—!" Tyler was ready. "What news?"

"I measure one oath against the other," John Horn said, "and I decide that your King is my King, and your foes Richard's foes, and mine." His face was hidden by steam falling from the brim of his hat.

"Yes, yes," said Tyler testily. "What news?"

Horn frowned, and pushed into the tent. "I'm a valuable friend, Tyler. Treat me well." Then, he leaned back and he laughed. "I was told to tell you not to come to London, but I believe I shall not. I shall tell you that half the city stands with you."

"The Brothers—"

"Of The Great Society? They're waiting for you."

"And the tower?"

"Put a third of your best at the tower," said Horn.

"The rest can call London an open city."

Horn, Tyler, me, we all began to laugh, so quietly. Only Ball huddled in his corner with the Bible. We rose and packed up in the heavy rain. Horn said there would be food and drink enough in London, and we left our scant supplies to rot at Blackheath.

We mustered in an instant. Women beat tabors with wet hands, and sputtering, smoking fires were stamped down. We marched through mud, onto the west road, to the time of the dirty, chilling rain. Ball lagged behind, and I pulled him forward, forcing the Maidstone banner into his hands, the banner of Adam and Eve. He dragged it and abandoned it after a quarter mile. All weapons were held high: axes, hammers, pikes, rakes, scythes, hoes, staffs. I had no weapon but my dagger and my voice. I raised them both.

> And who'll get the spare ribs
> Said Milder to Malder.
> Oh we may not tell you
> Said Festle to Fose.
> We'll give them all to the poor!
> Said John the Red Nose.
> We'll give them all to the poor!
> Said John the Red Nose.

John Ball's nose was red, but he didn't sing. The three miles seemed three days, made broad by mud and shouting, lost babes, thunder. We reached the bridge. The rain stopped, and London was invisible for fog. The bridge was down and the gate was open.

THREE

1. John Nameless

John Ball bore down on my arm till I thought it would break at the shoulder. The rain had turned to wet, thick wind and his hacking broke clean through, like thunder. The Thames was brown gravy, though the west was gilt, on fire. London itself we couldn't see, but we heard voices. Something arched toward Tyler—a bottle.

"You haven't seen the like of this before!" It was a swift, high voice, gone blunt with wine. Wat caught the bottle and looked up, squinting. "From the bloody Flemings on the Vintry. We knocked a couple down, just in the way of a welcome."

The London man waved through the fog. He looked like a wet, dirty sheep in a hat, and his face was black with ash. Wat held his eyes and tossed the bottle into the Thames. "We're here to see the King," he said. "Not to drink and quarrel."

The man shrugged, and looked at the bobbing bottle with regret. "You're from Kent, Captain. London's another story. Here you take what you can get."

Wat pushed past him, into the foggy crowd, into London proper. I strained up, steadied Ball, and followed.

I heard: "We've made a start on Gaunt's Savoy manor, even with the rain, Captain." I couldn't find Wat, couldn't hear his answer. The fog pressed, cold and soft as dung, and it made ghosts of us.

So that was Bridge Street, brothers, forty thousand ghosts pressed between high wharf taverns, five hundred standards milked of color. Is it any wonder we couldn't muster for a proper meeting? I saw Wat at last, on the steps of Saint Magnus with a guild of tilers. One blazing torch turned them into our center. The tilers bore a banner of a giant with a hammer; Wat was no giant, and as he grasped their hands their faces froze and fell. Still, they blazed back when they met his eyes.

We saw the tower of London. The turrets floated like high ship prows in the fog. Richard was there, penned in by traitors. Wat waved; the tilers backed away. Our eyes turned from the tower, turned to him.

"Today," he called, "we meet with the King. Do nothing that would make Richard ashamed. Still," and here his eyes searched for John Ball, "if the end is well, then all is well. Clean out this poisoned city with good, clean fire. Keep yourselves clean. Prepare to meet your King. For Richard and the True Commons!"

He stomped and raised a whoop that rolled off fog and cleaned the water.

We entered in the city in earnest, swelling London's own forty thousand till her walls near buckled. Some moved toward the lime-washed, moony tower, true as tide. Some bounded west to Fleet River, and fire. Alderman Horn stood at the Tower Street fork, in hazy scarlet, pointing stouter men to Tower Hill.

I saw Faith drag her babes past Horn; I saw Will Nettle and Stone risk a narrow, wandering alley. Wat waved me up Saint Magnus. Hugh and Martin had joined him there, and the three heads clustered, muttering. I started up the church stairs, bearing Ball. He let out a cough so rich and terrible that it near blasted life out of him. Hugh Smith met us midway, and carried Ball in his long arms.

Wat watched, shaking his head. Hugh set Ball against the wall and stepped back; the four of us circled him, like wolves, he must have thought. At last, Wat said, "Parson, this is no place for you."

Ball raised his head, opened his eyes slowly, and spoke: "Where is my place, Tyler?"

Martin said, "Well, there's a house not far, Captain." He spoke to Wat; he edged away from Ball. "There's the leader of the Cheapside Chapter of the Great Society, Tom Farrington."

Ball sat up. "No. Not Farrington."

Martin looked up and down, helpless. "Well, it's no

more than a hole in the wall, but it's safe. Good mooring point, I figure. Far from Fleet Street, far from the prisons . . ."

Ball pushed himself off the wall, against Hugh, and nearly lumbered down the stairs. "Not Farrington! No! I know Farrington!" His mouth twitched.

Hugh held him steady. "Now, Parson," he said slowly. "What's wrong with Tom? He's a townsman, yes, but they're all townsmen."

"Not . . ." Ball began, but then he threw up a weak hand and said, "Take me there, then, men, if you have no love for me."

"Right, then," Tyler said. "Best thing for everyone." He slapped me on the shoulder. "Jack," he said, "Farrington lives on Corn Hill. Buy your friend a meat pie on the way. Keep him happy." He turned to Hugh and Martin, then, and left me to help John Ball down.

The walk—oh brothers, I'd rather die right now than walk that mile again. West, east, folks tore fog with their torches, laughing, singing. To the west, the scribes' fine houses sizzled, and to the east the tower was ringed with wonder and delight. I struggled miserably north, bearing my burden of black cloth, bones, spittle, and blood. We had to climb many a steep mount of cobbles. Townsmen call them hills. Some streamed stink like waterfalls down clefts you call a gutter. Those guts of rain and dung would overcome the deepest gutter. At odd banks of these hell-rivers the merchants hawked their pies or caps or buckles. For the first time since Rochester I felt my purse and found only a farthing. I couldn't buy Ball his pie if he'd wanted one.

We turned a corner; all changed. We'd reached Lombard Street. The housefronts were high, clean and white; even the fog was clean. The doors were carved with ships, full sails, waves crashing, or with Saint Nicholas and his three bags of gold. Even the gutter here seemed gutless, a thin, clear line of water. One window opened, and a scarlet curtain parted. A man stuck out a bland, round face. His voice was hesitant.

"You rebels? You traitors?"

I shook my head. I pointed to the tower. "No, no. The traitors are all in there."

He snapped the curtain back, and we stumbled north. We passed one man, in purple trimmed with lush squirrel fur, staggering south under a chest big as himself. He met our eyes once and nodded greeting.

"Money lender," Ball said. He spat. I wondered if the stranger knew my brother, Alf.

We reached Corn Hill; Ball resisted feebly. He turned and set a hand against the wall. "Parson," I said, "where else would you go?"

He paused and let his hand fall to his side. "I wish I could die in peace."

"You won't die," I said. I took him under the arm and we stepped onto Corn Hill Street.

Corn Hill was wide enough to warrant a double gutter, so the water was no river, but an open, shallow lake. I saw what must have been two merchant's halls, dark shells for fear of us. Rain water dripped from ragged tile roofs, and I saw three black rats sporting in the puddles. I backed off, straining to remember where Farrington lived.

Ball smiled, and said, "Boy, follow the rats."

The smile gave me a turn. Ball led me now, up for a time and then down the darkest, leanest lane, a nameless lane. It was a breath between two rows of housefronts, a Joint Lane with the joint gnawed down to rotten bone. The stink of mold near blinded me. Ball wasn't blind. He struggled on and pointed to a low, lead door. I knocked.

"Hmph?" The door opened a crack. "What's the watch word?"

I answered without hesitation: "King Richard and the True Commons!"

There was a pause. Something made me seize my dagger.

Then, "You're from Essex?"

I hesitated. "Kent."

"Password enough." The door opened and I helped Ball forward.

The man behind the door was small and lean. His face was milk white, and his hair was black and sparse. He wore a false collar of sleek, brown fur on shaggy hemp-cloth. He looked me up and down. Then, he saw Ball. "Well, you might have said *he* was here," he said, turning the false collar round and round.

I felt Ball take my hand.

Tom Farrington went on. "I thought you were dead—that is, until a week ago." He stepped up and pushed us both inside. "We're meeting here, making plans."

The room was full of men. Squat candles set in their own tallow fought the dank and dark and won a little, but light didn't touch those men. They were cut from Farrington's cloth, little, tough, and dirty. I saw things hanging from strings, piled in corners. I fancied Farrington was a furrier.

All the while, Tom Farrington and Ball had circled one another, or rather Farrington had circled Ball and Ball had held Tom's eyes. Ball's cheeks blew out like a bellows. He spoke at last.

"Tom," he said, "I believe you owe me a favor. I need a place to die."

I turned, but said nothing. Farrington smiled.

"Talked yourself out, old man? Plague finally caught the man who carried her?"

"Perhaps. Or something like plague." He straightened. The effort was awful.

The men in the room chortled, but they were afraid of plague, in awe of Ball.

Farrington set his toe on a trap door. "There's a hearth there," he said. "This is the workshop, you understand, and the worker lives down under."

I forced the door open and climbed down, stepping into a pool of cobwebs. Ball followed; he near fell into my arms. I nosed flint from my rucksack and stumbled to the hearth. It held dry wood. It was uncanny—had we been expected? The wood kindled at once, and the room filled with smoke, but it was better than I'd feared. I saw spiders enough, but no rats.

Ball's eyes were closed. I wrapped him in my cloak and nested him just by the fire.

"You can't die yet," I said.

"Hmmm?" He looked up.

"We've got to turn Heaven to Earth, Parson. You've got to see Heaven and Earth—"

"Perhaps." He looked down again. "But first I'll see the end of the world by fire." He looked at our own, cloudy fire. "They don't listen to me now, Jack. Did they ever listen to me?"

I touched his shoulder and felt the old urge to work off his boots. It was hard to tell where boots ended and black cokers began. I turned away and started up to Farrington's common room.

First I heard sharp voices, snatches of a quarrel.

"Well, there's plenty who deserve bringing down. I say, we ought to give the word traitor a new meaning."

"But those lads from the countryside, they've never rubbed their faces in the dung. They're green as grass!"

I poked my head out, and I saw them huddled; a lad was keeping watch by the door. One man turned and saw me.

"I know you. You're Jack Straw."

I nodded, my head swimming.

"Well, you could help us, then," he said. "We need to know how far your men will go."

"We're King's men," I said. "We'll go as far as the King, talk to him, and go home with what was taken from us."

"So goes the tale!" There was some laughter and I wanted to leap out and knock them down. Then Farrington crossed over and pulled me from the cellar.

He shook his head. "You mean well, Straw, and you do well, as Long Will says, but what did we ever have for them to take? Remember Ball's words about hidden meanings. It's about time you lads and maids from Kent know that the horror goes far deeper than Gaunt's fools up in the tower."

Before I stopped myself, I called, "You know Piers Plowman!"

He nodded, and he said, "Look at our faces, Straw, and tell me about Piers the Plowman. You talk of taking back what's been stolen. We don't even know what they've robbed us of, Straw. Imagine Wat no tiler, Wat with no name, with no craft to master but the London craft of slow death. You talk of Earth and Heaven, of tales. If you tell tales, tell our tale then, and it'll have to be a tale without Heaven, without tilers, without windmills. You bargain for tales, Straw. We're done with bargaining. We do well to know it, better to taste blood."

He set a letter in my hand. It was damp; the ink had wilted through. I knew the script.

Farrington smiled. "I was Ball's pupil back in Colchester. He preached. I listened. He thinks I owe him a favor. Ha! He taught me to read and it's been nothing but a curse! I read these men the new laws, and they hate me for it—For all they know, I wrote them!"

I bowed my head and read.

> Iohan Schep, som tyme Seynte Marie
> prest of York, and now of Colchestre,
> greteth wel Iohan Nameles and Iohan
> the Mullere and Iohan Cartere, and
> biddeth hem that thei bee war of gyle
> in borough and stondeth togidre in
> Godes name, and biddeth Peres
> Ploughman go to his werk and chestise
> wel Hobbe the Robbere and taketh with
> you Iohan Trewman and alle hiis
> felawes and no mo, and loke schappe
> you to on heud and no mo.

I thought: why would Ball talk about Colchester when he was in Canterbury jail. The parchment was so brittle that it flaked off at the ends. I read on.

> Iohan the Mullere hath ygounde smal smal smal
> The Kynges son of heuene schal paye for al.
> Be war or ye be wo;
> Knoweth your freend fro your foo
> Haueth ynow, and seith "Hoo";
> And do wel and bettre and fleth synne,
> And seketh pees and hold you therinne.

And so biddeth Iohan Trewman
and alle his felawes.

I saw it then. The paper, the letter, was older than most of the men in that room. It was from Ball's Colchester days. The words we'd taken for instruction had been spoken since the years of the Great Plague. What had we followed? What had bound us together and made kin of us?

Farrington said, "It's all words with him, words inside his head. Heaven—what's Heaven? Words and tales!" He fiddled with his collar. I saw small heads, and strings, or tails. "And Millers, and bells, and plowmen. Gaunt's spies know all those words and the fool's tales you weave of them." He reached for the letter. "Ha! Keep peace! Now is time! And he waves parchment before your simple noses and you follow! We're fighting now, and we'll come up with new words—words of our own!"

"How about Bread and cheese?" someone called.

"Tell Tyler we're with him," Tom said, "but tell him there's more to Hell on Earth than John of Gaunt. We'll harrow Hell! The Flemings, the lawyers, the King!"

I must have gone white. I looked at the soft pile in the corner and I saw rats; Tom skinned rats. His collar was a loose, worn ring of tacked rat-skin. The hats piled by the trap door were rat hats, black and sleek. The hats and letters tangled round together as if we'd been trusting Ball's words without knowing them, as if, like rats, they had a secret, nasty life that met our own lives by an evil chance. Farrington watched me, smiling.

"The hats are for merchants," he said. "They don't know the difference."

I looked at the letter once more, and gave it to him. I thought, he'll crumble it, or set it on fire. No, he set it deep in his pocket and opened the door.

Three voices called out: "We're with you in the name of the King, Jack!" Maybe Farrington was another Ball; they listened and heard only what they wanted to hear. I felt easier, but leaden, and I walked into the narrow lane and out, to Corn Hill. West, the fires roared, clean and forceful. I watched them, wondering if I'd ever known John Ball.

2. Good Clean Fire

The Londoners had made a fine start along Fleet
Street. The fog had bloomed into a quarter mile of fire. You
could smell the smoke from Corn Hill, and once you
reached Fleet River your face was poacher-black with ash.

I remember ash, chiefly, floating down like snow, and
endless drifting prisoners we'd freed from Cripplegate, Fleet
and Marshalea. The whores of Southwark joined us, and
they sprung up, like red cockles, at all corners, taking up
axes and hewing beams apart like men. All swore their
oath to Richard and the commons by the river. Some
convicts were so weak they fell into the Fleet and the
whores fished them out with staffs.

The road between Ludgate and Gaunt's Savoy churned
like black water over a fire. Men stood on roof after roof,
splitting the shingles with hammers. Maids and lads scram-
bled up with rabbit pies and ale. All was cracking, spark
and laughter.

At first, I was edgy; I bounded toward the nearest
house and boomed out to the rooftop through cupped
hands:

"Now see here! We go after traitors only!"

The man threw back his hammer and looked down.
His smock was torn at the shoulder, and his red face was
ferocious. "This man's a tax collector—he's Gaunt's puppy
dog and he lives in sight of the prison so he can wave
good morning to the men he locked away!"

I gaped at the dripping, crooked roof. The house was
char now, but you could see a strip or two of white paint,
a brass latch hanging from a single nail by the door. My
eyes wandered back to that dark, sparkling face. I said,
"You won't steal anything."

"Steal?" He threw back his head and laughed. "I'd

take his life, brother—I'll take nothing less."

"Where is he?"

He laughed again. "Oh, where do you think? He's in the tower."

The door had been torn free, and I stepped in. There was more hole than roof and the floor was freckled with shards of tile. They'd split the wooden tables down to kindling, and the cushions were sopping with wine and water. Empty bottles lay scattered. I knew he'd poured the wine out; he hadn't touched a drop. Let them write that about us! Scribe, scribble that down! Write about the man who didn't drink a drop of wine!

Hundreds more perched on those houses. Two women settled on one roof, flicking tile off with dull knives. Lads and maids ducked through the blaze and out. Rows of these homes, finer than lords' manors, crumbled under us. Some had four stories, countless rooms. Near all were empty; owners fled down the bright Fleet or Thames by barge. They'd left furs, silk hats—these fed bonfires. Ah— those rich, saucy fires, stinking of singed fur! If some of the wine went into the men and women rather than the earth I forgave all for the sake of the man on the roof.

At dusk, I reached the Temple Bar. The home for lawyers was owned by Legget, a questmonger. Legget had packed Cripplegate prison with men who'd worked above the law-set wage. He'd kept the Temple of lawyers like a stew house of plump whores. Legget was in the tower, now, but we found the lawyers in their rooms.

Sergeants-in-law were slippery; I'd never seen old men so nimble. Before we could lay a hand on them they skimmed off on barges in their scarlet mantles, like red ducks with white heads. The law apprentices were left to shudder. We pulled them by the hair and made them watch the Temple burn.

We gathered every charter we could find and sparked a bonfire in the front hall. Turned tight, the parchment was prize kindling. Black, loose sheets fluttered up, carried the flame. We danced round the burning Temple, singed hair in our eyes, mouths gaping. One crack of the hammer and flame spurted from the roof—a fountain!

Londoners had their own kind of fun. We thought it well enough to wait for Legget and throw our hearts into burning, but two ice-thin men caught two apprentices by their collars. The boys squirmed in their blue surcoats, but the townsmen held them fast. They threw them into a heap of dung in the Bar's garden, and they tried to set the dung on fire. The grass caught, and the blaze spread north. I guess the boys died.

I thought of old John Nameless, Farrington, again. I wanted him to blow off London like the ash and fog. I missed Wat fiercely, and Wat was at Gaunt's Savoy Manor, so I hurried west.

I couldn't push through to the door—too many packed inside. All laughed, danced, dashed in and out of the broken monster of the Savoy despite fire. I looked up and despair spilled from my heart like water. There was Wat Tyler, perched on a milestone by the Savoy gate with one arm outstretched. His powerful voice and his stubby arm rose higher, higher, then swung to the Thames.

Soon Gaunt's Savoy was a shell, empty, save for fire and what couldn't be burned. Light flames grew all through the floor like grass. I wondered if the company was looting, but I knew better. I watched Wat's hand again. The crowd dashed, laughing, to the riverbank, and there they flung their treasures to the water. I watched their faces. They were dottling drunk with tossing off their fortunes.

Wat called, "Come on now! We'll have no Hobb the Robbers! The stuff is poison and we're here to force the poison out!"

A wind rose and blew off the last fog. The river came to life, full of the fire. It bore a heavy mantle, turning, turning in the water. Gold rode the river bottom; silk rode the top. I saw a nest of bubbles rise—wine?

Three men rushed out with kegs of something. Wat called: "Toss that into the blaze—and run—everyone!" They turned and gave a whoop! They tossed it to the fiercest corner and there was a noise like thunder and a flash— pure light. The wall cracked like a nut.

"Powder!" a man called. The blast drove the fire up again and we stumbled, blind with light. We'd never seen such light, or heard the like of it before.

Wat's face was red from fire and black from blast. He threw his head back, laughing. "Ah, bright wonder of God!" He smacked his hands together. "Enough of this— let's see Richard and deal with the traitors!"

He climbed down and the thousands opened for him like the Jordan. I ran and grasped his hand. I asked him how he'd kept order.

He cocked his head. "The London folk are queer, Jack, but they hate Gaunt and Hales and Sudbury and they have courage."

"Has there been any looting?"

He looked at the Savoy, grim. "No, but two men couldn't get their noses out of the wine."

I smiled. "You told them off, I expect."

"No sense in that," Wat said. "I left them there to burn. I don't suppose they'd hear me if I called them now."

I looked at the smoldering Savoy and felt the color run out of my face. Well, this will make a good tale, I thought, when we're through.

3. The Fast Man

There was a man named Jack who was very fast; he kept on his feet all day and skimmed across the sea as though it was dry land. He had long, strong legs and very bright eyes and there was no faster man alive.

One day, he met an old woman, and he hailed her. She laughed and said, "Well, fast man, you are not so very fast."

Jack said, "I can part a wind so quick that it doesn't show a seam and I can blaze through any storm and stay quite dry. Now aren't I fast, old woman?"

Again, she laughed, and she shook her head. "I know one faster—night."

Then Jack stood and stared off, thoughtful. The sun was setting and night was heading straight overhead. "I'll match night, if I can." He turned and ran west.

He ran and ran, sharp eyes on the sunset, jumping over houses and tossing himself over rivers, but after an hour night had overtaken him and he stood on the top of a far western hill and watched the dark sky helplessly.

His friends tried to comfort him, but he wouldn't be comforted. He said, "I'll count myself as nothing until I outrun this woman, night."

Jack spent his days practicing, running west as swift as swift. Folks looked for him but when he passed they saw no man, but a quick light and shadow. Still, every evening, night came and every evening he couldn't pass her.

Then, one morning, Jack got up very early with a firm heart and he said, "Today I will—today or never!" He put on his leather shoes and ate a good breakfast and ran and ran until he couldn't feel his legs. He ran so hard his sweat ran out and filled the eastern marshes and his hair flew off and formed the lines of reeds. Then, just past midday he looked back and his heart soared; he couldn't see his shadow.

"I've outrun night's spy," he cried, "And so I'm free of her!"

Then evening came and he turned to run again, but now the world turned bright, full of pure light. He'd overtaken night and he laughed because he knew that there was none faster, none stronger, in the world.

Jack settled in the place where he'd fought night, and there the sun never set. There the weather always is sunbright. There people never tire, though they run like water. He built a great city, filled with gifts from those who wished to do him honor. He lived in joy and happiness, ease and triumph, for half a year—but then night came.

Jack ran again; she overtook him. He ran and couldn't leave night. For six months more the sun could not be seen. He ran east, east, south, south, searching for the sun until at last Jack found his way back to his own country.

There, he found his own bed and there he slept. He was through with running. He opened his eyes and the sun was out and shining. He never returned to his city, which they call Scotland. There the sun rides bright for six months of the year and for six months the sun is gone. Some say this is why the Scots are so proud, and so unhappy.

4. Tower View

Saint Catherine's field lay east, circling the tower moat, and we left Fleet Street smoldering and headed for the clearing. Enough lay waiting, their chins up, packed tight and straight as bound corn. They searched for the King. By moonlight, we found a small crown, a white face, high, an acre off on the White Tower. We must have seemed a faceless bunch to Richard. What did he see, from his tower? What did he say? What did the traitors answer?

You'd know, Lord Mayor, for I saw you there; I saw a short man with a cloud of dark, curled hair, a square black hat.

A butcher pointed to you. "Ah, that's the cursed mayor, Walworth. King Richard might as well have Satan at his side."

Then Richard broke free and leaned toward us, calling. "I want you to go peaceably to your homes, and I will pardon you for all your offenses."

Wat Tyler had been standing at my side. He called now: "King, we've come for the traitors in the tower."

"Hales!" someone called.

"Sudbury!" Was that Thomas of Aldon?

"Gaunt!" Gaunt's name near split the tower. Folks pushed forward with their bows and pikes and kicked up clods of sod and green grass, shouting themselves inside out.

"Where's Gaunt's son, Henry Bolingbroke! Let him do for his father!"

One man called: "Storm the tower!"

"This tower can't be stormed, fool!" That was a Londoner. "Not with long bows and tiling hammers and butcher's knives!"

Aldon sang:

And what will do then?
Said Festle to Fose—

Wat ran up, pushing us back with both arms. "This is Richard's castle! This is Richard's—" He strained up to the tower. "You don't want to burn this place, men! Richard's our King!"

I looked up. Richard had turned to a tonsured clerk. You, scribe? He faced the firestorm of Fleet Street. I felt a neighbor press a flask on wine into my hand.

I brought it to my lips and drank deep. It was bitter, and brought on sleep. I wavered on my feet, wearing so thin that the world turned plum-purple, like the wine.

I turned to pass it on, and found Will Nettle. He took the wine without a word and pressed the flask to his cheek. He took a long drink. I turned back to Wat. He paced, now, twisting his helmet round his head. The tower gate opened.

"Another messenger!" a woman called. "And when will our King speak for himself?"

A lad stumbled out, awed, stone-pale. He fumbled at his red belt, drawing out a charter. He stood a ways from Wat and whispered.

Wat grimaced. "I can't hear a word, boy." He snatched the parchment from the belt and the lad jumped and tore back like a dog stung by a hornet. A few babes chased him, calling "Join us, Will Scarlet!" and "Swear to the King!" but Wat called them back. "Let him be for Richard's sake."

Then Wat broke the seal. The writing was neat as a needle; the bottom was dotted with wax. Wat whispered, "The King's seal . . ." His eyes sparkled and the paper quivered like a quick thing. "This is it, then . . . he's heard us and he's going to—"

"Read it, Captain!" A big Essexman drummed his bowstring and stomped.

Wat looked at me. "Jack—"

I took the parchment and began, but my voice couldn't carry. Aldon knelt and took me up on his shoulders like a lad. He rose, and nothing stood between me and the moon but Richard's tower. I turned my full wit to the charter in my hand. I read:

"Richard, King of England and France, gives great thanks to his good commons, for that they have so great a desire to see and maintain their King."

"We do!" they cried at once. I searched for Wat. He stood by Aldon's elbow, tears streaming, eyes on the tower. My eyes followed. The turret was empty.

". . . and he grants them a pardon for all manner of trespasses and felonies done up to this hour and wills and commands that every one of them should now, in haste, return to his home."

I stopped, and heard my breath grind like a millstone.

". . . He wills . . ." My voice lost itself. ". . . and commands that everyone should put his grievances in writing and have them sent to him; and we will provide with the aid of his loyal lords and his good council such remedy as shall be profitable both to him and to them and to the Kingdom." I looked at the waxed bottom, heavy, dull. I muttered, now. "It bears his signet seal."

I lowered the charter, sitting, dumb, on Aldon's shoulders. Aldon stood rooted; the still, sharp, waste of faces turned up, waiting. My eyes fixed on Wat's face. It was an empty, thinking face, a wheat-grinding face.

I sat straight, and I called, "This is a mockery!"

They stirred. I went on:

"It's a mockery written by a clerk—a clerk who'll only deal with lawyers!"

It caught like oil. They bellowed "Lawyers! Lawyers! Let them tell us false tales with their heads piked on poles! Let them talk with their heads on London Bridge!"

Wat revived, walking, in haste, round the field. Aldon set me down and joined the troop who flew down Tower Street like angels of death.

A man who kindles good fire doesn't burn. I watched them with a sinking heart. Richard was gone, and I was shaken by the words I'd read, so different than what I'd read in his own face on the barge. He had to stand with us! He was a prisoner. Yet we'd walked tirelessly to free a

King on advice scribbled by a mad parson before that King was born. Why were we in London? The floating, dirty moon milked away hope. I felt Wat's hand on my shoulder.

"Son," he said, softly, "what do you think?"

I said, "I think we're going to get another pardon, then another, and we'll go home."

He squeezed the shoulder harder than he had to. "You're wrong," he said. "We meet Richard tomorrow."

And I thought, the moon's rowing down and giving its cheese to the poor. I shook my head.

Wat went on. "At Mile End. Just east of here."

I looked at Wat's face and knew he spoke truth. "What did you hear—"

"By secret messenger, directly from the King. He got it past the traitors, I'll warrant. That pardon was a decoy!"

I took his hand, joy thickening my blood. Wat's ears were rosy with excitement; I could feel him tremble. I spoke despite myself, thin doubts: "Mile End's beyond the city gate. They could lock us out."

Wat heard me, and he smiled. "Ought we refuse to meet him then, son? We must be Richard's good servants, and we must trust and love our master. But canny servants . . ." The smile narrowed. "We'll leave a third of our best at the tower."

I spoke again. "Mile End . . ."

"You're about to fall over, Jack." He rubbed his blunt hand through my hair with love. "I'll need you fresh tomorrow. Take care, son. You'll tell our tale one day."

Thus goes the tale: I turned to Catherine's Hospice, where most camped that night. Catherine is the patron saint of millers, and we'd strung the standard of the mill over the door. Wat stood back, lone, waving. I was so weary that I'd forgotten how to sleep. I stood just past the hospice threshold, glazed eyes pinned on naught. Three hundred lay, packed like wood, beneath a pile of woolen blankets. Faith and her babes shared a single shawl, and Aaron Stone lay with his head on his arm, bow cocked by his shoulder.

I thought, if I could make a tale of this, I'd save Joe Billing, Dopey Joe, to curl up in this room, cozy as a white pup, snoring. A young man rested by the door; he looked like Dopey, the same white face, flax hair, gentle, hooded eyes. He struggled up on an elbow and smiled. He said, "You're Mike Row, aren't you?"

The name gave me such a turn I jumped.

He nodded. "I used to see you, you know, years ago, when you went to Dartford Market with your pack of brothers. I know your Jenny. Figured she'd be here."

He sat up and rubbed his square hands together. I'd never seen the man before. "My sister's never been out of Gravesend," I said. "She's lame."

"This is her sort of thing, I'd figure." He smiled a thin smile, no dope's smile. I'd misjudged him, and I felt uneasy. "Lame, you say? Well, I should have known that."

"And made lame coming from your Dartford market," I said. I laughed, and hoped he'd leave me be; doubtless, he knew what happened to my sister, and I didn't need to be told again.

"Market all right!" Again, the cat's smile. He rubbed his eyes like a weary man, but he spoke on. "Saw her there three years ago—she was just a little maid then. In the church square. I was bringing in my cart for market. She was all got up for traveling." He nodded, patting his own rucksack. "Carried a staff like a friar. And up on her toes, talking to just me about Heaven and Earth—no one else to see—like that Parson, eh? Thought she'd be here now. But you're right. Didn't think about what those men did to her."

He rose and eased his back against the doorway, now, nodding his dumb nod, smiling with gentle memory. I didn't move.

"The alderman, the parson—they took her under the shoulders like a straw-kin, through the commons. They knew her face, I guess. I guess they dragged her back to Gravesend. That's where you've come from, eh? How's life in Gravesend?"

I seized his shoulders. "She didn't. She couldn't! She was only fourteen!"

He yawned. "She looked younger."

I braced myself against the door. "They—why didn't

you stop them? Why didn't you?"

"Peace." He stared at me. "Hold back, Row. I'm not her brother."

I pushed him back and stormed into the open. I was dizzy, borne down, as though Jenny rode my shoulders. I looked up at the moon and saw her face, and then a vision of her, hair wild, dressed in parson's black, up in a market square ringing a bell. I saw her thrown down in a wood somewhere between Dartford and Gravesend, torn between the legs, the wreck they left of her tossed in the ditch. The picture was as salt and strong as blood. I pushed through high grass. There was a glow west, and London bridge snatched firelight till the Thames filled with blood.

I don't know when I found myself. Maybe I slept, yet when I shook the last horror from my head, I was sitting in the grass, hugging my knees. I was in a cold sweat. The Thames was black now, and I stumbled south, knelt at the river bank and threw handfuls of water on my face.

I near prayed, there, on my knees, but I held back. Who owned those prayers? I rose and my eyes cleared, or rather filled with tears and vision till they felt as powerful as stars. I wanted to drink.

There was a tavern by the wharf, a narrow crumble of a house called The Boar's Ease. They saw my face, pumped me a free draught. I balanced a pint of ale down an aisle like an alley. It was so dirty there that the crown of foam was gray. I was known, and ignored. I'd never felt so lonely. The men were pale as the tavern was dark, with ill starred faces and big, restless hands. John Nameless every one of them. I sat with my ale at my elbow and lowered my eyes in shame. Will Nettle walked in.

He was alone, and looked uneasy. He bought his ale and walked down, saw me. He paled and slopped most of his ale over turning back again. Worse, he bumped into three townsmen with mutton chops in their hands. They cornered him.

"You're one of those peasant lads, gone to visit Richard?"

He nodded, wary.

"You're one of them who spoiled the fine houses on

Fleet Street?"

He shook his head. "I was at the tower."

"He was at the tower. Isn't that nice?" The tallest of them waved his chop at him. "Playing ring-a-ring-a-rosy round Richard!"

Nettle shrugged his friendly shrug. "I'm just a simple brewer."

"You'd best do good here. Go after the Flemings. They're the ones making life hard in England." He moved closer.

I called, "Will—sit with me and help me write this list of London traitors!" My voice was stale, but it did its work. The men snorted and said, "He's Jack Straw's boy." Nettle walked back with reluctance. He sat across from me and poured the rest of the ale down his throat.

"Well . . ." he said slowly, "I guess you've heard about Mile End."

I nodded. "Will," I said, "Can we talk, just for a moment? Like we're in Gravesend? Like I'm Mike Row?"

He gaped and melted. "I . . . you need to ask? Has it come to that?"

I spoke at once. "Will, I did it. Lamed Jenny."

I looked at the table; I didn't want to see his face, or hear him answer. I went on.

I told him it was my fault, the lame leg, what the men did to her, her heart that snapped like a green branch. She'd followed fool's words, and now we rattled after those same fool's words like a pack of mad sheep. Like sheep, we'd be gutted. I babbled on, my voice a wandering pity, and I could have talked for hours but I stopped when I felt his warm, steady hand on my arm.

"That's a lot to put on your shoulders, Michael," he said softly.

"I used to put it on your shoulders, Will," I said. At last I looked up, and I met his eyes. They were round and wet, and they closed for a while. He spoke again.

"We're friends, Mike, and friends share burdens."

"Then I have another burden," I said. I looked up and down the tavern; we weren't watched. "I think we'll fail, Will. I think the King's enemies are too powerful. I think

Mile End's a trap."

His wide mouth worked back and forth, and his eyes narrowed. "I don't think so."

I sat up.

He smiled, then, and said, "In fact, I know we won't fail." He leaned back, and downed the dregs of ale. "You know why? Because of our wishes."

I was baffled. I watched Will nod his heavy head with warmth, and struggled to remember. Then I said, "Whitsuntide?"

"I wished that Jenny would agree to be my wife," he said. "And you wished to keep faith. That sun won't let you keep your faith in vain."

"I meant I didn't want to turn traitor to a friend," I said, and I dropped all caution and spoke my heart. I told Nettle about John Ball.

He listened, and I don't know if he had wit enough to hear the tale or if I had wit enough to tell it, but at the tale's end, he smiled again. "Ah—well that's settled, then. You'll live to be put to the test once more, and to prove yourself a true and loyal son to him."

The tavern grew a shade lighter, yet I shook my head. "It's not a world that lets us be loyal, Will." But when I said this, I saw Will's face and knew myself a liar. I took both of his hands. "And what about Jenny's wish, then, that I play tiler to her tiler's daughter?"

He mused on that, and said, "These wishes aren't tame things, Michael. They have their own ways of coming true."

"More likely Gaunt's men will turn tiler on us, and take a hammer to our thick heads." All the while I knew the spirit meant something. I trusted my heart, and Will Nettle's words rang true.

Will bought two ales. He took a sip and snorted. "Varnish!" he cried. "Undrinkable!" He drained the cup and belched. Then he asked, "Feel better?"

I nodded.

He looked at the window. "I haven't been much use to you, have I?"

"Nonsense!" I said, and then I laughed. He laughed

too, and we grasped each other's shoulders across the table, just to make sure we were really there, really talking like old friends.

"Ah, your sister's brother! You know sense from nonsense. Well, so do I. I swear, Michael, I'll make myself of use from now on. You've shared a burden, and so will I. When there's a dirty job, give it to me. I'll stick by you."

"Marriage or none, Will, you're my brother." The words rang with the Matins bell and we rose together and left the tavern. We walked toward the tower. Stars set behind us, and the black frames of the western houses burned as though with life. I walked and slept at once, dreaming of three wishes, and of Mile End.

5. Mile End

We started for Mile End long after sunrise. Wat sent the message round; men and women over fifteen years of age were to gather to meet Richard. They mustered, mute and wary. Fifteen thousand kept watch by the tower, and by dawn the vigil had borne fruit.

Faith was telling her Art a story when she saw a boat slip through a watergate to the Thames. It was Archbishop Sudbury.

"Traitor!" she called. Twelve bowmen had him covered. The pale little man slipped back into Cradlegate like a white rat. The glimpse was startling. There was the man who'd ordered Ball's imprisonment, and he was small and soft as a maid. I felt a lovely hatred bloom; I let it pass. Some of our folk edged the moat and hunted barges, lest other tower traitors try to float away. They hewed them till the gilt wood filled the Thames.

By late morning, we'd mended our dulled banners and gathered out by county. Wat and I led Kent. Nettle stayed close behind, straining at a man-high banner of a mill. Alderman Horn sat on his horse, bearing his alderman's mace. The low, cross crowd of Londoners behind him scuffed earth with their boots, eager to push on. Behind them rode a company of grocers, dressed like lords. A wind caught at our back, and sent us drifting like a fleet.

Richard came by carriage, with a scant half dozen of his council. How he trusted us! Earls flanked him on horseback; none met our eyes. Richard's face was hidden behind a blue curtain, and the carriage itself was a mass of carved and painted wood. I thought I saw him peer out, once. Our troop coughed up a man—Tom Farrington.

Farrington was backed by three Essex bowmen. He seemed to have made friends. He caught hold of the reins of the carriage, an act that turned us white for wonder and shame.

He twisted the horse-necks round and stopped the carriage short. The driver was mute; he stared at us with glazed eyes.

Farrington looked through the carriage curtain. "Where is Hales?"

No answer came. I couldn't see the King.

"Where is Hales of the poll tax? Legget of the Temple Bar? Sudbury?" His voice carried like a crow's. "What of vengeance, then? Avenge me!"

I heard Richard's voice, steady, clear. "Justice will be done," he said.

Farrington dropped the reins and stepped back. The driver hesitated, and then rode on through Aldergate. He left silence in his wake. We looked at one another and wondered why lightning didn't strike Tom Farrington on the spot. Wat stepped forward.

"Who are you?" he asked.

"I'm leader of the London Chapter of the Fellowship of the Great Society and I believe I'm strong enough to take justice into my own hands."

Wat looked him up and down and said, "You'd best stay at the tower. You'll be no use to us at Mile End."

"Gladly," said Farrington. He turned and a number of our men turned with him. They left a pocket of empty air I could feel in my stomach. They surrounded the tower with hungry eyes, as though it were a pudding.

Nettle put a hand on my shoulder and nearly lost the banner to the wind. I turned and smiled weakly. "Richard seems in good spirits this morning."

Wat boomed in. "Why shouldn't he be? He's about to meet a hundred thousand of his bravest countrymen!" He shouted, and we moved north, to Mile End.

We passed through Aldergate, past a straight-backed guard. At once we were in open country. I felt disarmed. They could well close the gate and leave us on the moor. The road cut across harsh, green grass and puddles white with sun. The puddles blinded our walk east; the wind whipped long grass round our shins and tripped us. I envied the Dukes and grocers on their mounts. I was so edgy that I walked on fire.

The carriage was slow, and we overtook it easily, circling Richard on all ends. An Earl edged his horse to the outskirts, and tore off to Whitechapel.

Then, the carriage paused. The knights dismounted and stood by the carriage door. We heard planks creak, a door shake, held fast by a latch. We were so still, the King's steps were distinct. Wat's hand snapped across mine, soaked in sweat. One knight worked the latch. We saw the King.

He was at ease. He held his hands together and smiled knowingly, a gentle smile that made me think of Holy Mary. He wore a mantle only, no fur, no gold. His pointed, downy chin was raised and his eyes found Wat Tyler's.

Tyler freed my hand and fell on both knees. The crowd rolled back like grasses in the wind; we bowed our heads. Only Wat's round head was raised. He prayed:

"May our King suffer to take us into his heart and deal with all traitors against him."

Richard turned; his moist blue eyes traveled the length of us and back again in wonder. He raised a hand. Tyler rose.

He said, "Tell me what you lack."

"We lack protection," Wat said. "False lords have enslaved us and false lords have taken our land from us."

He nodded, and said, "You shall have protection. What else do you lack?"

"We ask a fair rent for land, at four pence an acre," said Wat Tyler.

Richard nodded again. His gaze fell on me. At once I bowed my head, hot with wonder and doubt. As I bowed I felt doubt pour out like dirty water. I was empty, ready to raise my head, to meet his eyes.

"All this I grant you," Richard said, "and all who bring their grievances to me. I have a clerk here who will put the charter into writing and then I shall seal it with my seal."

Wat's voice was low. "We want to kill the traitors."

This time, Richard said nothing. He turned to the knights and Earls to his right and left. They might well have been made of Essex stone. He bit his lip, and silver drops of water gathered at the roots of his hair. He said, "Do as you please."

"You have a hundred thousand subjects here who love you," Wat said. "You'll never have to fear for your life, Richard, for you're our King and we're your Commons and we'll never betray you!"

A clerk came with the written charter bearing the King's seal. It was passed round to those who read and I read it. I read it, brothers, and felt myself turn upside-down. The whole sky turned to sun—the paper was on fire! I called, "It's come! It's come!" I turned, dancing, and my head swam with that old, triumphant psalm:

> If it had not been for the Lord
>   who was on our side
> Let Israel now say—
> If it had not been for the Lord who was on our
>   side when men rose against us,
> Then they would have swallowed us alive,
>   when their anger was kindled against us;
> Then the flood would have swept us away,
> Then over us would have gone the raging waters.
>
> Blessed be the Lord
>   who has not given us as prey to their teeth!
> We have escaped as a bird
>   from the snare of the fowlers;
> The snare is broken and we have escaped!
>
> Our help is in the name of the Lord
>   who made Heaven and Earth.

I couldn't see for joy. The world was on its head—I danced a blind dance, turning back to Eden, to Jerusalem, to London once again. Some turned for vengeance. Some started home with freedom's charters in their hands. If Eden had been opened, so had Aldergate, and I passed through for one reason; to tell the man who'd ended this Old Story before it had been written—to tell John Ball.

6. Jack the Giantkiller in Paradise

Jack the Giantkiller grew old and died in bed like any other man. He left his captured treasure to his son and mounted the ladder to paradise.

Jack was infirm, but he'd always been a mighty climber, and he overtook five swift saints on the way.

"My brothers!" he cried. "I'm on my way to paradise. I bid you tell me something of it."

They said, "In paradise you sit at the foot of the throne of God and sing his praises!"

"Baa—" Jack said. "That's no life for a Giantkiller!" He looked down; the earth was very far below. He could only continue on with dampened spirits.

After a while, he overtook a company of old beggars who'd thrown off their rags and were clothed in white.

"My brothers!" he called. "You poor devils look like you've taken a turn for the better. Now I bid you tell me something of paradise."

They answered with good cheer. "In paradise, the alms are given so freely that there's no sense in begging. They're thrown on your lap so thick and fast that you can't stand for the coins and bread and wine."

"Now that sounds like a better life indeed," Jack said, and he smiled. "Still, I've never been a beggar, and I fear that paradise will have no place for me."

The beggars went on laughing, drinking, singing, and they left Jack to climb higher. He was happier, but wondered if he'd done wrong to climb up without thought.

At last, he came to the high bright clouds of paradise. He stood and got his bearings and saw Saint Peter waving his ring of golden keys.

"Ah, Saint," he said, "I'm Jack the Giantkiller, and before I enter paradise I beg to know what I will find there."

Peter tossed his golden head. He was as tall as ten men and his deep shadow covered half of heaven. "We bid you enter and welcome," he said merrily. "For there's a Giant here who needs killing and has needed killing since the world's creation."

Jack flushed with excitement, but he looked through the gate and saw nothing but angels and poor folk rejoicing. "Show me the Giant," he said.

"The Giant is Lucifer, and it will take you an eternity to slay him."

Jack looked through the gate and saw Lucifer cursing, tearing clouds to tatters, stomping through paradise with clumsy cloven feet. "Ah—I have my task before me! I beg to enter paradise, Holy Peter, to gain new glory and new treasure!"

Peter turned the key, and Jack the Giantkiller gladly entered paradise. He follows the fierce Lucifer, eternally on his tail, eternally rejoicing in the spoil of earned victory. He's almost as clever as Christ, and one day he will trick the Devil into biting his own tail, and on that day, save us all.

7. On Tower Hill

"Now," said Wat, "we'll break into bands and scatter.
I say—five hundred search the tower and the rest hunt
Cheapside and the Vintry." He was backed by a row of
blithe men with axes, his flat face beacon-bright. I turned to
Corn Hill.

"Just a moment with Ball—" I said.

"There'll be time enough, forever time enough." Wat's
eyes moved over our folk. We were twenty thousand now,
those hot for blood, those washed in joy and peace who
feared to break the charm. They leaned like drunk dolts on
their neighbors, watched the tower, raised their pikes.

Nettle had been mute since Mile End, since he'd
known my will, that I'd meant to stay till we'd slain the
traitors. Aaron Stone had said farewell by Aldergate, and
Will had held him longer than he had to. Aaron covered a
guard's beard with kisses and bounded off with the charter
he couldn't read rolled tight in his big hand.

Now we stood at Byward Gate with our own charters.
Wat pointed his at a Guard's nose. "An invitation to tea
from the King!"

The guard bit his lip. Wat patted his cheek with love.

"Ah, brother, swear allegiance to him. Times have
changed. We're all kin now."

He whacked me on the back, and we led our troop
into the tower.

The still moat lay behind us now: before us there were
lime-washed walls, towers with names the men around me
knew: Bell Tower, Salt Tower, the tower of Saint Thomas. It
was the White Tower we were bound for. We crossed the
green and pressed through Bloody Tower gate. The walls
and gates, built to withstand High Doom, were no more
trouble to us than heaps of turf and straw.

I didn't stop to wonder how the world had changed, how we walked like nobleborn into the tower we'd gawked at hours before. It seemed natural as sunlight, bathed in Richard's grace. We'd prune the traitors from the tower like rotten branches from a tree and we'd rest in that tree's green shade ever after.

The hall was empty; the traitors were elsewhere. Wat passed through, and led us up into the gallery.

One old man blocked our way. "You can't go in there —Joan of Kent—"

"Ah, the princess of Wales," said Wat, "the King's blessed mother. Let us by, brother." He put his hand on his dagger. "Unless, of course, you're one of the traitors we—"

"I'm no traitor," said the old guard, turning his face away.

The room was draped in tapestries. They were so keenly dyed that it was hard to see a stick of furniture for crimson, yellow, blue. A woman mounted a white horse. Long birds shed golden plumes. A stag tangled his antlers in a rose-bush. A king charged the walls of a yellow tower.

"Hey ho!" Wat called. "Sweet Princess! We bring news of your son!"

No answer came. A big Essexman with rough, gray hair said, "I'll bet one of those stinking traitors is under the bed!" He took a bold step forward, knelt, and threw the bed curtain back. "No luck . . ."

"Oh, they're likely all in the chapel," said another, "buying pardon from Sudbury."

"And who will that traitor buy absolution from?" I laughed and took my first step into the chamber.

Its beauty turned me dumb. I sunk into myself, bashful, afraid to touch or smell or see. The red and blue light caught the silver in the bed curtain and the room jumped and quivered. Hesitant, I touched a corner of the curtain. My fingers climbed it, slowly, slowly.

Wat's voice broke in. "Princess!" he called again.

I moved toward the tapestries and touched the needle-work. The shadow of my hand turned green to blue. I turned a corner up, and heard a gasp.

"Princess!" I shouted. I threw the hanging up and she was sitting, curled tight as a nut. Her long face was buried in her hands.

"Hey..." Wat approached. "Hey now, dear." His voice was rough and wrong. His big hand touched her shoulder and she shook like she'd been struck by lightning. "Your son is safe, princess, and so are you." He knelt and kissed her hair.

She shook and shook, whispering over and over in a voice as smooth and thin as her hair, "Go away ... please go ... please go ... please ..."

I touched Wat's shoulder, and he jumped and turned. I said, "Leave her be. There are no traitors here."

He rose, scowling. "Lady, none of us have bared a sword. None of us will do you harm. We're all brothers and sisters now."

Joan of Kent didn't look up. She stayed behind her tapestry. Cowed and still, we left the room, and I turned to see the old guard push in to comfort her.

I said, "Richard shouldn't leave his mother alone."

"Well, we'll take care of her," said Wat, "but first, the traitors."

We walked down to Saint John's chapel, and I heard a whoop and a howl from the tower green. The Essexman dashed to the window. "Wonder of God!" he cried. "Look!"

Three thousand gathered in a deep circle and a man with red, bobbed hair knelt at its center. He was held hard by the shoulders and a man was working off his head with an ax. The neck split, and the head cracked onto stone. "For robbing us three times!" one woman shouted.

"Sweet mercy of God, it's Rob Hales!" The Essexman beamed, rubbing his hands together.

Outside, they called, "A pole! A pole!" A pole was found, and they worked the head on neat as an apple. They carried it toward London Bridge. I searched, and found two heads fresh-mounted there, staring.

"They're good men," Wat said softly, turning back. "We came here for the King's sake. They'll kill traitors only."

I nodded. I felt a wild rush of glee as I watched them pike the head of Hales beside the others. It was as if when that head left his shoulders all the harm he'd done would disappear, from Kate's encounter with his clerks to the French battles his tax bought, battles which cost me two brothers.

We hugged each other, laughing—Wat, uneasily—and hurried to the Chapel.

"Ah," said one man, "that would be a job for me, lopping off their heads."

"Oh, you don't have the arms for it," said another. "And it's dirty work."

He started back, and said, "You've done it?"

"Sure I have, in Erith!" He held his ax high, and tapped it with his finger. "It was this that ended the power of the Abbot!"

Wat looked at the men, nodding. "Yes, we'll build a new world on warriors like you."

"New Heaven, new Earth," I said, though I couldn't remember what the old ones had been like.

The man who held the ax was certain the chapel lay just above the hall. In truth, it lay below. We found a set of straight, lime stairs and met the door by way of music; moreover, we heard Latin: "... *omnes sanctic orate pro nobis* ..."

We pushed in. The chapel was empty, the music no more than the sun's hum through the east windows and a small, alabaster screen carved with the figures of the twelve, half-folded and quick with light.

Wat cried, "Where is the traitor to the kingdom? Where is the despoiler of the common people?"

A lamb's voice answered. "Good sons, you've come at last."

Wat crossed the chapel, and tossed the screen away. The archbishop was at the altar, on his knees. His white head was bowed and bare, and he looked up with friendly interest.

He said, "I am the archbishop whom you seek, but not a traitor or a despoiler."

It happened, then. I looked at his face and I knew all

he wrought. I jumped out and I cried:

"You threw Ball into prison and the third time kills him!"

He didn't look up, but he whispered, "I die in peace. I forgive you all."

I tore the ax from the hands of the man from Essex. "Let me do it!"

Wat turned cautiously. "Jack, you've never killed a man!"

"He dares to play the saint! Oh, Christ! He dares!" The ax was heavier than I'd suspected and the madness weakened me. I stared, blind, toward the window, thinking: Lord who made Heaven and Earth and who forsook my sister, give me strength, and then the ax grew light. I looked down; there were four hands on it. Nettle caught it fast and pulled it from me.

"This is my job," he said. "Dirty work."

We pulled the archbishop from his knees and dragged him out and down the stairway, through the broad door, onto tower hill. His face never changed, and he repeated softly, "I forgive you."

My own face was red and white and my hands cold and shaking. I was no help to them, no help. I looked, helpless, at Nettle, who held the double-edged ax as though he didn't know what it was for.

When our folk saw Sudbury they broke into a rumble and a cry. The earth split—sunlight broke to pieces—and all I could do was hold onto Nettle's shoulder for sweet life. I thought, I'm going mad, I won't be sound until his awful, gentle head is hewn from his body!

They set his head on a block, and held his shoulders down. Nettle stood in the white, noon sunlight, looking at the neck and at his ax and grinning nervously. The men and women shouted out "One blow!" until, at last, he raised the ax and struck.

Sudbury's body jumped. He slapped his hand onto his neck. "Ah! This is the hand of God!"

Wat tried to move Sudbury's hand from his neck, but it was rigid. "Don't bother with it," he said. "Chop right through."

Nettle nodded. This time, he put his shoulder into the blow. The fingers flew off the hand and fell into the crowd, but again the neck itself was only grazed. Will's eyes glazed over for a moment, and he ran a hand through his hair, and only afterwards saw the blood he'd streaked across his head. He tried again.

The men and women grew restless. "Get someone who knows his business!"

Sudbury himself was thanking God. The blood and water streaming from his fingers and his neck was endless, and his wretchedly stained lips still moved.

The next blow was a clean miss, and it caught the bishop on the head. Three more dug deeper—none struck home. Nettle looked at the sky and rubbed his eyes.

On the eighth blow, Nettle's eyes were clouded and he seemed to sweat blood. A big man whispered, "Aim for the big arteries in the neck."

Will squinted and struck—blood sprayed straight up and caught him in the eyes.

"Argh!" he cried, "Oh—someone help me! I can't see! I can't see!"

I pulled him toward me. "Will?"

"Is he dead? Mike, did I kill him?"

They swarmed around the body. Wat tried to pull them off in vain. "Yes, Will."

One man pulled off Sudbury's ring. Wat caught his arm. "We'll have no thieves!"

"Oh fool! That was before!" The man laughed in Wat's face and rushed away.

"After him!" Wat called, but no one bothered. They moved the limbs of the dead archbishop. Two little girls found his severed fingertips.

"We'll sell these as relics one day!" they called. "Ah, they'll make him a saint, and we'll be rich!"

I took Nettle down the hill, to the Thames. His eyes were rimmed in blood. "Wash them," I said.

His voice wasn't his own voice. It was wild and full of sorrow. "No . . . it's no good. It's God's vengeance. I'm blind!"

I forced him down and poured palms full of river

water into his eyes. He blinked and blinked. His eyes were clean as milk; the thin blood ran down his cheeks like tears. I laughed. "Ah, you scared me, you know? Well, it's all over. We're cleaning London of the traitors, now, and we'll head home."

He shook his head miserably. "I'm still blind."

I moved a finger past his eyes; they didn't follow. I paused and said, "Hey, look!"

"I can't look anymore," he said.

I sighed and helped him up. "You're just tired. You've had a shock, Will. You'll be fine."

Will said, "He was a saint."

"Sudbury?" I laughed uneasily.

"He died forgiving me," Will said.

I clucked my tongue and turned him north. Everywhere men passed with axes drenched in blood, and I passed London Bridge and saw Simon Sudbury's head piked with the others. It had no true face. I knew it only by the number and the violence of the blows.

Folk rushed ahead, faces full of will and fire. They'd behead John Legget at Cheapside. They'd burn Hales's new palace at Highbury. We were fighting God's war in London with the blessing of the King. Nettle dragged along behind, vainly rubbing his eyes.

8 . Bread and Cheese

They call it The Hurling Time, as if it ran an age. I know I passed through more than sun to sun that Friday after Corpus Christi. Will Nettle held my arm and I wandered, baffled, bone-weary, past smoldering buildings, over broken streets. Wat bounded up and nearly knocked me backward. "I'm losing order, Jack. Something's gone wrong!"

I turned toward the Thames, where ax-swingers flocked. "They're free men."

"Jack, something's missing." His steady eyes turned inside out. He held my shoulder. "We've got to work sense back in!"

"Oh, Wat, I don't have the heart." I bowed my head.

He looked me up and down, stern. "If good men don't have the heart, then Farrington and his lot will take back all we've won!"

"What have we won?"

"How can you say that?" He seized both my shoulders and pushed Nettle off, shaking and shaking, tears streaming. "Jack, if you say that again, I'll have your head!" Then he came to himself. He freed me and staggered back, breathing like a bellows. "Your friend looks in a bad way. You ought to find him shelter."

"In London?" I laughed without cheer. "Oh, the only shelter in this town is in the house of Thomas Farrington!"

The name summoned Tom Farrington from Hell. He marched across the cobbles, his little figure followed by two thousand. They all called: "Bread and cheese!"

Wat and I exchanged looks. I guess he thought I'd lend him strength, but I had none to give. I stepped back; Wat stepped forward. He puffed himself out like a toad and crossed to meet them. They carried loaves and rounds and cheese on poles.

"Hey! Captain!" someone called. "We're after the true traitors now—foreigners!" A man with red hair and a black hat pushed through. He held a blond lad by the hair and grinned. His free hand held a dagger. The lad's face was pulled forward and the man spat a command: "Say it, you Fleming turd—bread and cheese!"

The boy babbled through tears. "Brod and case . . ."

"Bread and cheese!" He ran a dagger just below the ear and drew blood. "I'll cut deeper, sonny!"

The thousands cheered.

"Farrington," said Tyler, "if we want to keep the grace of the King . . ."

"What does this have to do with the King?" There was a healthy rose red to his face, and his small hands were clean. They held an axe.

"There's been drinking, looting . . ."

"What would you have us do, Tyler? Sow corn on the cobbles? We're killing traitors!" He handed his axe to a lad and threw his arm back to the Vintry. "The Flemings, the Lombards, they've been tanning our hides for years, robbing us, trying to make London their city. Your lords take nothing when you set the whole of them beside one merchant. When Richard's dust, when Gaunt's dust, these worms will still crawl London unless we make High Doom today! There are two traitors for every honest man here—and today the traitors die!"

His sharp voice was more knife than drum. The men and women whooped.

Will raised his head. He whispered, "There are devils in the crowd. I see them . . ."

I shivered so hard that I thought I'd fall. "You're blind," I said.

He nodded. "But I see them."

Wat turned, mute, and walked up Bridge Street. I shadowed him, dragging Will Nettle by the hand. I stumbled over cobbles slick with old rain and new blood. I near lost sight of Wat. There was plenty to see. Doubtless you saw it, brothers. Men crowded the church of Saint Michael, forcing out a sea of Flemings. They plucked Legget from the church altar like a bit of lichen from a tree and made him watch the slaughter before killing him as well. They were neat executioners. One blow and the Flemings were headless.

Did you see them, Mayor Walworth? They lay headless in your city's swimming gutters, and it took a hard will not to turn your face away. I wanted to find Wat, to follow him. He walked as swift as horror, and I didn't know where he was headed. Then something happened that kept me from Tyler for a while.

Someone cried: "Christ! You can't! You can't! I'm your leader's brother!"

"And he'd want you dead if he knew you! You're a cheat and a traitor!"

I turned and saw Alf, God preserve me, my own brother, down on the cobbles with both hands twisted behind him. A tiler held a hammer to his head.

I called, "Don't touch him!"

"You think you're King?" The tiler's voice was full of dull hatred. "A merchant rents storefronts for a pound of flesh—and you say 'Don't touch him'!"

Alf's head was forced to one side, and his full black beard and merchant's cap hid most of his face. His black eyes were turned up; he didn't know me. I ran and knelt beside him and the tiler set the hammer down.

"Leave off," he said. "I'm not feeling too particular today, and you just may die as well."

I said, "I'm Jack Straw."

He said, "I'm Wat Tyler and you're keeping me from an important meeting with the King."

"Oh—damn you to hell!" I snatched the heavy hammer and pounded it again and again against the cobbles, but the cobbles, rather than the hammer, broke. Then I tried to lift it and managed to heave it over my head.

The tiler laughed. "All that trouble for a merchant! You wouldn't bother if you knew—"

I struggled the hammer up and tossed it the ten yards into the Thames. The tiler's manner changed.

"You steal a man's livelihood," he said, "and you're next."

He left Alf on the ground. At last, I turned his face. "It's your brother." I caught my breath. The right side of his jaw had caved in, and there was a deep, black hole in his temple. His beard was a tangle of dark blood. He'd been dead from the start.

My heart told me to take my dagger and run, to find the tiler and carve him into tiles! I turned, and was caught by Nettle's blind, traveling eyes.

"What?" he said. "What's going on, Michael?"

I grasped his hand. "I don't know." I looked past Saint Peter's and saw the rise of Corn Hill; I knew where Wat had gone and where I had to go. I seized Will's arm. "We're off to Farrington's."

He said, "I'm seeing demons everywhere, Michael. Will there be demons there?"

"Most likely." I dragged him on, sweating. "Get a grip on yourself, Will. Either you're blind or you're not blind."

He sighed a sigh with a sob in it, and we passed through the narrow way that smelled of ash and sulfur. I saw three apprentices dragging off their master, and I saw John Horn on mount like a Judgement vision, shouting: "Come to me for justice! Follow the grocers!" Three hundred followed, shouting countless names.

A man sat by the merchant hall, playing havoc with the strings of a harp, and singing:

> Oh she betrayed him in the morning
> And he forgave her at the noon.
> The rival's floating in the river.
> The babe is sleeping on a stone.

Then, from the distance:

> Oh that will not do
> Said Milder to Malder.
> Oh what will do then?
> Said Festle to Fose.

> Big bloody brass cauldrons
> Said John the Red Nose

Big bloody brass cauldrons
Said John the Red Nose.

I hurried from the harper and the song as I'd hurried
from the dead. I ducked into an alley, searching, searching
for the door. It was unlocked.

The big, dull room was empty. Even the rats were
gone.

I called: "Parson Ball!"

His voice floated up, thin. "Jack, we're down here."

I stared down into the cellar. There was Wat, fanning
the fire, and Ball, with my cloak round him, his long hand
on our Bible. His sharp face turned up toward my own; he
waved me in. I helped Will down. Wat turned; he looked a
world better.

"Jack," he said, "I've been talking to the parson and
he figures we'd got it all wrong."

Ball spat. The floor was drizzled over with pink spittle.
"Ha!—your charter's a sham! It doesn't scratch the surface!
If you want Heaven, you must follow Adam and Eve. You
must delve and spin. You'll have to dig and spin Heaven
with your own hands."

Wat laughed, the first honest laughter I'd heard all
day. "You understand, we've all been lazy-bones."

"You've been waiting for Heaven to descend like ash
after a fire, or be handed down from Richard like your
scraps of parchment. Ah—you fools!" His voice wandered,
and his lean face turned to the hearth. "You've got to build
Heaven out of Earth. What do you think I've been saying
all these years?"

"One thing I don't understand, Father," Wat said
slowly. "Without a King, who leads? Who knows what
Heaven is? Where does the Heaven come from?" He turned
his flat face up, eager, listening.

Ball answered without hesitation. "Listen to the words
of Long Will," he said. "Listen to Piers Plowman." He
turned to me and nodded. I began:

" ' There is a natural knowledge in your heart which
prompts you to love your Lord God better than yourself
and to die rather than commit a mortal sin. That surely is

Truth.' "

Ball's face was red through. He said, "Yes, my son. My son, truth is authority and leadership enough."

Wat had spread his copy of the charter face down on the floor. Half of it was already knitted over with Ball's writing. There was scant light there, and Ball's script had grown worse since the prison letters, but a glance and I knew it for a blueprint of Jerusalem.

"I've got to arrange another meeting with the King," said Wat. "Tomorrow at latest." He looked at me warmly. "Jack, we'll meet as brothers this time. No more pomp. That's the way the parson wants it, and he's the only sane man I've talked to today."

Ball nodded. He was yellow, and he quivered like hot oil, but the nod was vigorous. The two men looked at each other with real love.

I tucked Nettle by the hearth and moved the charter into better light. Wat and Ball moved close, and while London hurled, we three conspirators read and wrote and prayed.

9. Jenny Row

My twelfth summer seemed longer than a summer. I willed it to be long. I figured, after this they'll watch me. Will I labor for wages? Will I apprentice to a smith or cobbler and take on a trade? Will I leave, like many lads, for London? Worse, will I be chosen by the lord to serve in France? They'd need answers by harvest, and I held onto the last summer of freedom with both hands.

I took my brothers and sisters into my conspiracy and made them wander far from Gravesend. Some days we would play Robin Hood and some days Pilgrimage. One afternoon we searched for late strawberries. August sun had filled the corn to bursting; a week would bring harvest. I coaxed a final journey out of them, and we seven Rows walked south, fanning ourselves against the heat.

We walked in clusters. My two older sisters told Saint's tales; each laid a troop of icons by her bed at night. The middle brothers, Frank and Peter, had become prime bowmen. They pointed to high limbs of trees and bragged. That left me, my head full of summer, Alf, his head full of figures, and Jenny, who seemed too young to have a head at all.

She was just five, and still put anything that shined into her mouth. There wasn't much she wouldn't eat, and we tried to teach her caution.

That day we paused midway between Gravesend and Rochester to search for fruit. A ruby-tail fly settled on Jen's hand and she popped it straight into her mouth. She made a face.

Alf threw her, caught her by the middle, and turned her upside down. "Spit—Jen!"

"Phew!" The fly fell on the road. Jenny wagged her hanging arms and giggled. "Turn me over! Turn me over!"

Alf swung her by her short legs till her skirt turned inside out. "Not till you promise to tell us before you put things in your mouth!"

"Oh . . . Alfie . . . I will!" She giggled and sobbed and her fair hair flew.

Gently, Alf set Jenny on her feet. He rubbed his hands.

We sat on a knoll by the road. The grass was blue; we'd had sweet, long rain that summer. There were some marshlands near, and herons walked through bladderwort and pimpernel. "Jenny ought to eat a heron," Peter said. "Hmmm. I wonder how a heron would go down."

"Roasted, with garlic," said Marjorie, the middle sister. She was always hungry.

"Why don't you ask Saint Catherine to fetch one for you?" Peter slapped his knees, pleased with himself. Marjorie ignored him.

Jenny looked at Alf, squinting. "But what would have happened if I'd swallowed the fly?"

Alf shrugged. He sat back and rested his head on the grass.

"You would have died, likely," said Peter.

"Oh, hush! Of course not!" Ann cried. She turned to Jenny and smiled tenderly. "You just would have spat it up, dear."

Peter tore a hunk of grass and earth and threw it at Ann's face. It hit her shoulder. "Well, aren't you grownup today."

"Someone has to be."

Jenny's eyes were wide open. She stared out past us, her small mouth slack and her hands pressed together. "Well, what then?"

We looked at her. Peter shook his head.

"I mean, after I die what would happen?"

Marjorie said, "You'd go to Heaven."

Jenny asked, "What's Heaven?"

Marjorie pointed at the sky. Jenny's eyes followed her finger with small trust. "It's up there," Majorie said.

"But there's nothing up there." Jenny looked at each of us, hoping for a better answer. "You can't run around there and there's nothing to eat."

"There's all the food you want up there, and there's angels and saints and you can see God there and—"

Jenny said, "I don't see anything."

"That's because you're not dead." Marjorie was faltering. She looked at us for aid and we looked back with heartless glee.

"But I want to see it now." Jenny's voice wavered to the point to danger and the red was creeping up her neck. Alf sat up.

"What's your hurry, Jen? You'll get to Heaven."

"But if I can't see it . . . I want to stay here!" She leaned on Alf's long arm. Alf stroked her hair. He threw a dagger of a look at Marjorie. Jenny said, "I want to stay here after I'm dead."

Peter brightened. "You'd be a ghost!"

"No! No! I want Heaven here!"

Alf was the sort of brother who could bear a wailing sister for so long. She'd begun to weigh on his arm. "Now Jenny," he said, "quiet down!"

Ann said, "You're very spoiled and you can't have everything you want."

I looked round, past our lazy circle. The sun was high and the hills were feathery blue. The warm earth was so fertile that I could have taken it in my hand and stroked it into life. Then, I thought of Heaven. It was nice there, but very cold. I shivered at the thought of it. "Jenny's right," I said.

They looked at me. Frank woke from a stupor and said, "Well, it's the first time I heard you take a stand on anything."

"Well, isn't it nice here?" I paused and no one fought the point. "Why didn't God build Heaven here?"

Alf cut in. "Michael, can't you think as far back as last winter? We were all down to a little brawn and bone. And some folks never have—"

"But look!" I rose. I felt my truth brighten round my head like a halo, sprout from my shoulders like wings. "Look around. Now this place is a wonder. Heaven always seems like you have to sit with a straight back and speak

Latin and . . .''

Peter said, "The lad has a point."

Jenny put her arms around my leg and hugged it hard.

"But why didn't God build it here?" Frank asked.

"Well . . ." I said, "maybe it was too much for him. In Heaven . . . well, don't you fancy everything's one color, all in order, all simple? There's nothing simple about Earth."

Alf smiled bitterly. "Too much for God?"

I shrugged. The idea was beyond me now and I sat, nearly on Jenny. "Can God do anything?"

Marjorie nodded. "Anything he wants to do." She looked at the sky. "I guess he never wanted to put Heaven here. Or he never thought about it."

Peter said, "You know him so well, Marjorie, why don't you ask him yourself?"

Frank's eyes were on the sky as well. It was clear, and lines of cloud crossed like white tails. "If he doesn't want to put it here, should *we* try? Would that be like building the tower of Babel?"

"Ha! How do you make Heaven? In a smithy?" Peter snickered, and we all laughed at the thought of Peter at his bellows while the ornery blacksmith shaped Heaven in the forge. Then we wearied of talking, rose, and wandered on.

The birds had picked the berries clean long before, and we returned empty handed. Jenny sucked three stones; she swallowed one. No whacking forced it out. She was poked and prodded, hung upside down, and at last filled with milk and bread and ale. My mother led her to the hedge. She gave her a hard cuff and told her to come back with the stone. I went to comfort her and she put her soggy hand in mine.

"Michael," she said, "I'm not going to die till I can stay here. So I can swallow anything."

I nodded and left her with the stone in her belly. I looked up; the stars were full as fruit, but cold. I looked down, and dug my toe in the earth.

10 . Smithfield

We had to grant a bargain; we had to meet outside the city. Smithfield, a green croft ringed by trees, lay in sight of Aldergate and Newgate. Each week, it held the market of horses, and it smelled of mares, of dung, of leaves. Our folk didn't know why we'd called the meeting. Some said Gaunt was mustering an army in Scotland to attack Richard, and that the King had need of our strength. Others said Tyler was to be knighted, and the King was to grant lesser gifts to myself and Farrington and make Ball the new archbishop. They gathered, gossiping. There was no need to guard the empty tower.

We packed in, spreading onto Chicken and Cow lane. Smithfield's shade rounded our voices into silence. Faith held her babes by the hand. Art waved his broken stick. Little Mary swayed on her feet. Their clothing was in pieces, and they looked very happy.

"We're going to see the King again, aren't we?" the little girl asked. "Then Canter-berry?"

"We'll see the King," said Faith. Her voice was distant. "Hush, now, and keep your peace."

Wat stood apart, scratching his neck. He stared at the city wall, at the tower. I held the new petition in my hand, still scribbled on the King's old charter. Ha—old! True, Tyler had only gotten it two days before, but it was so stained and tattered he might as well have used it to clean Corn Hill. John Ball was absent.

Wat said, "Jack, after this we'll go home, live as best we can." He held his hand out, and I set the charter in it. He squinted at the script. "Could you teach me to read, or am I past hope?"

"I'd be honored," I said, "though you made more sense of Ball's old letters than this learned Jack Straw could."

He chewed his lip. He'd gone without his armor, that day, in good faith, and he seemed half the man without it. He wore a white tunic, and his bare arms were brick red with rubbing on the chain-mail and leather. He passed back the petition. "Well, after this, come live with me in Maidstone. We'll take Ball. Do you have family?"

"A sister," I said.

"Then we'll have her too." The leaves crackled like paper, and Wat turned his face up to the sun. "You, me, Ball, Kate, the sister . . ."

"But she'll be marrying." Then my heart cringed. Will Nettle stood close by, blinking. "Or maybe not."

"Have her marry. And you'll marry Kate. You'll be my son in earnest." He crooked his arm around me, and it shook so hard that I shook with it.

Richard approached on horseback. This time he was joined by a hundred retainers. Wat looked at me with hope; they let him meet us of their own free will, now, and maybe they'd accept us as brothers. Richard's men were armed with swords. Our folk had left weapons in London.

Richard was refreshed. He'd spent most of that morning in the Abbey. His clean face rose above the haze of horse sweat like a lily. He rode past Saint Bart's and paused at Smithfield's threshold, between two leaning trees. It took a real struggle not to kneel before him. We'd talked it out the night before; all that would have to change.

I saw the same struggle on Wat's face. He tried to summon up an easy, brotherly smile, but he looked abashed as ever. He stared across the empty place between the two companies and tried to look King Richard in the eye.

Richard spoke: "I would address your chieftain."

Wat started forward, but his legs had turned water. A butcher ran up, leading a pony.

"Here, brother," he said, slapping the creature on the side. "Here's the proper manner for a man who's to be knighted to approach the King."

Wat moved his lips in gratitude and let the butcher

help him mount. Wat was no horseman. He gave the pony a half-hearted kick. It walked boldly forward, as if the hundred yards were any hundred yards, until it rubbed noses with the King's horse.

It was hard to see past the press of retainers, and I stood nearer than most. Wat, then the King, dismounted. After a while, Wat took Richard's hand. He looked at the hand. Then he shook it, hard.

That helped. He had shaken the King's hand like any other hand, and he could speak to Richard like a neighbor.

"Brother," he said, with warmth, "be of good comfort, for you have more companions now than you would have hoped for a fortnight ago. We shall be good friends."

The King did not meet his eyes. "Why won't you go back to your own country?"

"First you must hear our new petition. You'll regret it if you don't, King. I think it'll please you mightily." He kept shaking the King's hand. I suffered for him. He seemed to think he could only talk to Richard so long as he shook his hand.

King Richard said, "Whatever points you wish me to consider, you shall have them freely and without contradiction, written out and sealed."

Wat freed the hand at last. He stared at the sky and tried to force the carefully set points out of his memory. Then he stepped back and spoke:

"First, there shall be no lordship in the future, excepting your own Lordship, Richard, and lordship will be divided among all people. Likewise, all land must be ours to hold in common."

All this was distant—I can speak the words in good faith because I knew them by heart, and held them in my hand. For once, Wat Tyler's voice was thin. The folks by me strained forward. One old man nodded his head slowly, as if he was remembering something.

Wat went on, red and dripping sweat, his hand stroking the side of the brown pony. "And likewise, all the lands and tenements and goods shall be taken from the abbeys and bishoprics and divided among the commons. And last," he said, "there shall be no bound men in

England, but all folk shall be free and of one condition . . ." He turned back, and struggled to find my eyes. He couldn't find them. He said, ". . . for Christ bought our freedom with his blood."

The King wrung his hands, nodding. "Well," he said. "You'll have all of this. And now you'll go back to your own homes without delay."

Wat's shirt was plastered down and the hot wind had stiffened it. He turned and called back. "Could someone fetch some ale?"

A lad ran toward him, stopped and whispered, "Oh—I can't approach the King."

I took the ale from him and walked the distance slowly. The jug weighed as much as a man. I handed it to Wat and he lifted it and took a long drought. Then he swirled a mouthful round his teeth and spat.

Richard winced. His face was dry as Wat's. I offered him the jug.

"Drink, brother," I said, feeling pleased with myself.

I thought I saw him hide a smile. He shook his head. I thought: I'm right to call him brother. Then I helped Wat mount the pony.

Someone from the King's guard called: "Wat Tyler, you're the biggest traitor in England!"

Wat stopped mid-mount. I whispered, "Go on, brother. Pay him no mind."

"Wat Tyler," he called again. "You're the biggest traitor in England if not in all Christendom."

Wat dismounted. He faced the King and his men. An old, old man, an old soldier by the look of him, stepped forward, and the color drained from Tyler's face.

The soldier said, "I know you, Tyler. You deserter! You coward!"

"You stop now, Henry. Now!" Wat held his dagger.

"You left us in the thick of it, didn't you? You left us and ran home, like so many, and we looked for you in Colchester and heard you'd deserted your family too, for fear of war—Oh! Now you strut before the King here like a hero in a tale! Like a soldier!"

I seized Wat's cold arm, but he broke away. "You'll

stop now!"

"I won't stop! I won't keep silent! Traitor!"

Wat lunged forward. Then you, Mayor, you Walworth, caught Wat by the neck. Three others caught his shoulder, shins, his middle. You cried: "You dare to show cold iron before the King!" You stabbed him in the stomach.

I ran. I would have run to London or Gravesend or Land's End if I hadn't been seized by anxious countrymen. "What's going on, Jack? What's happened?"

I twisted my head back, and saw Wat splayed and circled. I heard Richard's voice. "I have knighted your leader!"

Faith poked my shoulder. Martin held my middle. There were faces and arms everywhere. "Tell us, Jack? How did he knight the Captain? Did you see? Did they knight you as well? Oh, Sir Straw, tell us!"

"I . . . I . . ." My words stuck together. Had I only thought I'd seen the stabbing? No, I'd seen it. I near swooned and a few men read my face and placed their arrows. I looked up at a spinning, snow-blue sky and I reached for Nettle's shoulder.

"Michael?" His voice was calm, like he was dead or under water.

Then, Richard's voice, as I had never heard it—like a trumpet. No, I'd heard it once. "I am your King! You have no Captain but me! I am your leader—Follow me!"

His horse tore north, toward open country. They followed, and I was pulled forward so I had to run or be trampled. I looked back and saw Nettle far behind, on the grass, shielding his head with his arms. I wept and ran, and kept on looking back and charging forward.

Nettle called: "What?" Two knights kicked him in the side and rolled him over.

"Bastard! You don't follow the King!"

They laughed, and I thought I saw them drag him to Saint Bart's. He didn't struggle. That was the last I saw of him.

But I ran on behind my King. Driven, we were packed in Clerkenwell Field, among the low corn, penned in by armed men like sheep. There was something of sheep in the faces of my neighbors.

"Jack," said a young woman, a stranger to me, maybe from Essex. "You haven't told us whether you've been knighted."

"And why did they lead us here, Jack?" A man my own age, a bondsman by look of him, who'd seen twice my own hardship, stared now at me, now at the mounted Richard.

I eyed the King as well. I thought, could Richard want us to keep clear heads while his doctors tended Wat's wounds at Saint Bart's? If I told them the truth, of Tyler's stabbing, they might turn on him. So I played the King's fool, and his second voice. I said, "I'll soon be knighted. We're to wait here while they clothe Wat Tyler like a knight."

The woman held her own cloak close and shivered. "Will we all get new garments, Jack? It's turned chill here. The weather's turned."

I nodded. "New mantles," I said, "spun by Joan of Kent herself." I turned to face my folk, and the armed men with their high spears and their long mercenary faces were forgotten. "And England will be a garden," I said. "All those bones, all the blood we've strewn here will turn the good earth rich, like marrow. And we'll have bread enough to deal it free as air."

The man spoke now, the man my age with the hatchet face and hunger-thin hair. "Bless Richard, then, and bless you, Sir Jack Straw."

"No," I said, and now it didn't seem me talking, but another. "I'm not knighted yet. Tyler's knighted, and Straw will be knighted soon."

"You saw him knighted," he said. "How was it done?"

Again, the words came to me: "When you're knighted, you kneel low and they take a sword to you."

The woman laughed. "Sounds dangerous."

"That's the trust in it. You don't see the blade coming and you never know if it'll be the broad or bitter end. And when you rise, you're someone new. I'll be knighted soon."

I shivered hard. I saw it, my knighting, the block, the

folk who might have called my name with fierce love once, turned gray and watching with not fear, but faithless wonder.

"And you might see my knighting," I said. "And you might cheer. Well might you cheer, for it's the knight's heads that will watch over all of England, watch it turn into a good garden."

"And garden with us?" someone asked.

I shook my head. I felt my own doom wring me dry, and I asked, "You know the tale of the Straw-kin?"

Few nodded, so I told the tale.

And when I'd finished, when I'd kept them still and listening for a long time, a tall man walked through the wheat bearing something at the odd end of a pole. The King met the man midway, and he set his horse at a walk beside him. The lumpen burden seemed no bigger than a melon. Need I speak of how rough and blue round the jowls Wat's dead face was, and how they forced the dead eyes open. The King gestured toward the head again and again as if he wanted us to note the hair, the eyes, the chin, consider them. And he stood near, amount, and drew his small white hands together. My tale had thinned the wild world down to penny ale, and we did nothing.

Then I understood myself at last; that Wat could be a knight, yes, in Heaven. In Heaven, Richard would be called my brother. I'd been John Ball's fool—now I'd be the King's fool in payment for the bitter lesson.

Wat's head bobbed toward us, and I closed my eyes and thought, when they give me the peasant's knighthood, when they hit me with not the flat of a sword but the edge of an ax, I'd best be sure I go to Heaven.

That's why I make this long confession, so I can meet Richard in Heaven and thank him for the warning, so I can call him brother. Oh, brothers, pray for my soul, and pray for the soul of Wat Tyler.

11. The Straw-kin

An old woman lost her harvest through ill luck and weather. She had three things in the world: a loaf of bread, a pitcher of ale, and a son named Jack who loved her more than his own life. She knew that she would starve soon, and her son would starve with her, and she was very unhappy. Like many an unhappy soul, she was approached by the Devil.

The Devil said, "Pay the price of one of your possessions and I'll spirit it into a fine harvest."

The woman was a good Christian, but she accepted the bargain for her young son's sake and promised the Devil his price by morning. Still, she had so little that she was reluctant to pay. She looked at the loaf and couldn't deny it to her son. Neither could she deny him ale. She sat and thought all night, and as she thought she munched the loaf. Her throat was dry and she washed the bread down with ale. Before dawn, she'd finished the whole loaf and emptied the whole pitcher. Jack rose to greet her and found her weeping.

"My good son," she said, "I have nothing left to give the Devil. We will die of hunger."

"You have me, mother," he answered. Before she could contest him, he rose and left the cottage. She followed, but she couldn't find him. She saw only a broad, high, field of wheat.

She embraced the wheat and wept, and she was loath to harvest. The wheat stayed in the sun through that autumn, and the night of the first frost, she had a strange dream.

She didn't see her son, but she heard his voice, as clear as though he lived. The voice sang:

> Out in the cold I lie
> I die until the spring.
> In quickening the death.
> In death the quickening.

The woman rose at once, and harvested the wheat. She kept the corn on the stalk and plaited the stalk into a straw-kin. The body was formed all of straw. The grains of corn mounted up into a shaking golden face, and stray straw feathered off like hair. The woman loved the straw-kin and she resigned herself to the loss of her son.

The woman grew lean, for she couldn't bear to thresh the corn and take it to the miller. Her neighbors laughed and said, "Here's a woman with corn who goes hungry. She'll get no help from us." And so the woman could find comfort and fellowship only with the straw-kin.

Winter passed, and the woman took good care of the straw-kin. When he grew damp, she set him in a dry, warm place. When he grew frosty, she warmed him with her own hands. Sometimes she'd speak to him, and he would answer and she'd hear long tales about the ways of straw to charm her from her hunger. When March came, she had no seed to plant, so she left her strip of the field fallow and didn't plow.

One morning, she looked out the window, and saw the little straw-kin. He had yoked her oxen to her plow and he walked across the field, turning soil, and singing:

> The sowing-time is nigh.
> Prepare the soil for spring.
> In Quickening the Death.
> In Death the Quickening.

She helped the straw-kin turn the soil, and by April, the field was set for sowing. Alas, the woman thought, the straw-kin and I have worked for nothing, for I have no seed to sow. The straw-kin said, "Good woman, you have treated me well. The time has come for me to repay you in earnest. Cut off my head."

The woman refused. "You've grown dear to me," she

said, "and I couldn't bear to do you harm."

"Cut off my head," he said again, "and plant the seed."

Again she refused, but the straw-kin was insistent. At last she resigned herself and cut off the straw-kin's head with an ax. The seed scattered over the cottage floor and the straw body fell to pieces in her hands. She used the straw to mulch the turned field and sowed the seed. Then she returned to her cottage, weeping. She thought: this will be a fruitful and a joyless harvest.

That summer, she dreamed of the straw-kin. She thought she heard his voice singing:

> The bargain is reversed.
> I am a living thing!
> In Quickening the Death.
> In Death the Quickening!

She rushed out, expecting a full field of corn. Instead, she saw her own dear Jack, standing in the middle of the plowed field, his hair full of earth, looking sleek and brown and bright. She took him in her arms and praised him for confounding the Devil. The two lived together in peace and charity till the end of their days.

12. Ϩeaven anϸ Earth are One

The rest of the tale tells itself. It tells itself in this high, dripping tower. I saw Martin here, but not Hugh Smith. Tyler's head holds place of pride among the heads on London Bridge. I can't find Ball's. Have you spared him? Likely, you want to catch Ball, but you can't. You can't find him.

Have you looked for Ball, then? Doubtless you've threshed through Corn Hill looking for him. Farrington's yours. I clung to the high bars of my cell and watched them lead Tom up Tower Hill, to the block. I've seen his head piked up, skewed on the bridge. They didn't think Will Nettle worth the piking, likely, but he's dead, or good as dead, as dead as Sudbury. As for Jenny and Kate, any thread between their lives and mine has snapped so clean they may as well be dead. Leave them to the many trooping home with their bum charters. Leave them to their mercy, which is deeper than Jack Straw's.

Don't badger me about Ball. You'll find him without my help. The world's turned rightside up again and all we've won has spilled out of our hands. Richard disowned his charter, you tell me. Serfs remain serfs. Richard is a good King and he did right to break faith. Don't call me disloyal, brothers. That would break my heart. Richard only put us back where we must be till we die and go to Heaven.

I've parted with Ball's words entirely. It was a madness that made me confuse a tale and a confession, Heaven and Earth. You'll find Ball without my help. The man's doubtless coughing up blood somewhere. He may give himself to you, rather than die alone. Try to save his soul, brothers. He's sinned greatly, but so have you. I'd like to think that one day some pilgrim will enter Canterbury

Cathedral and light a candle for John Ball.

I see at last: You've sat through this confession, hot for word on Ball. I can't tell you, don't you understand? I've betrayed him once, twice, how many times? That's my limit. I can't break faith with this John Ball again! You're looking at me now, smiling a little—scribe, you smile like a snake, and you, Walworth, like a wolf. By peril of my soul, if this will push me into Hell to Hell I'll go. I've spent my life in Hell! But I can't think you'd throw away a soul like entrails—no, you wouldn't hold back yearly masses for the sake of John Ball's head.

My Whitsun wish! Curse it! I know I'm cursed unless I have your blessing. I bow my head, now, waiting. Maybe not you, Mayor Walworth. Oh—that's right, Sir William now. You told me Richard knighted you for knifing Tyler. Oh, not Sir Wolf Walworth—but you, scribe, you who write this. Bless me, father, for I've sinned and I'm repentant.

No, scribe? What have you written? Have you written what I've said? Your own damned version? Let me see the copy! What right do I have to see it? Christ died for my sake, Gentlemen! Am I damned then? Let me see what you've written!

Afterword:
The Confession of Jack Straw

". . . Since there would be no one left who was senior, stronger or more knowledgeable than ourselves, we would have founded laws at our own pleasure by which all subjects would be ruled. Moreover, we would have created kings, Walter Tylere in Kent and one each in other counties, and appointed them. Because this design of ours was hindered by the archbishop, our greatest hatred was directed against him and we longed to kill him as quickly as possible. Moreover, on the evening of the day on which Walter Tylere was killed, we proposed, because the common and especially the poorer people of London favored us, to set fire to four parts of the city and burn it down and divide all the precious goods found there among ourselves." And he added: "These were our aims, as God will help me on the point of death."

After he made this confession, he was executed and his head placed on London Bridge near the head of his colleague, Walter Tylere. And so we learn how the rebels conspired to destroy the realm. And if the evidence of this one confession should seem insufficient, many other captured rebels made confessions of a similar nature when they saw death before their eyes.

Walsingham, *Historia Anglicana*

On Accuracy

This novel is not a history of the English Peasant Revolt of 1381, though fine histories have been written. Unlike many popular uprisings of the period, the Peasant Revolt is well documented, and many of the documents are collected in R.B. Dobson's *The Peasants' Revolt of 1381*. Contemporary chroniclers, some actual witnesses, were taken with the drama of the uprising. Each "true" account was pruned into a tale. No two tales agreed, as writers shaped events and characters to suit their story.

I work in that tradition, and I never ceased to wonder at the resemblance between history and story. The more I knew about the history of the Peasant Revolt, the more this novel worked as a piece of fiction, but it remains fiction, grounded in research, but shaped by my imagination.

The Peasant Revolt spread as far north as York and lingered for weeks after Tyler's death. I dealt with a small part of a great uprising, that uprising itself inseparable from the history of fourteenth-century England. I tried to understand that history, and the more I learned, the more apt I became to make far-fetched, but educated guesses.

When I knew the peasants were at a certain place at a certain time, I tried to put them there, but when I had no facts before me, I asked myself what I expected of my story and my characters. Most of the characters are historical, but I often played havoc with popular conceptions of men like Tyler and Ball. There is no evidence that Tyler deserted in France, though many did, and some were traced to Maidstone. There is no evidence that John Ball had tuberculosis. As for Jack Straw, the chroniclers give us only his name and his confession. His life in Gravesend, his family, and his relationship with Ball, are my own doing.

I felt a deep responsibility to see the revolt the way the peasants themselves might have seen it, and to try to tell the story on Jack Straw's terms. This led me far from Walsingham and the other chroniclers, to folktale, song and, at last, to the Bible and Langland's *Piers Plowman*. Ball's letters are authentic. The song, "The Cutty Wren", is popularly associated with the revolt. The folktales are my own.

One month after Tyler's death, John Ball was captured, hung, and drawn and quartered. Eighteen years after Tyler's death, Richard was displaced by John of Gaunt's son, Henry Bolingbroke. He died five months later. We'll never know how many men and women died for their part in the Peasant Revolt. To twist the history of these people would be like killing them a second time. I've tried to be true to the accounts I've read, and at the same time tell a different story altogether—the story of the peasants.

Simone Zelitch was born in Philadelphia. She received her M.F.A. from the University of Michigan where *The Confession of Jack Straw* won a Hopwood Award. She is currently a lecturer in fiction writing at Southern Illinois University in Carbondale. She is completing a novel about Moses in the wilderness.